The
Gourdmother

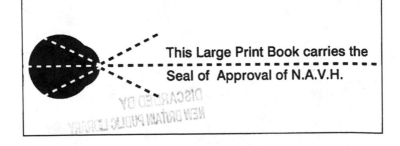

The Gourdmother

Maggie Bruce

Published in 2005 by arrangement with The Berkley Publishing Group, a division of Penguin Group (USA) Inc.

Wheeler Large Print Cozy Mystery.

The text of this Large Print edition is unabridged. Other aspects of the book may vary from the original edition.

Set in 16 pt. Plantin by Christina S. Huff.

Printed in the United States on permanent paper.

Library of Congress Cataloging-in-Publication Data

Bruce, Maggie.
    The gourdmother / by Maggie Bruce. — Large print ed.
      p. cm. — (Wheeler Publishing large print cozy mystery)
    ISBN 1-59722-131-7 (lg. print : sc : alk. paper)
    1. New York (State) — Fiction. 2. Gourd craft — Fiction.
3. Handicraft — Fiction. 4. Artisans — Fiction. 5. Large type
books. I. Title. II. Wheeler large print cozy mystery.
PS3602.R8325G68 2005
   813'.6—dc22   2005023468

For my mother, Lillian Weiss,
who taught me about unconditional love;
and for Arcie Wallace, always an angel;
and for Mitch Wallace, hero, 9/11/01

In loving memory.

As the Founder/CEO of NAVH, the only national health agency solely devoted to those who, although not totally blind, have an eye disease which could lead to serious visual impairment, I am pleased to recognize Thorndike Press* as one of the leading publishers in the large print field.

Founded in 1954 in San Francisco to prepare large print textbooks for partially seeing children, NAVH became the pioneer and standard setting agency in the preparation of large type.

Today, those publishers who meet our standards carry the prestigious "Seal of Approval" indicating high quality large print. We are delighted that Thorndike Press is one of the publishers whose titles meet these standards. We are also pleased to recognize the significant contribution Thorndike Press is making in this important and growing field.

Lorraine H. Marchi, L.H.D.
Founder/CEO
NAVH

* Thorndike Press encompasses the following imprints: Thorndike, Wheeler, Walker and Large Print Press.

Acknowledgments

My most sincere gratitude goes to Dyan Mai Peterson, author of the fabulous *The Decorated Gourd*, for sharing her thoughts, knowledge, and long experience with the gourd world, and especially her enthusiasm with me. And thanks to John Stacy, whose identity as "The Gourdfather" inspired the title of this book.

As ever, I'm grateful to my First Reader for the manuscript critique and for our friendship, both of which are essential to me. And I'm delighted to have the wisdom, humor, and energy of my agent, Deborah Schneider, to guide me.

Thanks to my husband, Bruce Wallace, for sharing the journey that brought me to gourds, but more for sharing a life journey that's the best I can imagine. And to our sons, Mark and Jeremy, who continue to make me proud and to teach me so much about the world.

Special thanks to my wonderful, smart, savvy, and blessedly *real* editor, Natalee Rosenstein, whose friendship and support are a source of true pleasure.

Maggie Bruce
Brooklyn, NY

Chapter 1

The scream that woke me from sleep sent my heart pounding and made it impossible to catch my breath. My eyes flew open and I sat straight up in bed in a single shot. I thought that only happened in the movies, but there I was, upright and shivering. The luminous face of my clock shone green and bright: ten minutes past midnight. I had been asleep an hour, no more. Outside, moonlight fell softly on the shed roof and lit up the back lawn all the way to the trees that trailed down the hill and disappeared into the void of night.

Nothing moved. The Kensington house, a quarter mile away and the only habitable structure I could see from my window, was dark and still. Surely if a living creature had made that sound Mickey Kensington or her husband Alan would have heard it too, would have clicked on the lights in their house. I consoled myself with the notion that I had dreamed it, but the tortured, strangled sound echoed in my head, the anguish in the voice magnified in my memory. An animal, maybe, caught in a trap. Could it be a fox or a coyote? Did bobcats roam the Berkshire foothills?

I slid back under the covers and waited, but except for a breeze stirring the wind chimes on the back porch and the ticking of my heart, nothing moved, nothing made a sound.

Nothing, that is, but the chatter in my head that wouldn't stop, questions about who or what had made that awful noise, and echoes of my friends' warnings that a thirty-four-year-old girl from the city wouldn't be safe living alone in such an isolated environment. Maybe they were right. After all, what good are street smarts in a place without sidewalks?

I tossed my old down vest over my cotton nightgown and headed for the stairs, flipping light switches as I went. Here I was, wide awake and spooked by noises I might have dreamed. If I were in Brooklyn, I'd phone my best friend, Karen Gerber, who would run her fingers through her pink- (or maybe this week it would be gold-) tipped hair, slide her feet into her favorite running shoes, and meet me at the all-night diner halfway between our apartments.

10

What would a real country woman do now?

Well, I wasn't a real country woman. I was an exile from Brooklyn, a captive of the weirdest business arrangement I'd ever let myself be suckered into, on the lam from Edward P. Thorsen and a love affair gone flat, and not at all familiar with night noises that weren't car alarms or party music. When a fast-talking client offered me the deed to this cottage in lieu of payment for the six months of work I'd done for him, I anticipated bee stings and power failures and frozen water pipes but not heart-stopping screams in the middle of the night.

I needed to make the shivering stop, but I had no brandy; besides, something in me wanted to be fully alert.

Tea. That was it, nice and herbal and soothing, sweetened with honey, to be sipped slowly while sitting in a rocking chair. I made a mental note to buy some — maybe that nice yellow, flowery mix in the health food store. I turned on the flame under the kettle and ground a scoopful of the Colombian Excelsior I'd bought in town last week. If I couldn't sleep, at least I could work.

What I had come to think of as my real

work still surprised me, after years of toiling for large corporations in their communications departments. There, I'd spent ten or twelve hours a day juggling deadlines to write pieces touting drugs that lower your social-anxiety quotient or shoes that make you feel like Carrie Bradshaw even if you have as much style sense as Courtney Love, explaining vacation policies and stock options, and writing newsletter fillers hailing the low-carb offerings in the company cafeteria. I was drawn to the work because I thought I could make enough money to support my real passions: gourd art and serving as a volunteer mediator to help people resolve their disputes at a local community center. After a couple of years I discovered that I wasn't willing to trade my time doing things I loved for my weekday morning stomachaches.

Tom Ford was my first client as a freelance writer, and my experience with him nearly sent me back into the familiar embrace of cash-rich but compassion-poor organizations. In spite of Tom, a mutual fund manager who hated sharing his name with a famous fashion designer, I persisted. Now I earn enough money writing the occasional corporate report to pursue my *real* work, which involves cutting, cleaning, burning, painting, drilling, carving, and otherwise altering gourds.

This is a strange thing to confess to total strangers at parties or in casual conversation when you're standing on the bank line waiting for a teller, but I adore gourds. I mean, I love people and sunsets and Aaron Neville's music and the idea of fairness and other fine, even majestic things. But I really am crazy for gourds. Not the kind that florists scatter among the silk leaves in their window displays, but the hard-shelled, smooth-surfaced, nut-colored things that have been used by people all over the world as bowls, dippers, musical instruments, and containers for the stuff of life.

Unlike most things in my life, gourds found me. I wasn't looking for anything more than a quiet road trip, a week of aimless meandering with stops in state parks, funky barbecue joints, and clean, impersonal motels when I got into my Subaru and headed south. By the time I'd passed through Kentucky and Tennessee and made my way to North Carolina I'd discovered gourds — nature's canvas, ready for anything from a Grandma Moses farm scene to an eye-boggling geometric pat-

13

tern, from Native American, African, and Hawaiian traditional designs to carved bowls that looked like leaves or grass. Within two weeks, my equipment took over a small bookcase in my living room and the gourds I'd ordered sat on every available surface of my one-bedroom Brooklyn apartment.

I learned from books — Dyan Peterson's *Decorated Gourd* and Jim Widess and Ginger Summit's *The Complete Book of Gourd Craft*. And I went to every gourd festival I could, which always meant days more on the road, because gourd events in Brooklyn were as rare as polite drivers. Along the way I met wonderful people and learned enough to eventually get several pieces into a couple of local craft fairs. But with my selection to participate in the juried craft show at Rhinebeck in June, I'd slotted four hours each day for gourds. I had to have twenty to thirty new pieces by late May, and I wanted them to communicate the magic of ideas, the possibilities for beauty and fun. Making forty or fifty to get my twenty really special ones was pretty realistic, and I needed to order about a dozen more gourds to have them on hand.

I sat at my desk and flipped open my notebook computer, woke it from sleep mode, and ignored the half-finished annual report for an Internet-based grocery that delivers brie and Perrier to city-dwellers' doors. No rush — today was Monday, and the Veterans Day holiday in two days meant that the first draft was due at headquarters in Queens on Thursday. Instead, I signed on to eBay, where I'd been tracking several items for days. Usually, I ordered directly from Welburn, Hurley, Wuertz, or other gourd farmers, but sometimes the thrill of the chase drew me to the auction site.

My fingers itched when I saw that the price for seven beautiful, cleaned tobacco box gourds had risen to thirty-seven dollars. For six days, nobody else had shown any interest in this lot, but now someone had raised the price fifty cents more than my last offer. I had a little more than eight seconds left to respond. Gourdgirl, my bidding nemesis, was at it again, lurking and then swooping down to carry away the prizes I was sure were mine. The woman had no manners. Her ruthlessness made my teeth grind in frustration, and I pictured her sitting in a dimly lit living room wearing only smeared mascara and a ratty bathrobe, a cigarette dangling from her bruised lips as she knocked back her tenth

Scotch of the night and cackled at my consternation.

Not proper form, I know, but I was tempted to write a snippy e-mail telling her that she was rude and annoying and wishing her bad luck.

On the other hand, the woman had good taste. Inevitably, whether it was a trio of penguin gourds with more attitude than a hip-hop band or two kettle gourds with so much presence they could charm a prison warden, she went after the very lots I most coveted. That this had been going on for three months only added to my frustration.

I signed off and sat at the desk, staring out into the night. I'd spent so much time at this spot that even in the moonlight I could see the pile of stones at one corner of the woods and the tree stumps that rose from the half acre of side lawn. Eventually, the coffee aroma drew me back to the room and I took a long, satisfying swallow.

The caffeine seemed to feed directly into my imagination, because in one single moment I had a vision that I knew would change my life.

Liberation was at hand.

Sweet freedom would be mine.

I nearly spilled the remaining coffee as I jumped out of my chair and danced my way to the front door and then out onto the porch. The November night sparkled in the autumn chill, starlight twinkling merrily above the patch of grass that would be Gourdgirl's Waterloo. By the following winter, I'd be free of Gourdgirl and her pals, RocksAnne and PaintEm. My own gourds, grown in my own garden, would set me free.

And then I stopped dancing and plopped in a heap onto the top step and leaned back against the railing, half listening for the sound of an animal in the woods where I thought I'd heard screams. My plan would never work. I'd never grown any-thing more than mold on the spaghetti in the back of my refrigerator. Unless raising one can't-kill-it philodendron counted as horticultural expertise. I'd read that the short growing season of Upstate New York wasn't long enough to get good hard shells on gourds. Most of the gourds I bought online came from Georgia, Alabama, North Carolina, and southern California — places with at least one hundred eighty good gardening days to let the beautiful plants fully mature. Here in the northeast we were lucky if we had one hundred good days.

All those hours I'd spent dreaming over

seed catalogs and gourd journal articles about growing gourds had delivered the same message. What I needed was a Headstart Program to make up for the lack of resources in the early childhood days of my gourds. How could I do that?

I wandered back inside, carried my coffee cup to the kitchen, and stared past the sun porch to the back yard.

That was it . . . the sun porch.

The sun porch and its wall of windows would be my greenhouse. This city girl would have dirty fingernails and gleaming little tools with sharp points, and my very own plants would help me declare independence from online competitors who beat me to the best gourds. I did some mental calculations and figured that I could put in two large tables like the ones I'd seen at Mountain Rock Nursery. I would start my gourd seeds at those tables, would heat them electrically with coils under the soil, and provide them with artificial sunlight from grow lamps to get my gourd babies going . . . when? Maybe in March, far enough in the future for me to put everything together. And then, when the seedlings were sturdy and the ground was warm enough, I'd transplant them, the way country people transplant their tomatoes. I would use the lawn beside the cottage and pray that screaming bobcats or those sweet-faced, round-eyed deer didn't savor Cucurbitacea *Lagenaria* as a mainstay of their diets. First, though, I'd have to wrestle those three old tree stumps out of the ground and devise some sort of trellis system to keep the growing gourds away from bugs and damp soil.

I'd seen the beautiful white tissue paper blossoms opening at night, and now that magic would happen right in my own backyard.

In the morning I'd phone Nora Johnson. She would know someone who could take care of those stumps. Nora was the first person I'd met after I moved to the cottage, and she'd become my mentor in all things local.

She'd been standing on the porch of The Creamery, a café that served spiced pumpkin soup and homemade quiches and pastries, when I pulled in to the parking lot a week after I'd moved. All I saw were a pair of long denim-clad legs and a stack of white boxes that might hold enough pizza for a townful of hungry fifteen-year-olds.

"You look like you could use a hand," I said. "Well, maybe two."

I was rewarded with the best laugh I'd

heard since I left Brooklyn. "If you'd get the door for me, that would be great," she said when her laughter subsided.

I followed her into the café, and she set the boxes down on the counter. I tried not to let my surprise show on my face. I was looking at an African princess, deposited magically in the very small town of Walden Corners. Nearly six feet tall, with cocoa brown skin, close-cropped natural hair, and a straight bearing, she had a regal air that seemed at odds with her hearty laugh and open manner. Over coffee, I learned that her family had lived just outside of town for nearly two hundred years, that her husband Henry, otherwise known as Coach, was the football coach at Walden High School, that her son Scooter, who didn't want anyone to know his real name was Severn, built model airplanes and played basketball, and that the boxes were filled with pies: peach, rhubarb, pecan, apple, blueberry, and her own secret-ingredient pear-custard pie.

We sat for an hour, talking about pie and life, gourds and dreams, and for the first time since I'd moved out of the city, the knot in my chest loosened. Nobody paid attention to the odd couple we surely were: tall, dark, lithe, and gracious Nora and me, five inches shorter, not-quite blonde, not-quite blue-eyed, with what my Grandma Becky extolled as womanly curves and I called a perennial need to lose ten pounds. The hour rushed by, my shoulders came down from what I'd feared would be a permanent place near my ears, and we chattered and giggled and traded stories about trying to make a living in a world too malled for its own good. I had made my first country friend.

Nora Johnson knew everyone within thirty miles of town, knew their special talents and their quirks and even many of their secrets. She'd steer me toward the person to remove those stumps.

But Nora, like most normal people in the country and in the city, was still sleeping, and I was too caffeinated and too upset by those screams to even consider going back to bed. I jotted a reminder on my to-do list and wandered back into the space that Tom Ford called the Great Room, giving the fifteen-by-fifteen-foot space an undeserved grandeur. I drifted over to the bookshelf, glanced at the titles that had become so familiar to me since I'd moved in. Tom's books covered everything from Asian art to Zero Population Growth. My original plan was to start at the upper left corner of the shelves and work my way through the three or four hundred books systematically, but my impulsiveness kept me from following so neat a project. I reached my hand out and pulled down the first thing my fingers touched.

Stepping into the Stream. I'd never met Tom, but I'd spoken to him on the telephone about a hundred times and he'd never mentioned an interest in trout fishing. When I flipped the book open, though, I realized that it was a collection of essays about Buddhism. The pages had that worn look, as though they'd been fingered many times. Where would he have sat to read this? I pictured him on the porch, bare feet planted firmly on the wood planks. The charcoal-gray buttoned-down Tom of an earlier fantasy floated off into a corner. The Tom of tonight's imagining was slender and brown-haired with wire-rimmed glasses à la John Lennon. Dressed in loose clothing, his dark eyes moved deliberately from word to word, his concentration complete.

Would Tom have known what kind of creature was capable of producing that scream? I shook my head, made sketches for some new gourd designs, ran out of steam, and just sat, staring out the window

22

into the velvet sky. The silence was deep and still and I started to believe I'd imagined that horrible sound.

Tired at last, I left all the lights on and went back up the creaky stairs. I'd call Nora in the morning. Meanwhile, I'd try not to worry about the hundreds of sheep I'd be force-marching over that rickety fence before I could fall into a light and watchful sleep.

Chapter 2

It took two days of playing telephone tag for me to connect with Nora, and when I did the conversation was stilted and abrupt. Something was bothering her, and if she wouldn't talk about it over the phone, at least she consented to a visit on Saturday morning so that I could bring her four kiwis that were in danger of spoiling if someone didn't use them.

The house was a surprise to me the first time I saw it, like so many things about Nora and her family. Four rectangles joined to form a quirky W in a wood-and-windows modern structure with tile floors and a cathedral ceiling. Nora and Coach had filled it with cream-colored furniture and African art. Those windows glowed with south light that would pour through the bare winter branches of the maple trees ringing the front lawn, but I worried that they were too close to Scooter Johnson's basketball hoop.

Scooter and his friend Armel Noonan waved as I pulled into the driveway. They were proof of the Opposites Attract rule. Tall, slender, and blond, Armel moved with the grace of someone comfortable with his body. At fifteen, Scooter was three inches shorter than his friend, his skin the color of toasted almonds, and he didn't yet seem to be entirely in control of his arms and legs. He still had the childish sweetness that a little chubbiness around the mouth gives to so many boys, but his smile was the shy smile of a young man just discovering the opposite sex.

"Hey, Lili." Scooter dribbled the ball, feinted toward the basket while Armel waved his arms to block the shot. Scooter stumbled, landing on hands and knees, and his laughing friend reached out a hand to help him up.

I looked away to give him a chance to collect himself. As though nothing had happened, I said, "Hey, Scooter. Your mom in the kitchen?"

He grunted something that sounded like an affirmative and tossed the ball into the basket in a single clean shot. I walked around to the back of the house.

Nora hollered for me to come in, and when I pushed open the door I inhaled the spicy aroma of nutmeg and sugar and pears.

"Well, look at you, half asleep and driving. How come you look like you need a nap at nine thirty in the morning?" Nora lifted a tray of pies from the oven and set them on a cooling rack, her movements slow and practiced.

Whatever I'd heard in her voice on the phone seemed to have vanished. I chided myself for not giving Nora the same kind of permission I'd give any of my city friends to have and then un-have a bad day.

"Some animal woke me a couple of nights ago and I haven't really slept soundly since then." When her eyes widened expectantly, I shook my head. "Don't you go imagining dangerous liaisons, Nora. I mean, I think I heard something in the woods. Are there bobcats around here? That's a real question."

"No panthers, no lions or tigers, oh my. But I have heard talk of bobcats. Why?"

"That scream that woke me up. It sounded . . . well, not human. At least, I hope it wasn't human. I can't make the memory of it go away." I realized how silly that sounded. "I guess it wasn't as bad as a police siren screeching down the street at three in the morning."

"You're just being a city scaredy-cat."

She moved with assurance around the kitchen, tossing bowls and beaters into the sink, running hot water into them, scrubbing spots of flour off the counter.

"Since I can't deny it, let's just change the subject. Kiwis," I said, setting the fruit on her counter, "and stump removal."

"Their pits aren't *that* big." Nora sniffed the furry skin of one of the kiwis and made an approving humming sound as she waited for me to explain.

"Tree stumps. I need my own personal Paul Bunyan to come and help me out. I'm going to put in a gourd garden, but the perfect spot is littered with tree stumps."

"So call Tom Ford. He used to have a landscaper from Chatham take care of the place. Probably can tell you all sorts of things about the soil. Just call Tom."

"I can't. I have no idea where he is. His mutual fund company is out of business or moved to Mars, but I sure can't find it. The phone numbers I have for the Ford Fund are all disconnected." Maybe Nora could help me fill in a few blanks. "What was he like, Nora? I mean, was he tall, young, nice, mean, rugged, what?"

She shrugged. "Never met the man. Never even saw him. Wasn't he at your closing?"

"He sent his lawyer. Funny, I spoke to him at least twice a day for five months. I got so I could tell just from the sound of his laughter whether he was making some sarcastic comment or was truly tickled by something."

She stared at me. "You worked for him and you never met him?"

"Weird, right? I should have known from that first breathless telephone call that this would be no ordinary business relationship, but instead I was charmed."

"Intrigued." She nodded.

"Flattered," I added.

"Nah, that's not why Tom Ford struck a chord in you."

I surprised myself by saying, "He made me aware of possibilities."

When she stepped closer and looked directly into my eyes, I knew that after four months of friendship it was time for me to tell her the rest of my story. In a way, I'd been protecting both Tom and myself by letting everyone believe the transaction that gave me ownership of the cottage was simple and ordinary.

"I guess my world had become unfamiliar territory. Lots of things, a combination of events that I think of as My Years of Living Dangerously."

"Starting with September eleventh?" she asked quietly.

"Yes. It was awful. A direct hit on my life and my work and my home and my feelings of safety. I saw those towers fall from my apartment in Brooklyn."

"The first time you told me, I didn't get it. I guess what I understand now is that the closer you were, the harder it must have been."

Nora was right, and I'd begun to believe that even if I talked about it for hours, I couldn't truly convey what that morning was like. Which was why I hardly ever talked about the images that had burned into my brain as flames consumed the tops of those buildings, or the dislocation that had lodged in my gut as I dragged gallons of water and a stack of paper cups to greet the exodus of stunned, dust-covered neighbors who poured across the bridge to get back to Brooklyn. I'd realized recently that I'd been driven to act that day, to help, to do something. That had seemed necessary, but maybe the real purpose had been to comfort myself.

Now I could only nod.

"So you decided to buy the cottage to fix what was wrong with your world." Her long fingers working swiftly, Nora peeled a kiwi and started slicing it into thin, even circles.

"It was such a queer, quirky place. I mean, it was like the Before picture in a slick magazine about home makeovers. The clapboards probably used to be white, but at first sight they reminded me of Aunt Millie. You know, the one who always needs her roots touched up. One of the downspouts hung by a thread, like a baby tooth about to fall out. But that house sat on three of the most beautiful acres I'd ever seen. And when I bent down and saw one purple hyacinth pushing through the melting snow, I took it as a sign that I could grow here."

"Outgrow Ed Thorsen, maybe?"

I nodded. "I'd accepted his marriage proposal out of duty, you know? Just like I'd responsibly finished every indigestion-inducing writing assignment on time. The cottage made me feel that something in me might bloom in different soil. Only, I didn't buy it."

"Well, I know you didn't steal it. And I also know you pay the taxes on it. So, how did you get it?"

"Tom Ford gave it to me."

Kiwi slices slid from her hands onto the counter. "What?"

"He gave me the cottage because he didn't have the cash to pay me for the work I did for him."

I didn't need to tell Nora all the details, didn't need to rob Tom, absent though he was, of the dignity he so obviously cherished. He'd said, "Listen, I'm starting a new mutual fund company and I want you to write a thirty-page insert for one of the industry magazines and bios for three financial analysts. They're stuffy, boring people and I need them to sound interesting. Katalina Negron says you can do magic with dry facts, so I'd like you to sprinkle a little fairy dust on their very sedate shoulders, all right?"

When I told him that most financial analysts truly were fascinating because they knew what *fiduciary* meant, he hired me on the spot and sent me a check for the first month's work and a thick packet of dry, nearly clinical biographical material on Mssrs. Chapman, Reston, and Payne by courier the next day. I wrote and rewrote those bios until Mr. Chapman had all the daring of a corporate Russell Crowe, Mr. Reston had acquired the panache of a financial Johnny Depp, and Mr. Payne, who was eighty-three and had bushy eyebrows that hid his steely glare, had achieved the *je ne sais quoi* of Denzel Washington. After that ordeal, the thirty-page insert practically wrote itself.

As for Tom Ford, it was his voice, assured and playful, and his pauses, in which I imagined him listening intently for nuances, that had intrigued me and made me do such good work.

And then I waited for the balance of my money. It hadn't taken long for the excuses to begin.

At first, Tom had invoked the ubiquitous cash-flow dilemma, and then he became apologetic. He was adamant that I'd have the money, that he was not the kind of man to walk away from a debt, and he even managed to convince me to finish the job — over the phone, as he did all his business with me. Finally, he told me that he had a cottage on a country road on the way to the Berkshires and if I would cover one year's back taxes, he would sign the deed over to me as payment for the money he owed me for my Ford Fund work.

I hung up on him the first time he made that offer and had walked straight to Karen Gerber's house. After I told her about Tom's proposition, Karen shook her brown spiky hair and grinned. "Sheesh, Lili, I swear you are the luckiest person I know.

You can freelance, for goodness sakes — generate a corporate client base that would cover you if you didn't have to pay rent and buy your groceries at some outrageously expensive bodega."

That sounded good.

Then she went for the kill. "And you can finally find out if you really do want to spend the rest of your life playing Gourdmother."

Better and better.

"Ed might like living in the country," I ventured. "I mean, they have middle schools upstate and they need principals there too."

Karen never said a word, never let a glimmer of scolding show in her dark eyes. She hadn't even crossed her arms under her small breasts. She just stood in front of me and waited.

"Okay, so he won't ever leave his job. Maybe that's the point. Maybe if I take this opportunity, it will be easier to explain that I'm not ready to get married."

"That you're not ready to get married to sweet, safe *him*."

We high-fived to starting over, to girlfriends, to inner truth.

When I called Tom to tell him I would accept his offer, he'd sounded relieved and tired. Four days later, I drove up to Walden Corners and saw the inside of my new home for the first time. Tom had left everything, every stick of furniture, every dish, spoon, pot, and scrub brush. Toothpaste still sat on a shelf in the bathroom, but not a stitch of clothing or a photograph was anywhere in sight. When I tried to phone him to ask him if he wanted his books, I heard that nasal recorded voice inform me that the number was no longer in service. Tom Ford had disappeared.

Now, sitting in Nora Johnson's kitchen, I wondered if I hadn't simply traded one set of problems for another. Screams in the night. A bathroom window that leaked water during thunderstorms. A boiler that might need replacing before winter. And three obdurate tree stumps that probably had roots two miles long in the very place I wanted to grow gourds.

"We can talk about Tom another time." Nora had turned the kiwi slices into a ring of emerald around the golden disc of sunshiny lemon custard. "Back to the intriguing topic of stump removal."

"Good. I need some. Stumps removed, I mean. Who can do that?"

"Bobby Benson. He's a kid, but he knows what he's doing." She frowned and shook another pie pan. "Custard's too runny. Better let it cook another three minutes."

"Just hand me a fork. I'll see if it's okay. No charge for my services." The aroma in the kitchen made my taste buds tingle.

She stretched out her arms and placed her body between me and the pies and grinned. "Stay away, Lili. Tomorrow is Ag Day. If we can sell enough pies, we can buy uniforms for six or seven kids on the football team."

"Ag Day?"

"As in agriculture. The basis of this town's economy, the foundation of its history, the pride of its citizens. You *have* to come with us. It's great — a combination harvest festival, carnival, and history lesson."

"In the middle of November? Why don't they do it when it's warmer?"

Nora sucked air between her teeth. "*Harvest,* get it? They've been doing it in November for over a hundred years. Truly, since the late nineteenth century. After all the crops are in and safely stored for the winter. Anyway, you haven't lived until you've seen a tractor pull."

"I can't imagine someone strong enough to pull a tractor. This I have to see."

"Good," she said, pushing a plate toward me. "Tell me if you'd buy this. If you didn't know me, I mean."

I lifted a forkful, sniffed the spice, admired the glistening plum that sat nestled in its gleaming syrup, and bit into the heavenly tasting fruit. "This one's perfect. Your jury didn't like it?"

"Scooter loved it, but Coach thought it was too sweet." Nora ducked behind the refrigerator door, but not fast enough for me to miss the cloud that came over her as she spoke her husband's name.

"Aha! Gotcha, Nora. What's wrong? Your whole face changed when you mentioned Coach. Where is he?" I might have been treading into personal space, but this seemed to be the morning for a little mutual secret sharing.

"Upstairs. Outside. In the shop. I don't know." She placed both flour-covered hands on the counter and looked at me with an expression that seemed more sad than angry. Nora's nose wrinkled as she sniffed the air and then let out a cry as she yanked open the oven door. "Darn! Burned. I haven't done that in years. I'm just so worried about him. He's been stomping around. Withdrawn. Growling. I've never seen him —"

"Three tree stumps!" I practically shouted, looking past her to the shadow that had appeared in the doorway. "If I can get those stumps removed, I can grow my own gourds."

"Where's Scooter?" Coach demanded. He was three inches taller than Nora, two shades darker, and his shaved head gleamed in the morning sun. A tiny gold earring caught the light when he turned his head. He nodded at me, looked away, and folded his arms across his chest.

"Hey, Coach. How's it going?" I smiled, but he only glanced in my direction.

"I need him to come with me to school," Coach said. "We have to set up the booth."

He wasn't the most talkative person I'd met in Walden Corners, but Coach's terseness and his social gracelessness amounted to weird behavior for this normally friendly man. I sat on the stool and watched Nora's face to see if I could pick up a hint of what was going on, but her expression remained neutral.

"Let him be," she said to her husband. "He's got basketball practice in an hour."

Coach wheeled and stalked out of the room, and I felt as though the world had spun out of orbit. Nora and Coach were the perfect couple. They didn't fight. They didn't sulk.

"What's going on?" my mouth said, although my mind knew I was intruding on a private situation.

"Two days ago he woke up on the wrong side of the bed," Nora said. "Went to work like a normal human being, came home, disappeared into his workshop, came to bed late. Next day, he woke up like he'd been trampled by the lions and the gladiators, both at once. He's been acting really closed off. He won't talk to me. 'Pass the salt.' 'See you after school.' That's it. I've asked him twice a day to tell me what's bothering him, but he just brushes me off. When he's home he sits at his bench in the workshop and he stares. He takes two bites of his food and then gets up from the table. It's like he's sleepwalking. I'm worried, Lili. I've never seen him like this before. Never."

I hugged her and felt her heart pounding against her ribs. "That *is* strange," I said softly, wondering that two days of withdrawal should translate into so much concern.

"I can come up with a million possible explanations. Not a single one is good."

I stepped back and tried to think. What

could I do to help? At once, my mind swirled with stories. Coach was having an affair. Coach was addicted to uppers, downers, cocaine, alcohol. Coach was about to be fired. Coach had some incurable disease. Nora was right. None of my explanations had anything good going on.

"How long did you say?" I asked, as much to turn off my brain as to get an actual answer.

"I told you. Two days." She wrinkled her forehead. "Which makes it three days after Scooter got a C on his geometry test. Two days after those screams woke you. Four days after I signed on to make desserts for that new French bistro in Rhinebeck. And three days after he came home late from football practice."

I only half-listened as she went on talking. Of all the people I'd met in Walden Corners, Coach Johnson was the one I'd never, ever figure to go off the deep end. He was too solid, too easygoing, too sure of his place in the world.

"Maybe he's having a midlife crisis," I said lamely.

"At thirty-eight?" Her whole body sagged, and all I could do was put my arm around her and hope that my gesture offered even a little comfort.

Chapter 3

The village of Walden Corners, set midway between the Hudson River and the Berkshire Mountains, bustled with activity on weekends, but on the Sunday of Agriculture Day it seemed that the whole county had converged on the Walden High School parking lot. Cars lined both main streets and snaked their way up the hill, parked at odd angles by people who hardly ever needed to fit into neat parallel spaces. I nodded hello to Charles Kimball, the high school math teacher, and to Elizabeth Conklin, whose sleek, pulled-back chestnut hair contributed to the pulled-together confidence she exuded. Elizabeth was an attorney who always seemed distracted by whatever knotty legal problem she was being paid to unravel. I wondered whether country lawyers, whose bread and butter I presumed to be real estate transactions and wills, had progressed to prenups and wrongful liposuction suits. But I'd probably never know. I'd met Elizabeth twice when I was in The Creamery with Nora, and she didn't seem at all interested in talking to me.

The mid-November energy was contagious. Hopefully, soon I would become one with the hundreds of people milling about on the six-acre high school campus having a grand old country time, instead of feeling like I was wearing a blinking neon sign announcing "City Transplant! City Transplant!" With few exceptions people smiled and nodded, chatting in small groups, all ages apparently connected by some invisible community thread. Which made the exceptions really stand out. One man, his ferretlike features pulled into a sour expression, stared at Nora and then turned his glare on me, muttering something indistinguishable as we walked past.

"Ira Jackson," Nora said with a laugh. "Believes that you, a white woman, are endangering the social fabric of America by being with me, decidedly un-white. He's had a rough time. You know, the old story — he needs to feel superior to someone, so he's picked the most visibly different family in town. He doesn't bite, though . . . at least not yet. He just blusters and everyone ignores him. Except his son, Will, who seems to be trying to follow in Daddy's footsteps."

Nora pointed out the Viking in jeans, muscle shirt, and leather jacket, standing beside a pert girl who hung onto his arm as though she were on a pitching ship on a rolling sea. "Will Jackson has been Coach's trial and tribulation for the past two years. Captain of the football team and he's always in a contest of wills with my husband."

"Anyone ever think of giving the Jackson men a one-way ticket to . . . I don't know, where do they still practice cannibalism? People are still walking around with those feelings? Creepy."

Nora smiled and shrugged as I linked my arm through hers. We wandered past the main school building, a U-shaped brick affair, following two dads pushing strollers. The smell of grilling meat and cotton candy reminded me of the dirty-water hot dogs and sugar-coated peanuts that vendors hawk from carts all over Manhattan. On this gorgeous fall day, memories of those familiar smells seemed like intrusions.

Nora seemed lighter, more at ease than she'd been in her kitchen the day before. We strolled among the exhibits — pan-

42

oramas of farms built in shoeboxes, fanciful animals made of vegetables and pipe cleaners.

"Where are Scooter and Coach?" I asked.

Instantly, her eyes lowered and a muscle in her jaw tightened. I wanted to take my question back, restore the sunshiny nonchalance, but it was like trying to put the juice back into the orange. Nora's step slowed and she turned to answer me, but before she could say anything, a slender man in his twenties stopped directly in front of her, blocking our way. He was burnished and gleaming, his skin scrubbed pink, his shirt well-ironed with a knife-sharp crease down the center of each sleeve, his boots polished to a high shine. The comb marks in his damp hair made his head look like an aerial photograph of a neatly planted wheat field.

"Hey, Alvin, how's your mother feeling?" Nora's voice was a little high, a little strained, but her smile was soft and real.

Alvin's lip curled into a sneer as he said, "She doesn't need anything from *you* or anyone in your family. We'll get what's ours one way or another."

My stomach churned from the hate in his voice. I glanced over at Nora's stricken face, grabbed her elbow, and steered her away from the scowling young man.

"Let's go that way." We veered off toward two large wood structures at the edge of the football field. "What was that about?"

Her face softened and she exhaled loudly. "I thought we were done with all that nonsense. An ancient property dispute. Alvin Akron's grandfather sold Coach's father a field fifty years ago, and Alvin claims the contract was never valid because Coach's father didn't pay the full amount and . . . never mind. He's just an angry boy, and I won't let him ruin this beautiful day."

"You ever consider mediation?" Having been part of the magic of mediation for five years as a volunteer, it was hard not to proselytize.

Nora frowned. "That's what labor unions do."

"Every county in New York has a community mediation center. You can go, meet with a trained mediator, maybe leave with a new way to deal with the situation." I had to be careful talking about this, or I'd start sounding like a televangelist on speed. "You talk, you get help to focus on the future. And you decide what will work and what won't. It's not foolproof, but when it succeeds, boy, it saves everyone a ton of grief."

"Too late. We've had at least a thousand pounds of misery already from Alvin. Come on, let's see the livestock." Nora led me to the open doorway of a green barn-like structure, and I dropped the pitch. Coercion and mediation are about as compatible as anchovies and blueberry syrup.

At the entrance to the building, the smells changed, becoming nothing at all that I recognized from the city. This was farm perfume — cows and pigs and goats and rabbits all giving off their very own very strong scents. I found it not unpleasant, especially in contrast to the cat boxes some of my city friends maintained in their apartments.

"Now you'll get to see real animal life. Not just dogs and pigeons and squirrels." Nora pulled her finger from the mesh of a cage in time to avoid being pecked by a chicken sporting stunningly iridescent feathers and a nasty attitude.

We strolled the length of the building, pausing to admire nervous calves with twitchy tails, a trio of white goats looking for mischief, and a mama pig and her litter of nine snoozing peacefully in clean hay. At each stall, two or three children between the ages of eight and near adulthood attended to their charges, grooming the animals, changing water buckets, scooping dusty feed into plastic troughs. One little girl with her hair in two thick braids sat peacefully reading beside a spindly-legged calf. She turned pages with one hand while the other stroked the smooth space between his eyes. I wondered what impact it might have on the lives of city kids if they had to take care of another living creature.

My rumination was interrupted by Nora's laughter. I turned to see her hug a lanky redhead in jeans and a brilliant orange sweatshirt. A second woman, whose perfectly cut bob and impeccable charcoal pantsuit made her look as though she'd stepped out of a magazine ad for gracious living, beamed at the huggers.

"Lili," Nora said finally, "meet my sixth grade buddies. This is Susan Clemants. Susan's just back from her honeymoon. A long weekend in New York City. Susan teaches high school social studies, and her husband is a science teacher in the middle school. They'll take the rest of their honeymoon next summer. Japan, can you imagine? And this is Melissa Paul. The proprietor of the Taconic Inn — you know, that gorgeous place about a mile east of here. Winner of the coveted Innkeeper of the Year award for last year, and very brave to take half a day off during Leaf Peeper season to come to Ag Day. Susan, Melissa, this is Lili Marino, gourd artist, freelance corporate writer, and owner of Tom Ford's cottage. And my friend."

The friend part warmed me, but I felt a little overwhelmed by all the new information and by the longstanding connections among the three. I stuck out my hand and offered a too hearty "Glad to meet you" and then found myself oddly tongue-tied. When in doubt, ask a question, my city instincts told me. I turned to the new bride and asked, "Did you see any plays in the city?"

"No, we just . . . well, we walked a lot and went to the planetarium and ate at some really, really good restaurants." Susan's fair skin turned pink and her red curls flamed around her head, reminding me that honeymooners don't need the theater to provide entertainment.

Rather than say anything silly to Ms. Bed-and-Breakfast, I decided to let someone else take the conversational lead.

Which Melissa Paul obliged me by doing. "I'd love to have you come by some time and see the inn. Deer season starts to-morrow, and our regular customers usually stay away until after Thanksgiving, so I'll offer our winter menu in early December. No sense in wasting all that creativity on the guys who drag their camouflage suits out of the closets once a year to come up here to guzzle beer and kill things."

"Thanks. I'd love to. I've passed the inn, but I didn't realize it was a restaurant as well."

Melissa took that as an opening to chatter on for a while about food and linens, until Nora tugged at my arm. "We've got to go see a man about tree stump removal. Maybe we can all get to-gether for girls' night sometime."

"Only if we can play poker again." The glint in Susan's eye brightened.

"And drink Cosmos," Nora said.

"And eat spaghetti." Melissa tossed her bob, grinned, and turned to me. "You'll love it."

Speechless but giddy at the prospect of what sounded like a grown-up version of a pajama party, I gave the idea and the three women standing near me a big thumbs-up.

"Let's not forget to tell Elizabeth." Me-lissa walked out into the sunshine.

Susan followed her, and I pushed away the flicker of annoyance at the mention of Elizabeth's name, a feeling that threatened to dampen my enjoyment of poker night. Nora and I headed toward the next stall, which seemed filled to bursting with a snorting, quivering mass of animal.

"That one's a bull," I said.

"Hmmm, even a city girl can tell the difference." Nora laughed. "So, you're well versed in bovine anatomy. Hey, wait, here's someone else I want you to meet."

A couple headed our way, the man tall and squarish, his shoulders, belly, and hips all the same dimension. He wore a plaid barn jacket and new dark blue jeans, and surprisingly, dark glasses. The woman beside him had one of those high-wattage smiles that lights up a room. Her long salt-and-pepper hair hung down her back in a single braid.

"Jane, Fred, this is my friend Lili Marino. I suggested she talk to Bobby about some work she needs done. Lili, aside from being Bobby's parents, Fred Benson is the master of the broken chainsaw, lawn-mower, snow blower; you name it, he can fix it. And Jane is the local expert on Africa. Visited six or seven times."

Jane Benson's handshake was as warm as

her smile, but her husband's felt like a perfunctory fulfillment of a social obligation.

"Nice to meet you both. This is my first Ag Day, and I'm a little overwhelmed. These kids are amazing."

Jane nodded. "They learn a lot from raising animals and doing all the research for those funny vegetable sculptures. We were just headed over to see Bobby. He should be up soon in the tractor pull. Want to join us?"

We wriggled through the crowd, past a booth where two young granola types were collecting signatures protesting the building of a cement plant on prime Hudson River waterfront property, to the baseball field. Fred and Jane Benson climbed to the top row of bleacher seats, and Nora and I followed behind. My face warmed instantly in the sun, and I watched the action, if it could be called that, with amusement. Tractors idled in a snaking line, waiting to be hooked up to a pallet loaded with heavy slabs of stone. At a signal from a coverall-clad official, the next tractor, a faded red behemoth, chugged forward a few feet. The driver, who looked about Scooter's age, struggled to keep his face from revealing his anxiety as he peered over his shoulder. Two men bent down, positioned a heavy hook into the tractor's ring, and then stepped back.

One man dropped his arm and the tractor inched forward. I could hardly keep from laughing, thinking about the yellow cabs idling at lights in Manhattan, screeching off in a haze of burning rubber as they raced to the beat the next light. In just a few seconds, the tractor was groaning, straining like an ant trying to carry off a hamburger.

The tractor huffed. Its wheels spun in a rut and it stopped dead. Even from forty feet away, I could see the driver's face flush with embarrassment so painful that I had to turn away.

"Poor Bobby," Nora whispered. "He should never have entered that broken-down old thing. His brother won eight years ago with that Farmall, but it looks like it's lost its juice. Now he's going to hide his face for weeks."

I glanced down the row past Nora and realized that Fred and Jane Benson were no longer seated beside her. Maybe they'd gone to console their son. Nora's mouth puckered with concern. "Coach had him playing starting linebacker for the junior varsity team last year, but whenever Bobby went into one of his Mr. Sensitive slumps he forgot to show up for practice. Jane married Fred just this past spring, and we all hoped that would help Bobby. He never seemed quite comfortable, but a boy raised without a mother, well . . . she took off about a year after Bobby was born. Anyway, Coach moved him to the varsity team this year, but only because he promised not to miss a single practice unless he was in bed with a fever *and* a broken leg."

"Maybe he'd feel better if I offered him the stump removal job right now. That might boost his confidence."

"Lili, for someone who claims to be mystified by kids, you are one smart cookie." She hooked her arm through mine and guided me to the edge of the crowd. "Just pretend you didn't see his . . . stuck-in-the-mud performance."

We headed toward the gate, where men stood leaning against the fence with their thumbs hooked into their belt loops in that classic I'm-a-cowboy pose. Manly men, Karen would say in her knowing Brooklyn way, the kind without complications. I groaned at how she would romanticize the locals, never considering that they might beat their wives or fart in church. And what would Ed Thorsen make of them? Dear, constant Ed, recovering nicely from the heartbreak of my rejection by dating a financial analyst. All this rough, good-natured joking and poking would be so alien to him.

"Hey, Nora, have you seen Ron? And Coach?"

I blinked myself out of my reverie and looked over at Nora, whose expression seemed to leap into neutral at the mention of her husband's name. No, I hadn't imagined that avoidance earlier. She was doing it again, offering a controlled smile to the smooth-shaven man with the dark brown eyes and warm smile. Nora shaded her eyes with her hand, her pink palm tilted slightly. "Last I saw them, they were talking over near the calf barn. Seth, this is my friend Lili Marino. Lili, meet Seth Selinsky."

This handshake was definitely not perfunctory. It had been a while since I'd felt a frisson of anticipation from a casual touch, but this man held my hand and my gaze a beat longer than I'd expected and I liked the way it felt. Of course, I told myself, he's probably happily married and this is just how he relates to women — one of those men whose job it is to charm you and make you feel as though you were most attractive thing in his universe. A quick glance at his left hand showed no wedding ring, but that wasn't always proof of anything.

"Nice to meet you," I said, really meaning it. "Is it true that everyone in town is here?"

"Only the best and the brightest," he said, smiling. "Listen, I'll see you later, Nora. Nice to meet you, Ms. Marino." He pivoted and marched toward the livestock display.

"Umm, brusque or reserved?" These displays of rudeness bothered me out of proportion to the offenses. I wanted my country folks to be kind and gentle and well-mannered.

"That's so not like Seth. He's always the salesman, always *Sweetie* this and *Honey* that. He's a mortgage broker with the biggest client list in the county. Maybe he's mad because his son's not getting enough time on the field. Coach told me Ron's been too swaggery lately, so he decided to take him down a notch. And from what I've seen, Ron doesn't come down very easily. But then he's a defensive tackle, so he shouldn't."

The boy who shuffled toward us stood at least two inches over six feet and weighed enough to give those tractors some trouble, I thought.

Nora leaned closer to me and whispered, "Here comes Bobby. He's looking pretty glum."

When he reached the fence, he lifted his head and mumbled something that sounded like "Glmph Nkjy."

"No, you did fine." Apparently, Nora was multilingual. "Do you know Lili Marino? She's the new owner of Tom Ford's place, out on Iron Mill Road."

Bobby's stare confused me for a moment. Was I supposed to extend my hand? Say something? Wait for him to acknowledge that I existed? This level of self-consciousness had long vanished, gone with my teenage skin problems, and I felt silly to be so confused. He was a sixteen-year-old boy who was embarrassed by his performance, and it wasn't even the kind of performance-failure men three times his age worried about. I didn't need to let his awkwardness intimidate me.

"Hey, Bobby. Nice to meet you. Listen, I don't know if you have the time, but I need to have some stumps pulled up out of my garden. Do you think you could come over with the tractor and do that? I'll pay you for it."

Nothing. This boy was redefining taciturn. Not even the offer of pay made him glance up. A smile twinkled in Nora's mischievous eyes, letting me know that she wasn't about to help me out with our grim-faced boy. I was on my own here.

"How does a hundred dollars sound?"

Nora's eyes widened and her hands waved like a Las Vegas dealer signaling no more bets.

I had offered too little money. Insulted him. I knew how much to tip cab drivers and doormen and waiters in fancy restaurants, but I should have asked Nora about what was appropriate to pay for stump removal services.

"Each," I said, my voice a little quavery with apology.

Bobby mumbled something that sounded like, "Rmjd ngenv drfl," and pointed to Fred Benson, who leaned against a fence rail looking a little like a refrigerator-shaped Marlboro Man. For a big boy, Bobby hardly made a sound as he sidled off into the crowd.

Nora's laughter spilled out. "You just paid twice what everyone else does for Bobby's time. And he said he couldn't do it for a while because he had to stay around the shop and help his father fix chainsaws and lawnmowers."

Chapter 4

Since daybreak, the woods had been alive with the crack of rifles, shots going off so frequently that I thought I'd left my popcorn maker on by mistake. The opening of hunting season had been discussed at length at The Creamery the last time I was there, and I was glad that its arrival hadn't taken me by surprise. Glad, too, that it meant that in three weeks Nora and I would meet Susan Clemants and Elizabeth Conklin at Melissa Paul's inn for lunch. None of them was Karen, never would be, but then why should they be? I wondered whether Elizabeth required a seven-year apprenticeship in country living before she would accept me as a real member of the community.

The weather, thank goodness, was still pleasant, hadn't yet shifted into the dark, blustery chill that heralded winter. I still had to clean the outside mold from thirty-two gourds, a messy job at best and a health-endangering one if not done properly. All those dried-out little fibers that cushion and protect the seeds could lodge in lungs and eyes and cause irritation, but the real danger was the outside mold. Still, it was all part of the process, and the fact was that I enjoyed even this task, the beginning of the gourd transformation. Working outdoors was by far the best way to avoid problems, and even then, wearing a mask was prudent. With four days of concentrated effort, I could get them all cut, get the gourd guts cleaned out, and be able to do it all on my deck. Another three days of sanding their bumpy insides and I'd be ready for winter.

I rolled the small wire cart that held my tools — miniature jigsaw; Dremel rotary tool and all its bits, sanders, grinders, and cutters; the handsaw I used as a last resort; the scrapers and the sandpaper and all the supplies for cutting and cleaning the insides of my gourds — to a spot beside the picnic table on the back deck, then brought out eight gourds. They were light, even with the seeds and pulp still inside, with medium-thick shells that would be perfect for making intricate cuts with the mini jigsaw. My heart beat a little faster in anticipation, as it always did when I began a gourd session.

At least Tom Ford had the foresight to put an electrical outlet outside. This time, I pictured a short, balding Tom working hard to impress some exotic dark-haired guest who lounged in a chair with a strappy sandal dangling from her pedicured foot. He had overcome his lack of movie star looks by becoming a Titan of Industry, and he talked about his deals while plying his guest with killer margaritas from the blender he used out on the deck — rural performance art that he worked hard to perfect.

Funny how much not knowing a person made me think about him.

I picked up a gourd, turned it in my hand, feeling the smooth hardness of the surface, enjoying its curves and the satisfying curlicue of the stem end. This one would be a lidded container. The pear shape was perfect — tapered on one end, the bottom a flat surface where the blossom had been. I set the gourd on the non-slip drawer liner I used to keep it from skittering away from me and picked up my Exacto knife, working the blade back and forth, back and forth. I held my breath until that awesome moment when the knife cut through the hard shell. My mind was an idea factory, designs and rim treatments and colors all pouring out, floating in the morning quiet. I felt myself edge into that state of complete concentration, of nothing else existing but me and and the gourd and a soft rain of ideas. Bliss.

As I pulled the respirator mask up over my nose, something rustled in the woods just beyond the house and I looked up. Despite the warm sun, I shivered, remembering the scream that had come from that direction more than a month earlier. I thought I had succeeded in putting it out of my mind, but here it was again, alive in my memory.

Better to concentrate on the work at hand. I adjusted the saw, flipped the switch with my thumb, and guided the blade along the cut line I'd drawn. It flowed through the shell like a sailboat slicing the green waters of the Hudson River. When I reached full circle, the newly cut pieces came apart with a satisfying crunch. The moment of truth, of seeing what nature had in store for me this time, made my breath catch, but this time it also made me grin. Instead of requiring hours of soaking and scraping, the fibrous matter had pulled away from the inner walls easily. A good gourd day. A *really* good gourd day.

The next gourd and the one after that

cut like a dream, and I hummed a Dixie Chicks song as I worked, enjoying the feel of the sun on my back and the breeze on my face. I picked up the next gourd, made the starting cut, and inserted the saw blade. I was right there, ready to slide along the gently curved edge I'd been seeing in my mind's eye, when I realized that my luck had run out. The saw stuttered and jammed against something hard. I pulled straight up to remove the saw, and as I did, the blade snapped.

This hadn't happened in a long time. I needed that package of replacement blades I'd ordered. And Jim Widess had assured me that the three new colors of Gilder's Paste that I'd ordered from the Caning Shop in Berkeley would be here by now. Maybe everything would be waiting for me at the post office in town. Sighing away my frustration, I packed up my tools and the gourds, rolled them back into the house, and grabbed my purse and car keys.

The drive into Walden Corners took less than ten minutes. I ran into the post office, thanked Martha McIntosh for my package — new blades, perfect timing, life was good again — and then headed for home. As tempting as it was to stop for coffee at The Creamery to catch up on the news and the gossip, my gourds exerted the stronger siren call. Happy in my skin — I finally understood what that felt like. Of course, it was skin that hadn't been touched in months, not by a man I cared about, but I had faith that that part of my life would someday change. No amount of speculation or planning could make it happen, and I was comfortable. Not waiting. Not seeking. Just enjoying the routine I'd established.

The trees along the road, bare of leaves except for a few bright red beauties that still clung stubbornly to spindly branches, creaked in the wind as I got back into my car. What would my first winter in Walden Corners bring? Icy roads. Isolation. Downed power lines, no heat, food supplies running low. I laughed at my pioneer imaginings. This was Columbia County, where twice weekly deliveries of bagels from the Upper West Side of Manhattan were a long-established fact of life.

As I approached a crossroads, a milk truck roared through the intersection, barely pausing at the stop sign. My indignation flared, and I nearly responded with a city gesture that would have embarrassed my country friends. I drove up the hill and noticed how the weeds at the edge of the road seemed to be grayer than they'd been a week earlier. The golden cast was gone. I watched a straggling V of geese, like a shower of confetti for a heavenly parade, and I nearly ran myself into a ditch following their progress.

Just as I was about to deliver a familiar lecture-to-self about keeping focus, a shape in the pond down the hill caught my eye. My heart pounded when it registered on my wandering brain that it might be human, a person whose outspread arms and long legs floated in a position that had nothing to do with swimming.

I swerved, pulled in to a turnout, parked beside a green Taurus, and got out of my car. The Taurus, empty except for a blue and gold cap tossed on the passenger seat, seemed familiar, but my brain refused to make a connection. Call the police. That was what I needed to do, but I'd left my cell phone home. Half a day could pass on this road without a car driving by, so waiting to flag down another vehicle wasn't going to get me help. I squinted to try to see better, wishing that I had binoculars in the car, along with my cell phone. Whatever was floating at the edge of the pond, I was sure it didn't belong there. Even without the binoculars, I knew that it was a person in Miller's pond. A chill silence covered me, and I felt very alone and afraid. Afraid to look, but more afraid not to.

I walked several feet into the woods and started down the hill, and as I got closer the terrible truth peeled away my disbelief. Even from fifty feet away, I could see the gleaming bald head, the darker hole blossoming in the dark skin. The tiny glint of gold.

Coach.

I stopped and looked again to make sure my eyes weren't playing tricks. The broad shoulders and narrow waist . . . my stomach wrenched. I screamed out his name and charged down the hill. I'd had CPR training. If he was still alive, I could save him.

Blindly, I crashed through the dry brush and plunged into the pond, shocked by the cold water. I slipped on the slimy bottom and nearly went face down myself, but I regained my balance and waded five feet to the body.

The wedding band, three rings of gold like a Chinese puzzle. It *was* Coach. My mind shut down as I tugged the heavy weight of him to the edge of the pond, slipping twice and gasping for breath. By the time I reached the flattened weeds and put my head to his chest, I knew that CPR wasn't going to do any good.

Still, I tilted his head back to clear his airway and lifted his shoulders. I released, lifted and released, hoping beyond hope to hear sputtering and gasping, to see water coming rushing out. Frantic, I lifted and released again, the cold from my wet clothes turning my skin to ice as I repeated my action.

Finally, I let Coach's shoulders down gently, still not looking at his face. I hated leaving him alone here, hated the thought that an animal might come upon his body. But my brain had started functioning enough to know that I had to get help, had to get the police to come out here. I couldn't drag a two-hundred-thirty-pound weight up the hill, and I shouldn't, anyway.

Shivering with the cold, my jeans heavy with water and my arms tired from my futile efforts, I managed to climb the hill. Somehow, my vision had sharpened and all my senses were on alert. I smelled the decay of the leaves as I skidded on a wet spot, and I heard the rustling of an animal in the brush on the other side of the road. I felt the slippery embrace of a wet leaf that had clung to the back of my hand, and I brushed it away. And I saw on the ground beside my car a scattering of rifle shells, some old and dented, others newer, almost shiny.

I knew better than to pick them up. As I let my gaze sweep the turnout — a space barely big enough for three cars — I noticed a tube of lipstick without its top, a cigarette lighter, two old buttons, a small, round wire brush. I bent to look more closely at the brush and realized that it was like the Dremel rotary tool I used to clean the insides of my gourds. An old gray sock with a red stripe lay beside a tattered blue bandana on the ground.

And then I started to tremble. That was Coach's body I'd pulled out of the pond. This was Coach's car parked beside mine. I had to get help, and right away.

Somehow, I managed to drive back to The Creamery and park the car without hitting anything. I stumbled up the front steps and pushed open the front door. As I stepped inside, my car keys fell out of my hand and clattered to the floor. I knelt and picked them up, then leaned forward, shaking my head to clear away the sight of the body I'd just pulled out of the freezing water.

Later, two people who were sitting and

having coffee told me that the whole room had gone dead silent at the sight of me. But I was unaware of other people, except for Frank Vargas, who rushed out from behind the counter and put his hands on my shoulders.

"What happened, Lili?"

I opened my mouth but nothing came out. Finally, I managed to say, "Coach is dead. Shot in the back of his head. Miller's pond. His car is in the turnout. Call the police."

One of the patrons phoned the police while Frank led me to the back of the café and handed me a white chef's outfit, baggy cotton pants, and a double-breasted shirt. Grateful, I wriggled out of my wet clothes and put on the dry ones, my mind racing to try to hold on to the details I'd seen.

Nora.

For the first time since I'd seen the shape in the water, my friend's face floated up in front of me, and I sat on an upturned plastic milk carton in the back of The Creamery and cried, my shoulders shaking with sobs of sorrow, my hand covering my mouth to keep from screaming out loud.

Nora.

Her beautiful, laughing face floated in front of me.

I wanted to bring her soup. Lead her down the hall to the guest bedroom. Fluff the pillows and tuck the covers under her chin. Do something. Anything. How would she bear it?

I wanted to hug her.

Coach was dead, shot by some drunken hunter who'd mistaken him for a trophy to hang on the wall. What a senseless, infuriating, mind-numbing waste. What needless and unbearable pain for Nora and Scooter. My frustration spilled over into more tears, and I sat in the back of the quiet little café and wept into the paper napkin someone pressed into my hand. In a daze, I listened to a woman talking into her cell phone.

"That's what I said. She found him in Miller's pond. Shot in the back of the head. Damn city people don't care about putting food on the table, just come up here with their damn hunting licenses and shoot any damn thing that moves. One year they killed Marty Shook's dog. The next year they killed three cows. Damn stupid people can't tell the difference between a man and a deer. What's the matter with them, anyway? They don't have enough ways to take out their aggressions in the city, they have to come up here for sport and drink beer and —"

She stopped and gulped back a sob and pounded her fist against the small wrought-iron table. I was surprised that the clocks kept ticking, the world kept spinning, surprised that I managed to drive myself home without running my car off the road.

Until a couple of years ago, death had only made its presence felt in my life in expected ways. My mother's father died when I was fourteen, my father's mother when I was twenty-eight. One kid from my old neighborhood suffered horrible injuries while elevator surfing and died, mercifully, within a day. But then three work acquaintances, an old college friend, and a cousin I saw at weddings and funerals, plus a score of people I'd met only a couple of times, perished in the World Trade Center attack. And that was the end of my belief that people who are old and sick, people who take stupid risks, are the only ones who die.

If someone had told me that I would feel emptiness, a hollow sensation as though my insides were made of air, I would have denied that. I expected to feel anger, sorrow, a deep and piercing grief. Instead, it seemed like I felt nothing, as though the world had been colored a tired, uniform gray.

By the morning after I found Coach's body, the gray had lifted enough for me to make a big pot of chicken soup, make chicken salad from the plump, boiled fowl, and bake a dozen banana-nut muffins iced with cream cheese frosting, load it all into my car, and drive to Nora's in the afternoon.

The driveway was jammed with vehicles, and the brightly lit windows gave the house a festive look, as though a party were rollicking inside. But when I knocked on the kitchen door and stepped into the kitchen, the hush made my throat close up. Familiar faces looked up — I picked out Elizabeth and Melissa first — and then bent their heads again to loading the dishwasher and wiping the counters. Mickey Kensington, my next door neighbor, walked over to me and lifted the pot from my hands.

"Does this need to be refrigerated?" She was already on her way in that direction. "I think we're going to need to freeze some of this. Let's find some plastic containers."

Three people moved toward the pantry, where Nora kept her food storage containers, and I wheeled and headed to the car to get the rest of the packages.

"Lili, I'm so glad you came. This is awful. Isn't it weird? Coach has been dead more than twenty-fours and I still keep expecting him to come walking through that door." Susan Clemants hugged me and shook her head. This would be a time filled with tears and headshaking, and the only thing to do was to accept that and wade through the hard parts until we all reached another shore.

"I still can't believe it. What was he doing out by the pond when he knew it was the first day of hunting season? That's what I can't figure out." Something about Susan made me say things that I'd otherwise censor — her openness, perhaps, or those big brown eyes that seemed to be totally focused on whoever was speaking.

"I know, I thought about that a lot. But Coach wasn't afraid of anything, so maybe he was just walking where he thought he wouldn't run into any hunters. Oops, that's my cell phone. Excuse me." She grabbed a phone from the counter and turned away.

Time to get the rest of the food from the car. I said hello to Melissa Paul on my way out, and had pushed open the door and headed toward my Subaru when I heard footsteps crunch the gravel behind me. As I turned, I nearly bumped into Elizabeth Conklin. Her blue cashmere coat and high heels looked out of place against the vista of rolling hills dotted with weathered barns. I smiled a hello.

"I can carry something," she said simply.

I nodded, handed her the muffins, hefted the bowl of chicken salad, and kicked the car door shut with my foot.

"Nora needs some space. She really needs the hubbub to slow down." Her back to me, Elizabeth strode toward the door.

Incredulous, I stood in the driveway and stared at her until she disappeared into the brightness of the house. I sniffled and told myself it wasn't about me, that I had come to offer my friend soup and sympathy, and whatever Elizabeth felt about me, that was her problem. I wasn't about to be stopped by some uptight lawyer who was afraid that I was intruding on the territory of her friendship. Elizabeth and I would have to confront this someday. Or not. Today, I wanted to leave the food and then go back home. But not before I gave Nora a hug.

The house buzzed with activity and low conversation, and I set the bowl in the refrigerator and threaded my way to the living room. On the sofa, surrounded by people whose faces blurred in my tears, sat Nora. She nodded in response to something the man on her left said, picked an invisible thread from her sweater, and then looked up.

When she saw me, she rose and walked right to me. I thought my heart would burst with sorrow when I took her in my arms, and she held onto me long enough that the wetness on both our cheeks seemed to mingle into a single river of sadness.

"Oh, Nora. I can hardly believe it. I am so sorry." We hadn't let go of each other, but the tears had stopped. "How's Scooter doing?"

Nora straightened her shoulders and her dark eyes searched mine. "Bad. He's really devastated. Couldn't sleep last night. I sat by his bed all night. If anything, it gets worse with each hour."

"He's in shock," I said, noting that if she was going to keep a bedside vigil, then she wouldn't be sleeping much either. "I know you have a lot of support right now, but I want to say it out loud: If there's anything you need. Anything. Anytime. You know that, right?"

She squeezed my hand and hugged me again. "Thanks, Lili. As soon as everyone leaves, I'm gonna need some one-on-one time. Right now, it's all I can do to keep being gracious to the well-wishers."

Maybe that's what Elizabeth meant. If I stretched my capacity for charity, I might even believe that she wasn't trying to tell me that I had no place here. I nodded and said, "You do whatever you need to, Nora. Mourn your own way, whatever that is."

She looked into my eyes, the cloud of blankness lifted momentarily. "Thanks. Those will be words to remember. Later. Now I have to play the part, at least for a couple of days."

That's what I believed this was about, the ritual visiting and the food. A woman whose husband had just been shot in the back of the head didn't have to think for a while. Didn't have to decide what to do next because it was clearly prescribed by custom and belief.

"I'll call you tomorrow," I said. "I'll do my part now to thin out the crowd."

"Stay." She said it quietly, a royal command. "I feel better hearing your voice. Do you know that the sheriff has ordered an autopsy? That they have to do that whenever there's a death that's not from natural causes?"

"I know I sound like a broken record,

but I'm so sorry. That's awful." Television dramas had given me too many terrible images of the aftermath of crimes, and now some of them applied to Coach's body. My impulse was to change to subject, but that was only for my own comfort. Nora needed to talk about it, I knew. "When will they release the body?"

Nora looked at her watch, then peered into the crowded room, hanging back in the doorway as the din of conversation clamored around us. "Six days at the latest. That's what they told me. I tried to argue them out of it because I didn't want to wait to bury my husband. That's his birthday. I can't do this alone, Lili."

"You don't have to." I was ready to put her in my car and drive away, if that was what she wanted. "Tell me what you need."

She took a deep breath and closed her eyes. "Okay, I'm ready. I'm going to be all right."

I linked my arm through hers and steered her back into the living room, glad to be her friend, glad my presence offered her comfort. And terribly sad that her world was about to undergo such painful changes.

Chapter 5

"Your mother wants to know if you're staying in Brooklyn for Anne's birthday. Your sister really was cheated being born on November thirtieth. Thanksgiving and Anne's birthday, always days apart." My father sounded strong, no tremors in his voice, no weariness. The effects of his Parkinson's disease seemed to come and go according to some whim, and I was always glad to hear something that indicated he was having a good day. "I'm only the messenger here, but I'd love to see you, Lili. It's been awhile. Oops, no guilt trips. That's your mother's department."

I looked at the calendar. My sister's birthday was less than a week away, and in the aftermath of Coach's death, I'd been so busy that I'd forgotten completely. And now I'd have to tell the truth — that once again, someone was more important than my sister. She would surely add this to the list of infractions I'd been accumulating since I spilled ink on her white carpet when I was four and she was seven.

"Dave Marino, don't you duck this one. You used Ruth's name in vain here. Mom didn't want to know anything. You better cop to the fact that you made this call all on your own. I can't stay in the city, Dad. You remember I told you about my friend Nora?"

Dad murmured an acknowledgment.

"Her husband was shot, we're pretty sure in a hunting accident. They haven't arrested anyone yet, but it was opening day of hunting season up here and he was shot in the back of the head with a rifle. Actually, I found his body. Face down in a pond. His funeral is next Sunday. I'll call Anne and she'll understand."

We both knew that was optimism at its blindest, but Dad let it pass.

"They get the autopsy results?" He knew the drill — unnatural deaths were followed by an autopsy. He'd spent most of his career as an NYPD detective dealing with commercial fraud, but he still knew his way around a homicide investigation.

"Not yet. Tomorrow afternoon, that's what I was told. Dad, I really am sorry I have to miss Annie's birthday. But I'll be there for Thanksgiving."

"That's great, Lil."

I could see him grinning as he thought about how mad it made me when anyone called me Lil. I liked my name. My whole entire four-letter name. This time I was the one to let an annoyance pass.

"Thanks, Dad. Kiss Mom for me. And yourself."

I hung up and called my sister, enduring her coolness, knowing that it wouldn't last, knowing, too, that we still had a lot of ground to cover if we were going to close the gaping hole in our relationship that had been created by the intersection of her standoffish nature and my need for independence. No matter what I did, she never let me past her well-designed armor; even the thought of it seemed to make her uncomfortable.

In my uneasy state, I would surely ruin any gourd I touched, so I rummaged through my scrap pile, tops cut from gourds, pieces of gourds that had shattered when I got a little too creative with cutting techniques, and found a thick piece to experiment on. I got my Dremel, selected a carving tip, put on a mask, and started carving a design that I'd been longing to try on one of the big gourds.

I was concentrating so completely that my whole arm jumped when the phone rang. The Dremel stuttered across the surface, ruining the design and nearly gouging the table in the process.

I let it ring until the answering machine picked up, but when I heard the caller identify herself, I reached out and grabbed the phone.

"Hey, Susan. Sorry, I couldn't get to the phone in time. I was working. How's it going? You're not working today?"

Susan Clemants laughed. "Ever hear of lunch? I have to get back to my kids in a minute. Listen, a few of us are getting together to talk about what to do for Coach's memorial service. I mean, for after the funeral. You know, make a plan about food and dishes and linens and things like that, so that Nora doesn't have to think about it. I expect most of the town will turn out, so we're going to need all hands. Eight o'clock tonight, at Elizabeth's. Can you come?"

"Of course. I'm really glad to be included. Thanks, Susan."

Her warm voice made it easy to understand why she was Nora's friend. "See you then."

Elizabeth Conklin's two-story gabled house sat on a rise in the middle of a manicured lawn that must have taken four gardeners three days a week to tend at the height of the summer season. Rocks curved along one side of the driveway, marking the edge of a stand of tall shrubbery. If it were spring, I could tell whether these were lilacs or forsythia, but I hadn't lived in Walden Corners long enough to know the difference in November, when all the leaves were gone.

Suddenly, the refrain of that old song that my mother played when she was melancholy, "California Dreamin'," rolled through my head. I knew it would take awhile to shake the Mamas and the Papas. *All the leaves are brown . . .*

Sad enough when that happened, but then they fell off entirely, floated to the ground, had to be raked. No wonder people dreamed of California. Green all the time didn't seem half bad. And if the skies were gray, then it only meant more rain and more green. I sighed and parked my car behind two others, rang the bell, and was glad when Susan Clemants appeared behind the gleaming oak door. Her apple cheeks lifted in a broad smile when she saw me, and that look of welcome turned my anxiety level down several notches.

"Lili, I'm so glad you came. We're still

waiting for Melissa. Come on in and let me take your coat." She moved about as though it was her home, with a familiarity that meant she probably had spent lots of time here. That spoke better of Elizabeth. If both Nora and sweet Sue, as I started to think of her, liked Elizabeth, then the woman had to be more than the cold and distant person she appeared to be.

But Elizabeth herself did nothing to dissuade me of my old notions about her.

"Please take your shoes off," she said as she passed from the far end of the hall into the living room balancing a silver tray laden with a graceful tea service, leaving behind a steamy cloud redolent with the scent of bergamot. Earl Grey. A good choice for this dismal fall evening.

Susan shrugged and stuck her tongue out at Elizabeth's receding back. "Sorry, I forgot to tell her."

At least I was wearing socks with no holes.

At least I was wearing socks.

But when I got to the living room, I understood the proscription against shoes. Except for a gorgeous abstract painting in orange, red, and pale gray, and a chunky red vase in the middle of a glass coffee table, everything in the room was white.

White leather sofas and wing-back chairs. White carpet. White-on-white curtains. A person could go snow blind in this room. A person could really catch a chill.

We'd arranged ourselves on the ends of the sofas, and Elizabeth was pouring tea when the doorbell rang again. Susan jumped up and ran to the door, and I smiled and accepted the porcelain cup and saucer from my hostess, who never once made eye contact with me.

"I love the painting," I said, following my mother's advice that saying nice things put people off the attack.

"But you don't like me very much." Her thickly lashed eyes met mine and she held my gaze. I'd be darned if I was going to look away first. "That's all right. Honestly. All you have to do is —"

"Elizabeth, let's understand each other. We're grown-ups. I'm not very good at listening to people tell me what to do. Never have been. Sometimes I make mistakes and I learn from them. But please don't tell me what I have to do."

She smiled. "Bad choice of words. Nora says you're a mediator. You want peace. I'm a litigator. I want to win. So, that explains it. Different strokes, different methods of attack."

"Except that I have no need to attack," I said softly. "Nora's my friend, and I'm here to help her. That's all. It's as simple as that. What do you want from this meeting? What do I want? The same thing. To make a proper memorial for Coach, to help Nora and Scooter get through it with some degree of dignity and comfort."

Her face was still too new to me to be completely readable, but I knew that I wasn't seeing gentle agreement. Still, I'd said my bit and that was as far as I intended to go. Before either of us could say something we'd regret, Susan and Melissa breezed into the room.

"Hi, Lili. Glad you could join us." Melissa plunked down beside me and sniffed the air above my cup. "Mmmm, thanks, Elizabeth. This is just what I need."

Nobody called this woman Liz or Beth or anything other than Elizabeth. That comforted me. At least I wasn't the only one kept at arms' length.

Susan pulled out a pad and brushed a handful of red curls away from her face. "So we need to talk about a menu, speakers, music, flowers. Nora chose the music and asked that the speakers be limited to one student, one person from school, one from church, and one friend.

She and Scooter have decided not to say anything. And she gave me a list of Coach's favorite foods."

Leaning forward, Melissa poured herself a cup of tea and rested the saucer on her knee as she sipped the steaming liquid. "What in the world is going on with you, Elizabeth Conklin? You are behaving like something bit your butt."

Did that mean that this frosty silence wasn't exactly business as usual? In a way, that made me feel a little better. How would she get out of this one, I wondered. How would she say that she resented the presence of an interloper?

Elizabeth ran her hand over her forehead as one foot jiggled nervously. "I guess I'm a little unsettled by all this. Let's get on with it. It's getting late."

Snippy. That's how Ruth Marino would describe the tone. Imperious was more like it. The attitude of someone accustomed to having things her own way. But Melissa, gentle Melissa, was having none of it.

"You're not getting away with that, Ms. Conklin. Maybe at work. Maybe even in the courtroom. But not with *us*."

With a pointed glare, Elizabeth made it clear that I was not part of any *us* to which she belonged.

84

"Look, I know we hardly know each other. I'm here because I was invited, and because I love Nora and Scooter. I'd like to help however I can, even if that means leaving so that you all can go on without the distraction of my presence." I hadn't meant to be quite so defensive, but the words had just spilled out.

"This is not about you." Elizabeth Conklin's voice was icy, and she wouldn't look my way. She poured a shot of brandy into her tea, handed the bottle around, and we all followed suit. The tension rose as we slugged down the doctored Earl Grey from delicate cups. Elizabeth took a deep breath and then said, "You cannot say a word until the news is made public. Sometime tomorrow. The coroner says that Coach wasn't killed by the bullet in the back of his head."

Shocked, we sat in silence and stared at her.

"He drowned. He was already dead when he was shot. The autopsy results are being written up right now. I made Alan Calby promise that if anything unusual turned up, he'd let me tell Nora. He owed me a big favor, and this was the payoff, knowing this early. I'm going over to Nora's at nine o'clock. She tried to beg off and say she was tired, but I told her I needed to see her without saying why."

I shuddered and hugged my arms to my body. My head spun with questions and a huge, fuzzy silence rang in my ears.

"What does that mean, he drowned?" Melissa asked the question that would make all the others make sense.

Elizabeth shook her head. "It means that he drowned. On a cold morning in the middle of November, Henry Johnson drowned in a pond at the edge of his family's property. He didn't have a heart attack, but he did have bruises on his face and his arms. Not likely, Calby said, that all those marks came from a slip — a fight, he thinks. One of the head wounds is the result of his head hitting a rock. Someone had a fight with Coach, and then shot a dead man in the back of the head. It means that hunters probably had nothing to do with this. It means that Nora is going to have to wrestle with this new shock just when she thought the worst was over."

We were speechless.

"That's all I know for the moment. That's all Calby told me." Frowning, Elizabeth stacked the saucers on the tray, busying herself pouring tea from two cups into the teapot, moving absently as though the activity itself were the most important thing in the world. "Nora's not ready for this. To think you know what happened, have a place to put your anger, and then have that taken away in a flash. She's not going to take this well."

The obvious question floated in the air until Susan, her flaming curls quivering, wrestled it down and set it in front of us. "So that means it could be someone we know. In fact, it probably is, right? Oh, sheesh, I can't even think about that. Someone we know."

"Someone we pass on the road every day," Melissa added.

"Not to speak ill of the dead," Susan said, "but some kids and some parents didn't like how he demanded certain behavior from the kids."

My hands shook as I set my cup on the tray. "Actually, I think that's praising the man. Isn't there some kind of ongoing feud with the Akron family? And Ira Jackson, who can't get over the fact that Coach, a black man, got invited to parties and had a good job?"

"Sheriff Murphy is going to talk to everyone. I wouldn't be surprised if he showed up on my doorstep. I knew the man, so I'm a suspect. As are you all."

Elizabeth rolled a napkin into a tight cylinder, her slender, manicured fingers pushing and twisting as though she might wring the truth from it. "Calby said that the funeral could go on as planned. The report will be handed over to Gene Murphy officially tomorrow."

"Then we still have work to do," I said quietly. "I know I'm new here, so I'll just do what you think I should. I can type up the programs and get them printed; I can help fetch and carry and set up the food and clean up. I'll do anything that needs to be done. I'm going down to be with my family on Thursday, but I'll be back late that night or early Friday. If there's anything important, you can call my cell phone or leave me a message. I'll be checking in a couple of times that day."

Melissa put her name next to the food preparation, including providing linens, tables, chairs, and utensils. Susan made a list of potential speakers and offered to make a memory board of photographs and mementos. Elizabeth volunteered to see to the music and get a couple of local kids to help with cleanup.

The hall clock kept ticking. I didn't envy Elizabeth the job she faced in the morning.

Susan, Melissa, and I left all at the same

time. I drove home under a hazy moon, through a fog that lay low over the fields and made driving a treacherous affair. Exhausted, I pulled into my own driveway and sat in the car, looking at the fairybook setting. A pretty cottage, warm and snug and lit from within by soft, golden light. A ring of pine trees. Those holly bushes and hydrangeas, and the apple trees. Despite this evening's grim mission, I felt safe here. Had Tom Ford ever done this, just stare out into the night and feel the peace of the place, and have that sweep away the questions of a difficult time? I realized that for the first time since I'd moved to Walden Corners, I thought of this place as my home.

Chapter 6

As if mocking our sadness, the day of Coach's funeral was sparkling clear, the air spicy with the scent of pears and pumpkins, and the redolence of leaves crushed underfoot. The day confirmed my belief that people should be buried in the rain, under gray skies. It seemed somehow obscene to stand in sunshine, feel the warmth seep through my jacket and silk shirt to my skin, feel my face lift upward involuntarily when I should be looking down at the casket that was being lowered into the freshly dug hole.

Nora stood with her arm around Scooter, both of them with lips pressed tight and eyes focused on the flowers on the far side of the mounded dirt. Her parents flanked them; her sisters stood behind them. They formed a circle, each one touching another so that they were completely connected. Nora's knees buckled once, but her dad held her up, she took a breath, and then straightened her shoulders. Support, literally. It was so clear that she had that from her family.

About thirty of us, family and friends whose names Nora had put on the list for the funeral service, shifted our feet in the sunshine and waited for the minister to finish his words. When he finally did, I started to step back, but Susan tugged at my jacket. Unsure of what her signal meant, I was about to whisper my question when a rich, throaty contralto broke the silence.

"Amazing grace, how sweet the sound . . ."

Her voice lifted into the blue sky gently at first, and I turned to watch her face. A large woman with dark brown skin, she stood with her eyes closed and her hands clasped in front of her. The voice grew stronger all through the first chorus, until it filled the empty spaces in the vast open cemetery and lifted to the tops of the trees. Her body started swaying and her arms reached skyward and others joined in. I sang along, my face wet with tears.

"The whole town's going to be here. Coach has been at Walden High for eleven years. Four regional and one state championship. And he and Nora grew up here, so that's half the town right there." Melissa adjusted the burgundy cloth over the table, smoothed wrinkles, and pointed to another table waiting to be set up. "I hope she's ready for this circus. Now that everyone knows it's murder, the gawkers and the professional mourners will turn out in force."

"Everyone from school, and from her church. And Scooter's friends. Even city people who know her from The Creamery. I hope they don't think this memory board is corny," Susan said, pointing her head at the easel set up in the far corner of the living room in front of a tall, healthy ficus. Photographs — of Coach and his teams, of Coach as a round-faced child, a gawky teen receiving an award at high school graduation, a handsome man beaming at his beautiful bride, the thoughtful, loving father holding a newborn Scooter — filled the four-foot square. On the table in front of the bay window the trophies gleamed in the sun.

"Nobody will think it's corny," I said. "And if they do that's —"

A truck skidded to a stop in the driveway, spraying gravel and just missing the garage by about a foot.

"Thank goodness." Melissa strode to the

door and let in what appeared to be a stack of chairs.

"Where do these go?"

Who had uttered such simple words with so much venom? When he set the chairs down I realized that I'd seen the man somewhere but couldn't place him. Actually, I wanted to place him . . . fifty miles down the road somewhere, far away from this house. Whatever was feeding his fire, it was the kind of poison that tainted everything.

Melissa pointed to the long wall where the tables were being set up. "There, just next to the tables. Watch out, Ira!" She jumped to catch a porcelain teapot that the man had nearly knocked over.

"Shoulda had these delivered before you put out the good china. Besides, what do you want to use the good stuff for? It's only a bunch of —"

"Ira!" A deep crimson flush spread across her face. "Don't say anything else. Just bring in the rest of the chairs and then get out of here. Not a word, you hear me?"

Muttering, Ira Jackson wheeled and left the room.

The thick silence shouted that Melissa didn't quite know what to do about Ira Jackson. This wasn't the time for me to ask why she continued to hire such a mean-spirited person when lots of muscular high school kids would have been happy to earn gas and movie money by schlepping chairs for her. Besides, we had too much to do. We spent the next hour cutting celery, carrots, red peppers, and radishes, arranging them on platters, slicing cheddar and Gouda, and making pinwheels of sesame crackers on a doily-covered tray. The ham in the oven and the beans bubbling in the pot filled the house with aromas that spoke of family celebrations and laughter, not the solemnity of a community gathering to remember one of its own.

Before the last platter was on the table, a car pulled into the drive and three people got out. The driver, a neatly dressed young man with perfect posture, stood beside the car as the other two approached the house. He squinted, folded his arms across his chest, but made no move toward the house.

"Alvin Akron," I muttered. Elizabeth, who had just set down a bowl of green salad and was arranging a red pepper ring in the center, looked up.

"How do you know Alvin?" She wiped her hands on the crisp white apron and reached up to pull it over her head. "I'm surprised he's here."

"Met him at Ag Day. Nora told me about the property dispute. It sounds like it's been going on forever." Glad to be having a civil conversation with my hostess, I arranged the forks in the pottery bowl and stood back to examine the table, which I judged to be worthy of a professional. "You think the old family feud will keep him from coming inside?"

"That's not all of it," she said sharply. "It's me he hates."

At that moment, I was on Alvin's side. Elizabeth Conklin was behaving as though she knew everything and should be in charge of the world.

"Why?" I asked, trying to hide my smile by bending to pick up a tiny sprig of parsley that had fallen to the floor.

"Because I handled Coach's case when Alvin sued him for that land he thinks his grandfather never got paid for. He's not the only one who won't talk to me. Ira Jackson — now there's a prize winner. I represented his wife in their divorce and got her the house and sole custody of the kids." Her voice had softened, and I thought I saw something creep into her face that resembled compassion. "He was a batterer."

I knew enough from my mediation experience to understand how it felt to help someone who had endured horrible life circumstances, and I realized that satisfaction was the expression on Elizabeth's face. A human emotion, and one that I actually recognized — maybe she had other secrets.

"It's great that she had you to advocate for her," I said. Two more cars pulled into the drive, a snaking line of vehicles following close behind.

"I was told to take the case by the judge." Elizabeth looked at me impassively. "We take turns around here doing pro bono cases. Florence Jackson happened to come up on my watch. She died a couple of years ago — cancer — but she had five good years at least. Now Ira and Will live in her house — let it go so that it looks like an annex of the town dump. But I'm still glad we won; glad that jerk didn't get away with anything. He'll never talk to me, unless it's to tell me to go to hell."

"From what I can tell, you're not missing much." The doorbell rang and I rushed to the hall, wondering what else I would find out about the people of my adopted town.

I introduced myself to Mack Honicker, the owner of Hon's Appliances, a big warehouse on the outskirts of Hudson that sold discount — and some said refurbished — stoves, refrigerators, dishwashers, and all the other conveniences that farm wives and city transplants coveted. Right behind him, Armel Noonan stood, his pained expression and stiff posture making me wish I could hug him and make him more comfortable.

"Come in, it's cold. You can put your coat in here." I led the way to the study, where a coatrack from Melissa's inn had been set up. "You okay?"

Armel looked at the doorway, then back at me. "I don't know what to say to them. I mean, it's bad enough when your father dies, but if he's murdered? What am I supposed to do?"

"You don't have to say anything special. Just being here is what they need. You can say anything at all. Or nothing, honestly." I was glad to share the lessons I'd learned after keeping myself apart when my Uncle Monty died, thinking that if I were a truly good person I would have access to some magic words, just the right things to say. "Don't worry, Armel. Be yourself, love your friend, that's what you can do."

He nodded, his expression still dubious but a little more relaxed, and then he headed for the door. By the time Nora and

Scooter came downstairs, the house was filled with people balancing plates and glasses as they chattered amiably. I was introduced to so many new people that I knew I'd never remember names. Martha McIntosh, the postmistress who had been sorting mail since the day after JFK's assassination, as she told everyone who met her for the first time, helped deflect the hushed speculations in each little cluster of people she approached.

"So, what's your favorite memory of Coach Johnson?" she asked. She listened to the answers, nodded, and then moved to the next group, repeating the question and the nodding, as though she were shepherding the memories, corralling them into the center of the room, so that Nora could gather them at her convenience.

As I carried a tray back to the kitchen with dirty dishes, I heard one parent talk about how pleased she was that Coach wouldn't let her son play because he'd gotten a D in math. By the time I'd refilled the tray with baguette slices and a bowl with pink, blue, and yellow packets of artificial sweetener and returned to the dining room, a man in another group was wondering aloud how anyone could think of hurting Coach, the man who had tutored his daughter during his lunch hours after she'd been out for a month with mono.

I surveyed the table, checking to see that the platters were full, and a voice behind me said, "You probably don't remember, but we met for about five seconds at Ag Day."

I turned and looked up into brown eyes that peered at me expectantly. The face that went with the eyes was pleasant, unassuming, unremarkable. What was noticeable was the utter sense of familiarity I felt, despite that five-second meeting.

"Of course I remember. You have a son on the football team, right?" I glanced around the room but couldn't spot the boy I vaguely remembered.

"Ron, yes. He'll be here in a few minutes. You live in the Ford house, don't you? I live about a mile past the Kensington's in that white colonial with blue trim. I've been meaning to stop by and introduce myself but, well, you know how intentions can get waylaid. How's Nora holding up?"

"She's still in shock. She spent all day yesterday cleaning the windows. Moving. She needed to keep moving. She's got a lot of support, though. I guess she'll need it a week from now, a month from now, all through the first year." I'd said more than

I'd intended, but something about his eyes and the attention he paid to my words made it easy.

"It's all those firsts. After my wife and I split up . . . well, anyway, those firsts are all hard. Listen, I hate being a pest, but is there any salt?" He smiled, and a dimple flashed on the right side of his smile.

"Got the brie and the pesto butter and the hothouse tomatoes. Forgot the basics. Sorry. I'll get some."

The kitchen was bustling. Even there people were talking about Coach, about how he never took lip from kids or parents, about how he held himself to the same high standards to which he held everyone else. I threaded my way to the counter, where one unopened cardboard box still sat. Melissa must have been interrupted by something. Inside, a dozen small glass salt and pepper shakers sat beside four sugar bowls, four creamers, and a jumble of pie servers, cake cutters, and assorted serving pieces.

I distributed the salt and pepper shakers, looking for the man wandering around with a plate of tomatoes and mozzarella. When I spotted him, he was standing in a corner, his arm around a boy who was an inch taller than his nearly six feet, with a face that looked like it had been copied from his father's, a paler image, less formed, more indistinct. Whereas the father's eyes were deep-set and dark-lashed, the boy's were less so. The strong, straight nose on the son looked still childish, and the mouth especially wasn't quite grown-up.

"It's now safe to eat the tomatoes." I handed him a salt shaker and was rewarded with that dimple-flashing smile.

"Thanks. Ms. Marino, I'd like you to meet my son Ron. Ron is . . . was one of Coach's projects this year. Turned him into a first-string tight end."

"Pleased to meet you, Ron." I smiled and thought that it was the father who might have earned that description, but I wasn't thinking football at that moment. "You know, I didn't even ask Nora. What's the school doing about the rest of the football season?"

Finally Ron looked up and said, "They're going to have Mr. Kimball, the math teacher, coach for the rest of the season. We're going to dedicate the whole season to Coach Johnson."

"That's a lovely tribute." I looked around and noticed that the cheese tray was empty again. "Well, it was nice to talk to you, but please excuse me. I have to take care of a couple of things."

As I turned, I nearly bumped into Bobby Benson, shuffling along as though he had lead weights in his shoes. "Sorry, Bobby. I guess I was in a hurry." He nodded, then kept going toward an empty chair in the corner of the room. There went any hope that his behavior on Ag Day had been a blip. Still, I was committed to having him remove those stumps, and it would be over if not painlessly then quickly, I hoped.

Once again, the kitchen buzzed with conversation, but the groups were different this time. Elizabeth fussed with ham slices while a man in a pinstriped suit leaned against the counter with his arms folded across his chest. He was reminiscing about a golf game with Coach where he was caught doing some creative scorekeeping.

"Coach said to me that if I kept my business books the way I keep score, I'd be losing money like crazy." He looked at me appraisingly, then said, "You must be Lili. I'm Richard Conklin. Elizabeth described you very well."

So this was the famous spouse, the real estate developer who could buy and sell all of Walden Corners ten times a day for a month and still have cash left over for his wife's diamond trinkets. I offered him my hand. "Nice to meet you."

Unexpectedly, he took it, raised it to his lips, kissed the top of my hand. "Always glad to meet someone with the good sense to move from the city to our little bit of paradise."

"I love it here," I said, hoping to avoid inane conversation. "Excuse me, I have to fill this plate again." I pulled open the refrigerator and shook out the cheese cubes onto the tray. Richard and Elizabeth Conklin seemed a perfectly matched pair, snobby little bookends, dripping self-possession and attitude in a place where cow pie bingo was one of the entertainments. I arranged the cheese in a pyramid, then hustled back out before anyone else could snag me.

The dining room was even more crowded than it had been just a couple of minutes earlier. I glanced to the corner where Bobby Benson had been seated alone and saw Will Jackson hunkered in front of him, talking animatedly. Bobby's face burned with a red flush, and although I couldn't hear what they were saying, the Jackson boy seemed to be speaking through clenched teeth. Mesmerized, I stood in the middle of the crowded floor.

Bobby jerked back as though someone had gut-punched him and then shook his head violently. The other boy's smile was more a sneer; he tapped Bobby's shoulder, then stood, brushed off his pants, and headed for the French doors.

Bobby, mouth agape, lifted his plate and moved like a sleepwalker to the table, set the plate and glass precariously near the edge, and kept walking toward the same doors through which the Jackson boy had disappeared moments before. The odd little dance sent a shiver through me.

"Did you see that? I wonder what's going on with Bobby Benson and Will Jackson," I said as Susan gathered empty plates.

"Will Jackson. Captain of the football team. And a danger to teenage girls everywhere. Not much of a student, but he's one of those kids you don't worry about because he's got such confidence in himself he'll always land on his feet. Funny, Bobby's practically his opposite."

But I didn't have time to wonder about the exchange between Will and Bobby, because Nora and Scooter, who had been tethered to one another by an invisible thread all afternoon, came up to us.

Nora hugged Susan and then me. "Thanks. You two are the best."

Scooter just stood there, eyes red and puffy, his face wreathed in a stoic resolve that I knew would soon give way to the predictable pattern of anger, abandonment, loss, and finally acceptance. His father wouldn't be home for dinner tonight, would miss his high school graduation, his wedding, the steps of his first child.

I was about to ask if I could get them something to drink when Armel, dressed in gray slacks, gray shirt, and pearly gray tie, materialized at Scooter's side.

"Hey, Scooter, you want to take a walk?" Armel shifted uncomfortably in his shiny leather shoes, but the sight of him brought a relieved half smile to Scooter's face.

"Go on," Nora said. "Just don't go too far, okay. And put on coats, boys. It's cold out there."

I watched them walk away, touched once again by how much the small gestures matter. "You know they're going to forget about the coats by the time they hit the door. When I was a kid, wearing a coat was like having homework on Fridays — I did everything I could to avoid it. It's great that they have each other."

Before she could answer, Nora was grabbed up into a swirl of hugs and handshakes as a cluster of parents and kids came in. The sheriff's deputy hanging around near the doorway cast an extra weight on the room. I had managed for a few minutes to put the notion out of my mind that someone in this very house might have been responsible for killing Coach. Now I looked at everyone with that thought and it made my head spin.

What would make any of these fairly ordinary, unremarkable people step over that line? Anger that a favorite child was benched because he'd failed geometry? Fury that a black man had a big house, a wife, child, two cars, and a life of productive, energetic contribution to the community? Boiling resentment over a land deal generations old? A person would have to be twisted to let any of these push him — or her — over that edge into the realm of murder. So, who said my adopted little village of Walden Corners didn't have its share of twisted people?

Thankfully, the crowd thinned after two hours, and by four o'clock Nora and Scooter, both exhausted, were happy to be driven home by Susan. The only sounds in Elizabeth's stately house were the clinking of glass and the footsteps of people loading cartons into Melissa's van. I walked the perimeter of Elizabeth's dining room,

106

picking up napkins and glasses that had been left on windowsills, sweeping a handful of cake crumbs into the trash, until the room seemed ready for the vacuum.

"Elizabeth has a crew coming in tomorrow to take care of the rest. Don't bother with anything else. We all need to go home and just . . . well, just *be*." Melissa hugged me. "Get some rest, you hear?"

Somehow, it felt good that she hadn't thanked me for helping, as though being part of the effort was natural, expected, beyond comment. "You too. I predict you'll sleep fourteen hours tonight."

"Or three," she said, smiling. "Where are our coats?"

I led the way to the study, handed her the camel-wool coat, shrugged into my own black one, and looked around for the scarf I'd worn. It wasn't on the rack, or on the floor, or on the desk.

"That's funny," I said peering behind the desk and then scanning all the surfaces in the room. "I had a burgundy, blue, and gold plaid chenille scarf, but it seems to have gone missing. I'll have to ask Elizabeth to put it aside if she comes across it. It's not the kind of thing someone would easily mistake for their own. A friend made it, a weaver."

Melissa frowned. "Not likely someone stole it. You sure you had it with you?"

"Positive. I hung it on the hanger with my coat. No big deal, I'm sure it will turn up."

When I got home, the quiet and the small space seemed a great relief after the demands of the day. I changed into sweats, plunked down in front of the television, and watched two old episodes of *Friends*, letting the knots in my shoulders unkink. I made a cup of mint tea, sipped it, let the heat further relax me. I was about to doze off when bright headlights made their way into my driveway. A figure got out of the car and marched to the front door, rapped sharply three times.

"Who is it?" I asked, a little nervous that I'd so easily gotten over my city ways and joined my neighbors in leaving the doors unlocked most of the time.

"I found your scarf," the voice answered.

Without thinking I opened the door and was startled to see Ira Jackson standing under the porch light, his narrow face grinning. He held out the scarf as though he were a page handing the queen a tiara on a pillow.

"Thanks." The cold air nipped at my fingers, frosted my cheeks, but I had no intention of inviting this man inside. "Where did you find it?"

Shrugging, he said, "Over by the umbrella stand. In the hall. When I was carrying out the chairs. I knew it was yours. Saw you come in with it."

And then drove here at eleven at night to return it to me? My warning flags flapped furiously in the breeze, sirens sounding the alert. I reached for the scarf, but he dropped his hand to his side. I gritted my teeth and said, "Yes, I did come in with it. Well, thank you for —"

"You're the one who found the body, right?" He leaned against the door jamb, the scarf dangling from his hand.

"Yes. Listen, it's late and it's cold. I need to go inside now. If you —"

"You see anything? You find anything, you know, that you didn't tell anyone about?" His eyes bore into mine, and he smelled of alcohol.

"That's none of your business," I said firmly. "And I'd like you to give me back my scarf and then get out of the way so that I can shut this door."

He smirked. "Or what? You'll call the cops?"

"If I have to." My heart pounded wildly

as I grabbed the scarf and shoved him, not gently but not hard enough to hurt him. He stumbled back, and I slammed the door shut, locked it, then ran around to the back door and locked it, too. By the time I got back to the living room, Ira Jackson's car was pulling out of my driveway.

Again, I slept with all the lights on. That was not a habit I wanted to cultivate.

Chapter 7

A woman in a brown uniform stood on my front porch, her right hip tilted and her left hand resting on the porch rail. With her blonde hair trailing down her back and green eyes that crinkled in the corners, she was about as far from the mirrored sunglasses and mean, thin lips of the stereotype of a country cop as I'd ever seen. She looked more like she should play a television mom who's always exasperated at her cute teenagers and their homework problems.

"Miss Marino, I'm Undersheriff Michele Castro. I need you to come down to the sheriff's office and give me a statement about finding Coach's body. If you could do that now . . ." Her pretty mouth didn't smile, and she hardly blinked as she waited for my response.

What was so hard about finishing that sentence? I hate when people are indirect. It rouses my inner rebel like few things can. I stood my ground. Still tired from the emotional events of the funeral and the reception despite ten hours of sleep, I was beyond caring that my annoyance was probably written in neon all over my face.

"Well, I could, but I'm in the middle of something. I can make it at about four this afternoon." I wasn't sweet, nor was I challenging. I simply told her the way it was.

"It would be better if you came now." Her hand rested lightly on her hip, very near the holstered gun that hung there.

I could have said, "Better for who?" or even "Better for whom?" but I needed to get this out of the way so that I could go on with the rest of my life. I told her I'd be there in an hour, and she raised her eyebrows, then nodded and went back to her cruiser. Through the bare trees, I followed her progress for half a mile, until she turned onto the county road and disappeared from sight.

If I was going all the way into Hudson, then I might as well make the thirty-six-mile round-trip worth the gas. In Brooklyn, I used to plan my errands. The wonderful greengrocer and Mrs. Liu's fish store were on the way to the bank, and the cleaners and the bagel place were in the opposite direction, one block past the drugstore.

Life in Walden Corners wasn't all that different, except that here it was my driving route that I planned. I gathered up my vehicle registration renewal form to take to the Department of Motor Vehicles, stuck my shopping list in my purse, pulled my straight hair back into a ponytail, and grabbed my jacket.

As I stepped onto the porch, I heard a slow, deep rumble that got louder and louder as I watched Bobby Benson's red tractor roll into my driveway. Like a tired old bear that would rather be snug in a very large cave for the winter, the tractor turned wide and then juddered to a crawl several yards from my car. Two figures sat, one behind the other, reminding me of my college days, when I'd ridden on the back of Tom Gatti's motorcycle and felt the exhilaration of speed and the pleasure of wrapping my arms around a strong body.

Bobby Benson, in jeans and a red plaid jacket, muttered something angrily as he slammed the gear shift three times, then again, and finally found neutral. The whole tractor bumped and clattered, and he glared at it before he jumped down. A slender girl whose hair was tucked under a watch cap swung her legs over and then stepped down too. Bobby looked at her and she nodded and said something I couldn't hear, gave him a gentle shove, and watched indulgently as he trudged the twenty feet to the porch.

"The stumps. You wanted me to pull them out, right?" His ears glowed red from the cold and he rubbed his chapped hands together. Stocky and broad shouldered, he looked like he could simply push the stumps out of the ground with the sheer strength of his body.

"Absolutely. Your friend is here to help too?"

A rush of red burned his cheeks, and he started to say something, then turned and waited while the girl came to stand beside him.

"I'm Laura Miller. I'm a friend of Bobby's. Pleased to meet you."

"Lili Marino. Hey, we have the same initials. Call me Lili." I took her offered hand, shook it, and tried not to stare at the odd couple before me. "Let me show you where the stumps are."

"I know where they are. Mr. Ford had my father cut those trees down last year. I told him he should take them out then, but . . ." He broke eye contact, as though he was embarrassed that his fifteen-year-old self hadn't been able to convince a very grown-up and totally controlling Tom Ford to listen to his advice.

"So, Mr. Ford showed you where they were?" Maybe Bobby would be the one to fill in some facts about the former owner of the cottage.

He shrugged and ducked his head. "Nah, just left us a note pinned to the door."

I almost laughed. Of course he'd never seen Tom Ford. I was beginning to doubt the man's existence.

We started toward the west edge of the lawn, wondering about their connection. Beauty and the Beast — what was the lumbering Bobby Benson doing with Laura Miller, whose china-blue eyes, long lashes, pert nose, and generous, smiling mouth added up to a package that made her look like a Breck girl. I reminded myself that just because a couple seemed unlikely to me, that didn't mean it wasn't working for them.

Turning to make sure they were following me, I nearly stumbled on a tree root. The three stumps loomed like those concrete car barriers that had sprouted around all the courts in lower Manhattan and in front of corporations and office buildings a few days after 9/11. The bus stops had to be moved, traffic patterns changed, and —

"Okay, you want me to start now?" Bobby's voice pulled me back into my yard.

"Sure. I have to go into Hudson. About finding Coach's . . ." I couldn't say the rest. Bobby flinched, and Laura paled, and I felt my own stomach lurch remembering that morning. "Do you need anything? A glass of water? A bathroom?"

What was the protocol? I wondered. Should I leave the door open so that total strangers could come and go as they pleased while I was on a mission that I'd rather forget? That seemed the neighborly thing to do.

Bobby shook his head and Laura smiled and thanked me. Evidently nobody needed anything.

"All right, then, if you want to get started, I'll . . . oh, hold on a minute." Surely things worked the same in the country as they did in Brooklyn. I should be giving Bobby one-third of the money now, one-third when the job was half done, and the final third at completion.

"Do you mind if I get a drink of water?" Bobby frowned, glanced over at Laura, and jammed his hands into the pockets of his jeans. Laura followed me to the door.

"Of course not. Come in." The house seemed too warm when I pushed the door open. As I walked to my desk to get my checkbook, Laura followed me.

"I, um . . . I just wanted to say thanks." Her voice was light and musical, even in her hesitancy. "Bobby's a good worker. He'll do a great job for you. He's just not a great talker."

I grinned. "Well, I didn't hire him to make conversation. That's okay, I'm glad to have him here taking care of things. You're a good friend to him, I can see that."

"He's kind of . . . you know, he's taken Coach's death really hard. Anyway, I just wanted to say. If you want to ask him stuff, you can, you know, just tell me and I'll find out."

Unaccustomed to third-party communication, I thanked her, wrote out a check for one hundred dollars, and started to hand it to Laura. But she wasn't his keeper, she was his friend, and it would be a sign of disrespect to Bobby if I did that.

He was bent forward, peering first at one stump, then the other, walking around them as though they would reveal some great secret if only he looked hard enough.

Finally, he grunted. "Got a hose that reaches out here?"

"I don't know. I have a hose, but I've never tried to drag it out this far. What do you need a hose for?"

"Ground's wet, stump comes out easier. Run the water for a couple hours, then I can push it out. Either that, or we could just wait for a rain." He shrugged, glanced over at Laura, kicked at the stump.

Laura's tinkly voice chimed in. "Well, we don't want to depend on the weather around here for anything. Ground could freeze up hard before there's a good soaking rain. Let's try the hose."

Sensible girl, I thought, as I pointed to the coil of hose against the side of the cottage. I glanced at my watch. I would be at least an hour later than I'd promised in getting to Hudson. "Good idea. You guys set it up. I really have to get to town."

Bobby nodded and Laura smiled, giving him a playful shove. "Go on, Bobby. Let's get this started. You don't have to wait around here. It was really nice to meet you, Lili."

Despite my unease about Bobby's reluctance to talk to me directly, I was warmed by the notion that my gourd garden would have a place of its own, that Bobby knew what he was doing, that all would be well. I said good-bye and drove off to Hudson.

The county seat, known long ago as a stop on the railroad where easy women and gambling could be found for entertainment, had, in the prosperity of the 1990s, turned itself into the antique capital of the Hudson Valley. The main drag offered Hepplewhite this and Louis the umpteenth that and architectural salvage rescued from some of the grand old homes in the area before the historic properties started bringing astronomical prices. Restaurants — good ones — nestled among the shops, waiting for the weekend crowds.

But on Monday, with all the weekenders gone back to the grinds that allowed them to afford to buy extra virgin olive oil at the local gourmet shop for nearly as much as they paid in the city, I expected the town to move at a slower pace. The holiday lights blinked for the few with time to run afternoon errands, including sitting in some dingy, official room and writing out a very short, very sad, but necessary statement for the sheriff's department.

But when I turned onto Warren Street, I was stopped immediately by a crowd that appeared to be about two hundred strong, people milling in the street and shouting. My stomach twisted and my heart banged in my chest. For a moment I was confused, ready to flee to safety, aware in some dim place that I was reacting to an old fear, not to the situation before me. I sat motionless in my car until my breathing finally slowed. A cordon of uniformed officers formed a barrier that kept the crowd from marching down the street, and as my car idled I began to see the placards waving above the heads of the assembled.

STOP THE RICKLAND PLANT. Most of them bore the same message, preprinted in bold white letters against a green background. I became aware of variations — a circle around the word *Rickland,* with a diagonal slash through it; RICKLAND POLLUTES MY BACK-YARD; 10 JOBS=100 CANCERS. The noise swelled as people blew whistles and banged on drums, a sea of churning energy being channeled down the main street and blocking my way to the sheriff's office.

I spotted Michele Castro, knew she'd be too busy to worry about me, and then turned around and headed for home. Under other circumstances, I might even be out there with them, trying to head off the finality of a coal-burning cement plant coming to the shores of the Hudson River. Experts had been testifying for weeks that the plume of pollution from the plant would cut a swath twenty miles wide on both sides of the river, lowering property values and increasing the risks of environmentally induced illness. The owners of the plant had been working hard to convince the ordinary folks that the plant's environmental impact would be negligible compared to the economic benefits of creating hundreds of jobs.

To me, that wasn't like comparing apples and oranges, as one newspaper editorial called it. It was more like comparing apples and arsenic. But at least this demonstration meant that I could put off talking to the undersheriff until morning. Which left me the surprise gift of an unscheduled afternoon. I knew just how I wanted to spend part of it.

Two weeks had passed since I'd pulled Coach's body out of the cold pond. I'd stopped by Nora's house every other day. Susan dropped by after school many days, Melissa came in the late morning during the week, and Elizabeth planned to spend part of each Saturday trying to get Nora and Scooter out of the house. Visits from the four of us seldom overlapped, and although we never consulted about schedules, I suspected the others did what I did — if I saw another car in the driveway, I just kept on going, not wanting to overwhelm Nora with too many people who required her attention.

Which was just what I intended to do when I saw Elizabeth Conklin's massive green Land Rover parked under the basketball hoop. Except that Scooter was standing on the road at the mailbox examining a thick pile of envelopes, and I couldn't very well just drive on by. So I pulled over, engine idling, and rolled down my window.

"Hey, Scooter. How's it going?"

He was wearing the same expressionless mask that I'd seen on most visits, and his voice was barely audible when he muttered, "Fine."

"How's your mom today?"

His forehead wrinkled and he shrugged. Finally he said, "Okay, I guess. You want to come in?"

I couldn't tell whether he was just saying it because he had good manners or he thought a visit from me would be useful, but either way I could hardly say no.

"Sure. You want a ride?"

He shook his head. "I have to find the cat. She ran out of the house when Elizabeth came. She never does that, just run across the road like that."

I was about to ask if he wanted help, but he'd already turned and was crashing through the brush on the other side of the road. I pulled up beside Elizabeth's car and got out.

When I rang the doorbell, Elizabeth appeared. She was wearing a beautiful gray suit with a yellow silk blouse underneath, shoes with heels just high enough to show off her shapely legs, and a gold pin on the lapel that looked like the key to some secret society. On the streets of Manhattan I might pass scores of Elizabeths every day, but in Walden Corners I couldn't get past the sense that she looked a little silly.

"Hi, Lili. I was just leaving. How are you?" She stood aside to let me in, and her perfume, which I didn't recognize, drifted in my direction.

"I'm good, Elizabeth. How's Nora doing?"

Her expression softened, and she leaned closer to me, speaking softly. "She's cleaning again. She's totally wound up today. It's like she flipped a switch and now she's got triple energy. I'm glad someone's here.

I have to go to Albany for a case, but I was afraid to leave her alone. Scooter's spooked by her behavior too."

Unfortunately, I'd seen enough mourning to be familiar with the need to do something, to move, to not be sitting and thinking and drowning in memories and what-ifs. The best thing I could do would be to simply be with her, not try to stop her or force help on her, but be open and take my cues from her.

"You go on. I'll stay for as long as it makes sense."

To my surprise, her face lit up with a huge smile, and she reached out and patted my shoulder. Then Elizabeth Conklin marched to her car and I went inside.

"Noraaaaahh," I called into the quiet house.

In response, a crash resounded from the kitchen, metal against metal, the clattering like a waterfall of . . . pots. By the time I reached the kitchen, all the pots from Nora's cupboard lay on the floor, some tumbled one atop the other and others scattered to form an obstacle course to the stove. Nora stood, hands on hips, laughing so hard the tears began to run down her cheeks.

I laughed with her, but her laughter kept

on, gales of it, great gusts of it, and I began to worry that she might never stop. It came close to hysteria, and I was about to do something when I became aware that the laughter had turned to sobbing. I crossed the room in four steps and grabbed her into my arms and held on while the wracking sobs heaved through her body.

"I do that every once in a while," she said. Wiping her face with the back of her hand, she seemed to direct all her will to making her breathing slow and calm. "It only happens when Scooter's not around. Thank God."

"He's across the road looking for the cat. What's going on here? I walked in just as the Great Pot Calamity occurred."

Her crooked smile melted away. "I thought today would be a good day to change the shelving paper, and I had the pots on the counter and then one slipped out of my hands and the rest, as they say, is history. Maybe I should just leave it and come back tomorrow and the Pot Fairy will have taken care of things."

I raised an eyebrow. "Be careful with that kind of talk or you'll have the narcotics squad banging on your door."

The thought of a narcotics squad in Walden Corners made us both giggle as we

125

bent to grab the strewn cookware from the floor. "Elizabeth looked spiffy," I said as lightly as I could, practicing friendly feelings toward a woman who thoroughly confused me.

"She was off to Albany. Hearings on the plant start today." Nora shoved the last frying pan back into the closet and stood, brushing invisible dirt from her knees.

Elizabeth rose another notch in my estimation, until Nora said, "That's one part of her I cannot understand. She's a good friend, generous, passionate about a lot of important things. But then she goes and takes a job working for the Rickland people."

My head spun, and I could think of nothing to say.

Nora saved me from the awkwardness of the moment. She set the roll of shelving paper on the counter and said, "I don't think I'll do this right now. You want to come with me to the basement? I guess all this activity has been a way to avoid what I really have to do. Coach's basement lair — I have to clean it out. He keeps all the papers, bills, insurance, everything down there, and I don't want to get into trouble for not paying the mortgage. He's done all that financial stuff for years."

I started to say something, amazed that Nora wasn't the equal partner that I expected her to be in every aspect of their lives. But it wasn't my place to offer should-haves. I wanted to give her can-dos instead.

"Sure, let's go." I looked around her spotless kitchen. "We'll need some plastic bags, right? And a pad to write down things that need to be done. And a pen. Rubber bands maybe, and paper clips."

"And a bottle of bourbon." She grinned. "No, I'm not that far gone. Just the garbage bag. I'm sure Coach had all those other supplies down there. Let's move out, troops."

So we headed down the stairs, the basement greeting us with a mushroomy odor of dampness, and although I couldn't see a thing, I imagined the scurrying of thousands of hairy, spindly legs. Twenty centipedes or hundreds of silverfish — either way, the idea gave me the shivers.

"Why men actively seek places like this to hang out in is beyond my understanding. Has anyone ever studied whether testosterone flourishes in damp, dark spaces?" I nearly bumped my head on a beam as I waited for Nora to find the light.

Suddenly, the room was bright, and

when I looked around, the presence of Coach filled me with sadness. Everything was tidy, the desk surface clear of papers, pens and pencils sprouting from a ceramic jar, and the telephone at a precise right angle to the obviously homemade hutch with cubbies for envelopes, a jar of paper clips, a stapler, and the other necessities of Coach's personal and professional record-keeping and planning. Tools hung according to size on a pegboard behind a massive work table. A tall bookshelf was filled with health textbooks and Walden Corners yearbooks going back more than a decade.

The cement floor was painted pea soup green, and an old braided rug separated the office portion from the workshop. Coach's chair, an oak swivel, gleamed gold under the light. A small chest and can of paint stripper sat on the work bench awaiting attention.

"Okay then," Nora said too brightly. "I can't stand this. He's here in the air of this room, and I can't stand it. So let's get this over with."

I wanted to say something cheery, but the words stuck in my throat. Of course she couldn't stand it, but she would, and I would help her through it.

"Looks like a good place to start would be that mesh basket in the corner of the desk." Envelopes lay piled unopened, and that surprised me. I was the kind of person who could hardly wait until I got into the house to tear open anything that arrived from the post office, but I understood that this wasn't a universal compulsion. "Let's make four piles. Do it now, do it later, need more information, and best of all, toss and destroy. Then we can breeze through the do-it-nows and see where things stand."

Nora sat in the chair, reached for the first envelope, peered at the address, and then slit it open with the letter opener. "Friends of the library want money."

She tossed it into the do-it-now pile and reached for the next envelope. "Mortgage payment is overdue, late fees incurred." Frowning, she lay it atop the first papers. She went through three more envelopes, mumbling about late fees and finance charges as I handed her papers. Finally, we got through the stack in the basket.

"Now," I said, "all we need are some checks and some stamps, and we'll be finished with the first round of stuff."

Nora pulled open drawers, stuck her hand into each cubby, frowning as she continued her search. Finally, she waved a blue bank passbook in the air.

"Checkbook's not here, but this is our savings account. I need to find the checkbook, the bank statement, something that tells me what's in that account. Hey, this can't be right." Her voice was sharp, as though the papers in her hand were impugning Coach's character and she would have none of it. "I know it isn't. It says our savings account has one hundred three dollars and fifty cents in it."

Playing Pollyanna wasn't my strong suit, but I had to give it a try. "You're right, let's find the checkbook. Maybe he moved the money to a money market account or something."

Before I could finish the sentence, Nora was waving a blue check register in the air. But when she opened it, a frown knitted its way across her forehead. "The last entry was two years ago."

Laughing, I gave her shoulder a playful shove. "The computer. He's either been paying the bills online or he keeps the accounts on one of those computer programs that lets you see things in four colors and every which way."

She laughed with me and paced the room, stopping to flip open the laptop on the desk. She pressed the button to turn it on, dancing away to pull a broom from the rack on the wall. With short, rapid strokes she began to sweep the cement floor. "Of course. And thank goodness he told me that he uses the same password for everything. Scooter's birthday. You're smart, Lili, but then that's why I love you."

"And here I thought it was my gourds that you loved." The computer beeped and blinked and fluttered to life, and I stared at the screen as the boot routine continued. "And my lasagna. And my extensive knowledge of the human condition."

"And your modesty." Her laughter rippled across the room, a sound more natural than anything I'd heard from her in weeks. Sweeping her way toward me, she must not have seen the cord from the pencil sharpener, and her foot caught and she stumbled forward.

I leaped up to catch her, instinctively reaching out without being aware that I was standing near a teetering pile of wood. The wood went crashing to the floor, and one piece hit the tines of a garden rake, which then flew from its corner resting place to the other wall and hit a brick.

Which immediately disappeared.

Nora stopped laughing and together we

approached the space where the brick had been. Nora reached into the hole and pulled out the brick.

"There's something else in there, something metal," she said as her arm disappeared again into the now-empty space.

I grabbed a flashlight from the work bench and pointed the beam at the hole. She felt around for another second, still frowning, then withdrew her arm. "Here, pass me that screwdriver."

I watched as she poked into the hole two times, three, and then finally extracted a metal box, green and nicked and dented. She carried it to the desk as though she might burn herself if she touched it. I held my breath as she flipped the latch. The lid opened to reveal a single piece of paper.

She never looked at me, just stood there staring at the paper. I knew whatever was written on it would matter, could change everything, one way or another. Nora was overcome with a momentary shudder, and when the trembling stopped, she reached inside and pulled out the paper, and said aloud, "Sweet Jesus."

Chapter 8

I had never seen a check for so many dollars. Eighty thousand of them.

Eighty thousand dollars made out to the Ford World Fund.

"This check was cashed two years ago," Nora said in a barely audible voice. "My husband took our entire life savings and turned it all over to Tom Ford two years ago."

Her face was still, no longer the animated, almost frantic expression of manic energy that had sent her into a cleaning frenzy. This new bit of information was taking its time, registering its impact on Nora's life slowly as a new reality replaced the old one.

"He never said a word to me. I can't believe it. He kept saying that he was working on something that would take care of Scooter and me. That . . ."

If that money really had evaporated, with no cushion of savings and only the barest of life insurance policies, Nora Johnson was going to have to figure out how to pay the mortgage, provide medical care, and put food on the table sooner than she'd expected. But there was another possibility, and it would take a bit of work to uncover which truth she'd have to learn to absorb. Not that I expected that anything involving the Houdini act of Mr. Tom Disappearing Ford would lead to something good. It just felt better to keep the embers of hope from burning out entirely until we knew more.

"Maybe this means that you're rich. If that money has been invested well, it could be worth lots more. The existence of this check isn't enough to tell where things stand. Let's get back to the stuff on the desk. Maybe as you make sense of the bills and all that, you'll find out more."

I watched as she stuck her arm back into the hole, felt all around, her eyes closed and her face expressionless. When her empty hand reappeared, she plopped into the desk chair and sighed.

"I can't stand being down here. It's too much his place. I can feel his round butt on this cushion, you know, and smell him in the air. It's like he left pieces of himself behind because he spent so much time down here. Maybe some other time I'll be able to, but not now."

She upended a carton, banged out some specks of wood shavings, then grabbed papers from the desk and shoved them into the box, tossing in envelopes and receipts, emptying the wicker basket that appeared to house all the unpaid bills. She pulled open a desk drawer and started to rummage through files, tossing one in every now and then and talking all the while.

"You'd think that a man as careful as Henry Johnson would have kept all his important papers in one place, but no, he's got them scattered among these files, and it's going to take me forever to figure it all out." Two more file folders went sailing into the box. "I guess this is what my mama meant when she said that men shouldn't be left alone for too long or they'd create trouble where none existed. Oh, Coach, why did you have to go and die on me? I'm not ready for this. I am so mad. I am freaking furious." An envelope skittered to the floor and she stooped to retrieve it. "I can't breathe in this place."

I waited for her to make the first move, not sure that in her rambling she meant a single thing she said. But she grabbed the carton and marched to the stairs, not glancing back until we were in the kitchen. She closed the cellar door with a swift kick and then dropped the carton on the table.

"You want to go for a walk?" I offered. Her energy level was way up again, and I figured if I could wear her out, she might be better off.

For a moment, clarity of purpose shone in her eyes instead of the too-bright glitter I'd seen for the past hour. "Thanks, Lili, but I need to make myself a cup of chamomile tea and sit down and take a whole lot of deep breaths. Scooter's already scared by my behavior this morning, and I want to get myself calm for him. He'll be coming back inside soon. I guess what I'm saying is —"

"I'm outta here. I can tell when I'm getting the boot. I'll talk to you tomorrow." I smiled to show her that I understood, hugged her, and then grabbed up my coat and my backpack. "If you need anything, call me."

"Thanks, Lili. For everything." Her movements were slower and more assured as she filled the kettle with water and lit the stove. I let myself out and drove off wondering if I would have the grace and wisdom that my friend was displaying in the face of such shocks to her life's foundations.

★ ★ ★

So many vehicles were parked in my driveway that I thought I must have stumbled into a mechanic's convention. The red tractor still skulked at the edge of the lawn, an unfamiliar silver pickup truck was parked beside it under the bare branches of the shagbark hickory tree, and my brother's little red Fiat had pulled up practically to the back door, looking like a toy carelessly tossed onto the gravel by a willful child.

Bobby Benson turned his head as I walked toward him, and Laura jumped up from her perch on the stump. From behind me, a voice said, "I figured you'd have to come home sometime."

It took me a couple of beats to put name to that craggy, pleasant face. "Mr. Selinsky, hi. I didn't recognize your truck."

"If I were a good ole boy I'd shuffle my feet and say, 'Aw, shucks, ma'am, I reckon to change that.'" He rested against the fender of his truck, crossed his lean legs at the ankles, and smiled. "You've got lots going on, I can see. Just wanted to know if you're a B.B. King fan. I'm going to get tickets for next Thursday night in Poughkeepsie and I was hoping you would join me."

A date. This good-looking, apparently solvent, blues-appreciating man was asking me out on date. I could make excuses or I could jump into strange waters.

"That sounds great. Who knows how much longer he'll be performing? But I can't say yes until you answer one question."

"Shoot." As he smiled, the floating life preserver receded into the distance. Such nice warm eyes, such ease in his body. His hands, surprisingly rough for a man with an office job, looked strong and calm, like the rest of him.

"Your first name has gone out of my head. What is it?"

He laughed. "That'd be good to know, I guess. I'm Seth. And you're Lili. Four letters each. That gives us something in common right there. Great view from the cab of my truck, so I'll pick you up at six."

Decisive. I liked that. Not like Ed, who would have asked how I wanted to travel, what time was good for me, whether I wanted to eat first or later, and would have ended up making me feeling both stifled because he was so solicitous and responsible for everything because he could never say straight out what he wanted and left everything to me.

"That's great." I cast a glance at Bobby, who was doing mysterious things with the hose — moving it, poking the toe of his boot into the soil. "Listen, I have to go talk to Bobby. Excuse me a minute."

"That's okay. I have to get going myself. I'm glad you said yes." Seth Selinsky didn't shake my hand or squeeze my shoulder, and I felt a little bit of disappointment.

"See you next week." I turned without waiting for him to get into his truck and walked directly to where Bobby and Laura stood. As I got closer to the stumps, my shoes squished in the swampy morass that used to be my lawn.

"I'm going to try the small one here," Bobby said, tapping a stump with his scuffed boot. "I been digging around the roots and she feels pretty loosened up."

Laura glanced at her watch. "I have to get going soon, Bobby. You said two hours, and it's more than that now."

Bobby wouldn't meet her eyes. Instead, he poked at the mud. "I can't keep coming back. I need to get this done."

A sharp wind rattled the dry grass at the edge of the woods, and a lone bird called out in the silence. I wasn't touching this discussion with a tractor blade.

"All right. Do the small one and then take me home." The bite in Laura's voice matched the chill wind as she sighed and flopped onto the other stump. "I'm freezing."

That little display of attitude surprised me. Whether it was brought on by several boring hours in the cold November air or something else, I bit back an invitation for her to come inside. I wanted to see my brother, and I wanted to have this job over with as quickly as possible.

"Here, Laura, you can borrow my gloves. Bring them back when you get a chance. Okay, Bobby, so you'll do the small one now and come back for the other two. You know, if you give me some warning I can run the hose out here and start it going so it's ready for you to just come and yank out the stump."

Bobby checked the front blade, nodded, and then climbed up onto the tractor.

I did not want to watch, did not want to have to hold my breath while he pushed, pulled, and otherwise moved those stubborn tree stumps. I glanced down at Laura and felt a little sorry that I was being so inhospitable, but not sorry enough to invite her in. I wheeled and headed for the cottage, dark except for the beacon of yellow light at the rear. By the look of things, Neil was in the kitchen.

I shed my jacket even before I pulled the door open. Neil stood by the sink, washing a glass. He turned and opened his arms, hugged me, then for good measure and old times, punched my arm.

"Who's Mr. Adonis?" My brother smelled good, clean and herbal, and his brown eyes twinkled with mischief. "You looked mildly uncomfortable, but I couldn't tell if you wanted to be rescued or not."

Neil always surprised me with his observations, which meant that I was still thinking of him as the infant whose diapers I used to change instead of as the twenty-three-year-old fielding sensation for the Brooklyn Cyclones.

I peered out the window and nearly cringed at the sight of the tractor attacking the first stump. Bobby seemed to know what he was doing, even if I didn't understand the physics, the botany, or the cost to the beauty of my carefully tended lawn. I turned away, unable to watch. "Rescued from my dateless existence is more like it. He's a nice man. And he's taking me to see B.B. King. To what do I owe the pleasure of your unexpected company?"

"I was in the neighborhood. Albany, actually, and I thought your sofa would be better than driving off the road out of fatigue and boredom. I forgot to tell you at Thanksgiving. Wow, look at that," he said, looking out the window. "Those roots are huge. Shoot, now I'm going to have dentist nightmares." He stood transfixed, and I couldn't keep myself from turning to check out the sight.

The tractor rumbled in reverse, like a bull backing up so that it could charge again. In front of it, the stump now lay on its side, a thick tangle of brown roots looking too much like nerve endings now that Neil had put the tooth image in my head. Bobby yanked on the gear shift and the machine roared forward in very slow motion. The blade hit the knot of roots with a clang, and the tractor pushed another foot of roots up and then came to a stop. Laura stood off to the side, her arms waving wildly, anger wrinkling her pretty face.

I was about to pull my boots back on when the tractor chugged into reverse again, made a broken U-turn, and headed for the driveway. One stump down, two to go — if my heart could stand the suspense.

"Well, after all that hard work, I'm

hungry. Sloppy joes?" He grinned. "I already checked out your larder."

How could I refuse such a cute growing boy? I pulled open the refrigerator and pulled out two plastic containers, onions, and half a green pepper.

"So, maybe he's the new man in your life. But you'll wait and see if he knows what fork to use, right? I mean, I don't go leaping into things. I don't know, a man who drives a silver truck . . . he seems to be straddling a couple of different worlds, Lili. And those two kids out there, where did you find them? She's a piece of work. Man, remind me to be in another state when she turns nineteen. She's gonna be dangerous."

"Dangerous? As in lock up the boys, Mabel, there's trouble ahead?" His grin told me that was exactly what he meant. "I guess there are some things men see more easily than women do. You talk to them?"

"Only long enough to convince them that I wasn't coming to this deserted spot to rob you or worse. That boy was very protective, and the girl, well, she had that *look* in her eyes when she saw me drive up. Must have been the car. Gets to all of them."

But I knew better. My brother Neil is the kind of man who little boys wish they could be when they grow up, even if they don't know enough to understand why. Much of it has to do with his effect on women, which is to make each one feel that his smile and his attention were gifts that he was delighted to offer. The other is his fabled ambidextrous throwing talent, which makes him an exceptional shortstop. Neil would pay to play for the Mets, something he has been restrained from trying to accomplish. Meanwhile he has a berth on the Brooklyn Cyclones, the farm team for his beloved Amazin's.

"So, how's your friend, the one whose husband . . ."

"Whose body I found," I said softly. "She's having a hard time. I feel like I should just stay away from her whole family because I keep discovering bad news. Today we found out that her husband wrote a check to Tom Ford for eighty thousand dollars. That's every bit of money they had in savings. And we know that Tom's company went bust, which is how I ended up here. So we're assuming that she's flat broke now."

Neil stopped pulling open cupboards and folded his arms across his chest.

"Your mystery man sounds like he should be the subject of the attorney general's attention."

"From the things Tom told me, his activities were foolish, not illegal. He invested heavily in a pharmaceutical company whose magic cancer drug killed people, and in an insurance company that covered major hotel chains, and had to pay out huge dollars, I mean maybe three hundred million, after that series of hurricanes last fall."

"Maybe you want to believe that about him. Would you give him your life savings, knowing what you know now?" He poured himself a glass of red wine and handed me one.

A new vision of Tom Ford appeared, as a leering, potbellied bald man with sausage fingers and liver lips, sitting on a beach in the Caribbean as beautiful women brought him umbrella drinks. This Tom Ford deserved only scorn, and I had plenty of that to offer him.

"I wouldn't give him a safety pin, unless it was to keep his lips permanently shut. Thanks for asking that question, buddy. You do know how to put things into perspective. Now, can we talk about something else, like Mom's drinking or why my younger sister hates me or something easy for a while?"

While Neil chopped the onion and pepper, I opened a can of tomatoes and crumbled leftover Italian sausage into a pan and we chattered about baseball and the fundraiser for Habitat for Humanity that he'd driven up to attend. My two brothers and my sister and I hardly ever had the time to see each other one on one, always carving time out of our busy lives for family gatherings but seldom sitting down to catch up on what was going on beneath the surface. It felt good to have him here in my kitchen, and even better to share a meal with someone I didn't have to protect or get to know or figure out how to communicate with.

"Oh, I forgot to tell you," Neil said as we were about to sit down to eat. "Right after I got here, you got a call from someone named, I think it was, Castro. Sounded a little huffy. A woman. She wants you to come to her office at four tomorrow afternoon."

After Neil left the next morning, I went straight to my studio. Just being there surrounded by gourds in all stages of completion and my tools was at once calming and energizing. I felt like *me,* the true me, in this room, and I worked blessedly free of interruptions for four hours and finally finished the contemporary skyline gourd I'd been working on. That made it four done and thirty to go. I turned the gourd over gently, amazed that the picture in my head hadn't come even close to the finished gourd. This was better, the rich blue of the sky along the rim something I'd added at the last minute. This was how I wanted to feel every day, flooded with designs and ideas and happiness. But instead of new designs, my mind kept filling up with questions about Tom Ford, Ira Jackson, Alvin Akron. About Elizabeth Conklin and her hot and cold running emotions. About Bobby Benson and his apparent emotional shutdown. About Nora and Scooter.

Bobby wasn't a question, exactly. I just wanted make sure that his parents were aware of how affected he seemed to be by Coach's death so that they could get him help. My broken lawnmower might give me the perfect excuse. If I took a right out of my driveway, I could pass directly by the Benson house, drop off my wounded lawnmower for repair, have a casual chat with Fred, and then continue into Hudson to see Michele Castro. I wrestled the unwieldy monster into the back of my Subaru and hoped that when I got to my destination someone else with the brawn to toss around heavy equipment as though it were a Tinker Toy would be around to do the heavy lifting.

Fred Benson's shop, at the far end of the crescent-shaped drive, was a metal shed with red metal shutters and a neatly lettered sign that said *Benson's Mower and Mobile Repair.* No other cars were in the drive when I pulled in, and the place had a peaceful air about it, sun shining through the branches of three maple trees that formed a natural fence between the house and the shop.

I knocked on the door and then pushed it open. A tiny bell tinkled, but since the shop was essentially one big room, I wondered why that was necessary. Boxes overflowed with mysterious-looking parts and cans of oil, tools hung on pegboard racks, and a long wood work table with a large vise on one end and a small one on the other took up half the floor space. Four chainsaws, two lawnmowers, and some other odd-looking piece of equipment were strewn about in various sates of disrepair. Unsure of the etiquette — should I beep, knock on the door of the house, holler out into the cold afternoon? — I stood shivering and finally decided that I'd go up to the house and see if Fred was there. But before I reached the door, it opened, and the large man clomped in.

"Help you?"

"Hello" would have been nice, but I was so relieved that I wouldn't have to buck the lawnmower out of my car by myself that I said, "Yes. My lawnmower has a problem. It's in the back of my car. Do you have time to fix it, Mr. Benson?"

He cocked an eyebrow. "Nothing but time these days. Lemme carry it in. I can't do it now, have to go pick up Buster from the doctor's. So if you can leave it for a day or two I can see what's wrong. You're up at the Ford house, right?"

How long would it take until it became the Marino house, I wondered.

"Yes, I'm Lili Marino. We met at —"

"Ag Day. I remember. Car's open?"

I nodded. I was going to say that we'd met at the reception after Coach's funeral, but he was right, technically. I watched as he opened the hatch, lifted the mower, and carried it into the shop. He set it beside the workbench and then turned to me, a frown creasing his forehead.

"Something else?" he said finally.

"I, uh, no." I walked to the door, turned the handle, then realized that I was letting discomfort stand in the way of my mission. "Actually, yes. I just wanted to let you know what a good job Bobby is doing for me. He's got one of those stumps out and he does what he says and sees things through. I'd hire him again in a minute."

"Boy always does a good job," Fred muttered, as though he was offended that I even thought to comment on such a thing.

Did this man even see his child as a person? My concern grew — he had no idea what Bobby was going through. I smiled and said, "He seems so, I don't know, maybe the right word is *thoughtful*. Quiet, as though he's worried all the time. I have the feeling that Coach Johnson's death has been hard for him. He seems to be having a hard time."

"What do you mean, a hard time?" The frown, which had never really left Fred's face, deepened, and a red flush rose from his neck to his forehead.

I was right. This father wasn't even aware of his son's emotional state. "I think a lot of the kids on the football team are having a hard time, from what I've been told. When I see Bobby, he's either quiet and a little sad, or else he seems jumpy."

With a noisy intake of breath that expanded his barrel chest, Fred Benson shook his head, then exhaled and said, "You don't know anything about my boy. He's fine. That's just his way. He's not talkative."

Which he obviously inherited in a direct line from his father, I thought.

"Well, okay. I guess I'll wait to hear from you about the mower."

Fred only nodded and then turned his back on me. I was glad to get away from the shop. Until I remembered that my next mission would surely make the visit to the Benson shop feel like a stroll in Prospect Park.

Surprisingly, the town of Hudson was bustling with cars, people strolling the sidewalks, the holiday lights spanning Warren Street lending a festive air to all the activity. I parked behind the squat concrete block building, went to the front desk, and was shown at once through a dimly lit hall to Michele Castro's office by a woman who looked like a Hallmark grandmother, but who chewed gum so furiously that I could hardly understand when she told me to follow her.

The undersheriff was displeased, and she

didn't bother to pretend otherwise. Her eyes glinted with annoyance, and her mouth drew thinner as she pursed her lips, reminding me how glad I was to have parents who communicated in words instead of making me guess by the expressions on their faces what was bothering them. I probably would have run away at ten, instead of waiting until I was seventeen, if I'd been raised in such a household.

"Please write a full statement describing that morning." She slid a yellow pad and a pen across her desk to me. "Don't leave anything out, even if it doesn't seem important to you. Details count. Times. Objects. People. What you saw, heard, smelled."

I nodded. "You want me to do that here?"

She pointed to a chair and turned her attention to her computer. I started writing, stopping twice to blink back tears, and once to catch my breath, which still grew ragged whenever I thought about the moment that I'd realized that the body in the pond was Coach. Finally I stood, set my three pages on her desk, and waited for her to tell me what happened next.

She read quickly. "So when you got back to your car," she said, "you noticed a gray sock with a red stripe, a tube of lipstick, a cigarette lighter, a Dremel wire brush, about eight or nine rifle shells, and a blue bandana. Did you move or touch anything?"

"I told you, I didn't touch anything near the body. And I didn't know it was a crime scene or else I wouldn't have parked in the turnout — and I didn't touch anything there, either. I saw what looked like someone in trouble and I stopped to help. That's all."

"Then why did you wait so long to come in to give your statement, Miss Marino? You were supposed to be here yesterday."

Indignant, I said, "I *was* here yesterday. *You* weren't. I was a few minutes late and when I got here you were out on Warren Street. At that demonstration. But here I am. And I've given you a written statement and I've answered all your questions. I don't really want a lecture too."

"You didn't answer all my questions," she said, her voice flat and emotionless. "And it's not a lecture, Miss Marino. It's my job."

Maddeningly, she said nothing else, once again leaving me to wrack my brain as I tried to figure out what she meant. What question did I fail to answer? Where had I gone wrong in my terrible life of crime? That opened a whole universe of possibilities.

"Are you telling me that I'm a suspect?"

Michele Castro's eyes narrowed. "Look, if you stop thinking of me as the enemy, we can get on with what we have to do. How long did it take from the time you parked your car until you got back to the café? That's all. You said you left the post office at ten fifteen. It takes pretty much six minutes to get to that turnout. Based on what you said, it took you about ten, twelve minutes to get down the hill, drag the body out of the water, try to administer CPR, give up, climb back up the hill, and get into your car. Let's say you drove a little faster on the way back because you were in a hurry. Make it five minutes back. That's six and twelve and five, twenty-three minutes. But witnesses in the café said that you came in at five after eleven. And the call to my office came in at exactly seven after. That's twenty minutes longer than I figure. So, how do you explain that?"

For the first time in memory, I was speechless. The room dimmed and my heart banged in my chest. "I . . . this is . . ." I inhaled slowly, deeply, waiting for calm but my soupy brain swam with confusion. "I don't have a clue. Probably I was in shock and kept trying to revive a dead man. I told you everything that happened, exactly as I remember it. I'm not hiding anything, and I don't know anything more than I already stated."

The wind had gone out of me, and it had taken some of the fight along with it. The idea of squaring off against this woman no longer held any attraction for me, and I just wanted to go home, work on a gourd, go to sleep, and start my round of work-filled days and quiet nights again.

"You work with Dremels, Miss Marino?"

"I told you I did. I told you that's why I recognized the wire brush when I saw it."

"And you weren't the one who dropped it? And then realized it was missing from your tool kit?" She was the kind of person whose voice got quieter as she moved in for the kill. Her manner was unnerving, and her line of questioning confusing.

"Look, I told you that I saw it on the ground. It was there when I left. And I didn't touch it or move it or disturb it." I pushed my chair back and rose. "If you want to come with me back to my house, I'll show you my wire brush. And if you don't, I'm sorry I couldn't help you any more than I did. I discovered the body of a friend, and I told you everything I know, and that's the whole story."

She waited until I got to the door before she said, "He was my friend too."

Chapter 9

"Things are a jumble, as my mother would say."

Melissa, Elizabeth, and Susan sat at my dining table and nodded their agreement. Melissa glanced at Susan, Susan bit her lower lip, and I felt the tension rise in this small room. Elizabeth, doodling on a legal pad, seemed oblivious to the charged atmosphere, and I groped my way forward. I was, after all, the one who had called these women together, to see whether our collective wisdom might help me better understand what was happening and what we could do about it.

"She loves setting the jumbles in order. So Ruth Marino found the perfect job. She's the events coordinator for Mayor Silver's office, and one of her talents is soothing huffy caterers, florists, limo drivers. She thrives on dealing with cultures as different as Iowa and Indonesia. But I'm having a hard time with this particular jumble."

When I complained about not being able to settle down to my homework, my mother used to say, "If you can't concentrate, then at least make your desk clean." But even though my desk was tidy and the tools of both my trades ready for action, my mind kept circling around the events of the past couple of weeks. Coach's death, the revelation that he'd drowned before he was shot, the discovery of the transaction between him and Tom Ford — complication upon entanglement upon confusion.

"The only things that are clear to me are that Nora needs to find another way to support herself and Scooter, and the police are stretched thin by the demonstrations against the Rickland plant."

"We need to leave the detection to the police," Elizabeth said calmly. *Icily* wasn't quite right, but not too far off. "Sheriff Murphy does not take well to interference in any kind of case, much less the second murder of the year in Walden Corners. The first one was different. Order of protection violated, domestic disturbance culminates in murder, end of story. This one isn't so straightforward, and Gene Murphy knows it's going to take more time and energy to solve it."

I marveled at the clinical description of what she'd called a straightforward murder.

"Well, if the police weren't overwhelmed by the demonstrations . . ." Susan rolled her eyes, then straightened her back and said, "Elizabeth, why are you supporting the Rickland plant? We grew up together, we did Earth Day projects together in fifth grade. I can't believe you'd sell out to a company that's going to turn this beautiful valley into a cancer cauldron."

I nearly stopped breathing.

Melissa lay her hand over Elizabeth's. "We didn't intend to bring this up here. But since it's out, well, we were going to find a time to talk to you about what you're doing there, so let's not let it sit there like a huge fart nobody wants to talk about. That cement plant is so bad for the area. I don't understand how you can work for those people."

Elizabeth's eye twitched, but her face remained otherwise impassive. For a moment, I almost felt sorry for her. Her best friends were angry, and although they may have intended to confront her when I wasn't around, it had slipped out in my presence. I stayed silent, my eyes on the table top.

"It's so good of you to harbor your resentments and then throw them at me when I least expect it. I'm not going to defend myself to you. If you want to have a trial, you can convict me in absentia." She pushed back her chair, tossed me a glance, and then rose.

"I'll leave the room, if you three want to talk. Maybe that would be better." I stood next to Elizabeth, close enough to see her hand tremble. My stomach lurched with the pain in the room. "I was hoping we could talk about whether there's something we can do to help Nora, but we'll never get to that if all these bad feelings are getting in the way."

Elizabeth glared at me, her jaw jutting defiantly. Melissa nodded and blinked. Susan, who had been unable to meet anyone's glance since her accusation, looked up at Elizabeth.

"I didn't mean to ambush you," she said softly. "Sorry."

Elizabeth nodded. She didn't sit down, but she also didn't make any moves to leave.

"I guess we were so, I don't know, surprised, maybe even shocked, that we didn't know what to say. But I can't stand it anymore. I feel like it's this thing between us and I can't bear to see our friendship . . . I want to understand, Elizabeth. I really want to understand. Why are you doing it?"

If I had been conducting a mediation, I couldn't have done any better. They'd vented some feelings and now they were asking open-ended questions to gather information.

Still standing, Elizabeth placed her graceful hands on the table and leaned forward, her eyes steely. "You let this bad feeling build up for how long? And bring it out in front of a stranger? And then expect me to sweetly explain myself away and make you more comfortable again? Well, that's not very friendly, now is it?"

I'd forgotten about *both* sides needing to vent.

But Elizabeth surprised me by sitting down and pulling her chair up to the table. "You're right, of course, about what Rickland is up to." The edge was gone from her voice, and she looked at each of us before she continued. "When I took the job, I didn't know it was going to be so bad. Part of what I figured was that if I didn't do it, someone else would. Someone who would be ruthless, cutthroat, someone with no conscience. I thought I'd be doing something noble, keeping them honest. They approached me, they flattered me, they told me that their technology was up-to-date and the impact on the environment would be minimal and the impact on the local economy would be positive. So I became the local mouthpiece, the front for what they were hoping to accomplish. They needed someone like me to say to people I've known all my life that I was behind this so that they could sway what they knew would be initial negative reactions. But then I read the reports."

Nobody said a word. I held my breath and waited, wondering where this was going.

"The anti-Rickland group has hard data that show that the plume of pollution will devastate the river for fifty miles in either direction. I resigned today."

Susan whooped and hugged Elizabeth, Melissa leaped up and planted a kiss on her cheek, and I grinned and tried to keep in the background.

"I'm sorry." Susan sat down. "I mean it. I didn't mean to pounce that way."

Elizabeth opened her mouth, and for a second I thought she was going to launch into another attack. "Apology accepted. And since we're getting all warm and fuzzy here, I have my own apologies to make."

Sarcasm aside, she sounded sincere. The smiles on the faces of the other two indicated to me that this was vintage Elizabeth and anything too sweet would be suspect.

"I'm sorry for being so dense about Rickland." Once again, she made eye contact around the table, like Atticus Finch connecting with each member of the jury. When she came to me, she stopped. "And I'm sorry for putting you on the spot. I guess since you've become Nora's friend, I was a little suspicious, a little worried about how an outsider would be with her and her family. You know, like waiting for signs of condescension, waiting to see if she was going to be your token minority, a way to make yourself feel like you were being a good New York liberal. I didn't even give you a chance, actually. I just attributed all those things to you. I was wrong. I'm sorry."

Stunned, I counted to ten as I tried to get my mind to settle back into the place where I had access to words. Some kind of response was required. "I'm not sure what to say. Well, yes, I am. Apology accepted. For one thing, I'd much rather have you on my side than against me. For another, I'm glad we got this out in the open. I'd be really happy to let it go and move forward."

Melissa poured herself a glass of wine. "Can't be easy to walk into a town the size of Walden Corners, into a group like this one that's been together since second grade. Cheers to you, Lili, for your courage."

Now I felt my face flame. This wasn't courage, but I couldn't spoil the moment with an argument about semantics. "And yours for accepting me, city ways and all. Now, what are we going to do about Nora?"

Elizabeth's eyebrows arched. "Do? What needs doing? *Be* is more what I think she needs. She needs to find her way and not be treated like a child incapable of taking care of herself."

Susan bit off a burnt edge of cookie. "Helping a friend get on her feet isn't making her into a child. God, Elizabeth, you know you can carry this self-sufficiency thing too far. What did you call it when you and Richard were having problems and you were so confused you didn't know what you wanted and we all sat in kitchen of the inn for six hours, listening and talking and laughing and crying? Was that a bad thing for us to do?"

"No." Her voice was barely audible. "I am totally grateful for that night. It

164

changed my life. I just want to go carefully. None of us has ever been through anything remotely like this."

"I have."

It was like watching other people watch a tennis match. Suddenly, all heads swiveled in my direction and then stopped.

"And?" Melissa said finally.

"A good friend in Brooklyn lost her husband in the World Trade Center. She was eight months pregnant and they had just bought an apartment in Park Slope. She totally shut down for three weeks, then went into labor, came home with a beautiful baby boy and a terrible case of postpartum depression."

"She earned it," Susan mumbled.

"What did you do?" Elizabeth passed me the cookie plate.

"I sat with her at first. A couple of hours each day. I played with the baby, helped her bathe him, didn't say a word or lecture her or anything. And then one day I said, 'You think Mitch would want you to grieve for him this way?' Just that. And she understood." I sipped my tea. "This isn't the same, but maybe there's one quiet, simple thing that Nora needs to hear. Any one of you knows her better than I do, and can probably come up with that thing. She doesn't need pressure and she doesn't need lecturing and she doesn't need to be turned into a lifelong victim. She needs her friends."

Nobody spoke, and as I looked around I felt a sense that together we'd find a way to ease Nora's journey. Finally, Melissa cleared her throat.

"Okay, so after all the drama here this evening, I think we've learned a couple of things. We each need to call Nora and say that we'd like to help her, but we don't know exactly how, don't know what she needs, and we'd like to spend some time just being there. Listening. Talking. Whatever."

"That sounds perfect." Susan was grinning. "Maybe it's too soon to do poker night. But we can tell her we want to get together and let her pick a date. We should do it someplace familiar. Comfortable. Not the inn and not where kids or husbands can walk in. Sorry, Melissa. Sorry, Elizabeth."

"Here," I said. "There are no interruptions and no old memories. I'm going to the city the day after tomorrow to take care of some business. I won't be gone more than three days. So any time after that is fine with me."

"Next Tuesday night is best for me," Susan said, unfolding her long legs and pushing up out of her chair. "I have parents' night on Monday."

"I'm pretty open . . ." Elizabeth glanced at her PalmPilot. "Now that I don't have Rickland briefs to prepare, there's so much more time."

"Well, it's too late or I'd say we could play a few hands of five-card draw. Nora might not be ready for poker, but I am." Melissa looked around. "You better watch your assumptions, city girl, because these country folks might surprise you."

I laughed and poured more wine into Elizabeth's empty glass. "They already have."

They left at 10:30, after finishing two bottles of wine and all the chocolate brownies I'd made. We agreed, in a vague way, that we'd speak to Nora and make a date to make dinner together, see what else she might want to do. As I cleaned up our glasses and dishes and thanked goodness that nobody smoked anymore because dirty ash trays would have been more than I could face, I kept thinking there must be something more we might do, but nothing came to mind. Instead, I went upstairs, read the latest copy of *The Journal of the*

American Gourd Society, marveling at the pictures of projects other people had completed, enjoying the hints readers shared in "The ABC's of Gourds" column, and finally drifted into a restless sleep.

The phone rang at five minutes after seven, as I was stumbling through my morning routine, a little worse the wear for the wine I'd consumed the night before. My heart pounded, and in the two seconds it took me to cross the room and lift the receiver I thought about my father and his Parkinson's, my brother and his Fiat, my chronically overworked mother.

"Hey, Lili, I know you're an early riser. Scooter just left for school, and I've got something here I want you to see. I don't know what to do about this. It's way complicated, and I don't want to talk about it over the phone. I mean, don't worry, nothing to worry about but . . . can you come over?" Nora sounded as though she'd been up for hours, her voice thoughtful if not exactly calm.

"Can it wait an hour? A shower and a cup of coffee will make me a much more rational person." I poured hot water into the one-cup filter and stuck a piece of seven-grain bread into the toaster as I spoke.

"Sure, no problem. Thanks, Lili. I'm glad you're coming. See you later."

I slathered the toast with cottage cheese, then stood in front of the window watching the sky brighten as I took huge bites of toast in between giant gulps of coffee. The bushes on the far side of the walk looked sturdy, patient, strong enough to wait out the long, deep chill of winter. I wondered if I had that same hardiness. Whatever news Nora needed to share, it didn't sound as though it was going to make anything in her life easier.

After a quick shower, I pulled on jeans, cotton camisole, turtleneck, thick cotton socks, and my knock-off suede shoes that the catalog called moccasins but I thought of as clodhoppers and then drove the back roads to Nora's house. The lights were on in the kitchen, and I rapped on the door and then pushed it open.

"Hey, Nora, where are you?" I called out into the quiet.

"Right here." Nora appeared in the doorway, her smile a little wobbly. She hugged me, and I felt her heart racing. Her fingers tapped on the counter. Nora Johnson was in her high-energy state again. I braced myself for an onslaught of chatter, but instead she said, "I won't drag this out,

Lili. I found two letters. One from Coach to Tom Ford, the other one Tom's answer. Here, read them for yourself."

I took the first pages she handed me and glanced at the date as she paced from stove to sink to butcher block island and back. October, more than a month before Coach was killed. Coach's letter, neatly typed, started with a description of how he'd trusted Tom because of his experience, his much-touted philosophy of fiscal prudence, his commitment to growing a company that would be around long after its founder left. But the tone became increasingly angry.

You betrayed my trust and put my family in danger, the last paragraph began. *I will not stand around and watch while you rip me off and go on your merry way without a care in the world. Believe me, you will regret stealing my money.*

The first part of the letter confirmed that the entire eighty thousand dollars was, indeed, gone. The second half told the tale of Coach's roller coaster of emotions, from despair to fury to resolve to set things right. It mentioned how frustrated he was at not having a way to reach Tom by telephone, at having received no communication from the man into whose hands he'd put his faith and savings, at the fact that the letter was being sent to Tom's last known address in the hope that it would be forwarded.

"That's so not like my husband," Nora said when I handed her the letter. "He must have been even madder when he first sat down, because he wouldn't send something impulsively. I bet his computer has three or four other versions that are even angrier. Here, read the response."

I gasped when she handed me the next paper. A single line, written in straight, bold script was the only message.

I do not respond well to threats. Tom Ford.

"Wow, that's harsh." A clatter of thoughts whirled through my brain. Nora had called me because I was the one with the connection to Tom. But I didn't know him, not really, not in any way that would tell me whether he was capable of murdering someone. Had there been other communication between them, phone calls, visits? And what should be done with this information, now that all those questions wouldn't go neatly back behind their brick in the cellar wall?

Like one of those blow-up dolls with sand weighting the rounded bottom, the more I tried to knock down Tom Ford, the more he kept popping back up.

"So, I have to call the sheriff, right, and have them follow up on this." Nora's statement was really more a question, the reluctance in her voice stronger than the conviction. She squeezed out a sponge and started wiping the already clean counters. "I hate for everyone to know our business. This is such a small community, and maybe I have too much pride, but I don't want all the tongues clacking. Still, if he —"

"If he can be found, then he can be either crossed off the list or moved right to the top." What I hesitated to say was that perhaps the eighty thousand dollars could be restored to Nora and Scooter, although that seemed more wishful thinking than anything else. It shouldn't be so hard to find him, really, because he would have had to register his company with the regulatory agencies — SEC, NASD, the attorney general's office. So, even if he'd moved thirteen times and left no forwarding address, if he was still in business someone should be able to track him down.

"I don't know. I don't think Michele Castro would say anything, but other people in that office . . . it's Gossip Central. Everyone would know that Scooter and I have about twelve cents to our names. Oh, the pity and the charity events — I couldn't stand it. I can't believe Tom would kill a man for being angry at him. But then I couldn't believe Alvin Akron would nurture an old hate and I couldn't believe that Ira Jackson would . . . What should I do, Lili?"

I wasn't sure that in her present state Nora would hear anything I said, but if I kept things simple my words might penetrate later.

"All I can tell you is that I'd turn the letters over to the sheriff's department. They seem relevant. Talking to Tom seems important. Finding out where he was on that Monday seems necessary."

Nora's eyes lit up and she grabbed my hand. "You're right. All of that is relevant, important, necessary. You dealt with Tom for months, right? You're going to the city soon to bring down some gourds and talk to a corporate client, aren't you?"

"Yes, to that new gallery. Thanks for reminding me. The gourds are all signed and dated but I still have to print out an invoice." For a moment I let myself be carried away by the thrill of actually making money — it was even approaching what Karen would call *real* money — at my gourd art.

"Well, maybe you can track him down there. If you can get hold of him, maybe you'll find out that he was in Timbuktu or something. And then I won't have to tell my tale of woe to the entire Eastern seaboard."

My groan could have been heard on the West Coast. "What if he says something that makes me suspicious, or if I can't reach him, or —"

"If you can't find him, or if you do and you aren't convinced by what he says, I'll turn the letters over to the sheriff." She got out a bottle of window cleaner and started spraying the chrome of the stove hood, squirting little bursts of blue liquid onto the shiny surface. "Thanks, Lili. Honestly, I'm glad you're going to try. That's all. Just try. Just give me a few days."

Later that night, I Googled the company name and came up with only the same address and telephone number in New York City that Nora said was no longer in service. One article said that the Ford World Fund was defunct. That would surely make finding Tom more difficult.

A gentle rain started to fall, and the sound on the roof made me glad to be snug in my cottage. I lay in bed wondering how I would feel returning to the city tomorrow, aware that each trip back taught me new things about myself and my choices. I couldn't anticipate what would happen, which was what had made living in the city so exciting and so stressful for me.

I fell asleep ten minutes after I recognized that the same was true about living in the country. I'd never been involved in a murder before, never had to navigate what amounted to an unfamiliar culture. Never had to wonder if the man who used to live in my house or the one I was supposed to have dinner with later the next week might have something to do with Coach's murder.

Chapter 10

"Fabulous!"

I did my best not to laugh aloud at the exaggerated enthusiasm of the woman holding my cannonball gourd up to some imaginary light source and turning it in her magenta-tipped fingers. She resembled Cruella De Ville, black hair pulled back into a tight chignon, her lips a crimson slash in a flour-white face. But she was good at what she did, which was to sell handmade objects to people who sported real Rolexes and vacationed in Bora Bora.

And she paid me outright when I handed her the invoice, instead of taking the pieces on consignment. I thanked her and strode out into the bright and windless day. Sutton Place, a neighborhood I only visited when business brought me there, was quieter than midtown, but I still felt assailed by the constant clang and roar of traffic, airplanes, machinery. Even the clicking heels of a woman in a Chanel tweed suit offended me.

I had almost two hours to kill before I was to meet Karen in Brooklyn. Another time, I would have ducked into the Morgan Library to see the exhibit or walked across town to the American Craft Museum. But I'd taken the address of the real estate lawyer who had represented Tom Ford in the cottage transaction, and my plan to track him down started there.

The building's security, as in so many public and commercial establishments in New York City, required that you show picture ID and state your destination. I flashed my Walden Corners driver's license and dropped the attorney's name, and the gentleman in his epauletted uniform smiled gently and said, "Second elevator. You have a nice day."

I still couldn't understand why people who had never been here persisted in thinking that New York City was a cold, cruel test of how thick your skin might be.

Until I met the receptionist on the thirty-sixth floor.

"Sorry," she said without a trace of regret in her voice. "You cannot go inside. Call Ms. Bogel's secretary and make an appointment if you want to see her."

She bent her head to whatever paperwork she was attending to, shutting me out as though I didn't exist. I was about to argue when the heavy wood doors leading to the inner sanctum swung open and a harried young woman with an armful of files trotted to the glass doors. Before the receptionist looked up, I slipped inside, congratulating myself on my quick reflexes, which often took over when my wit failed.

The question of which office in this stately warren was the right one was soon answered by the nameplate beside the eighth door, the corner office, announcing Margaret Bogel's name. This time, the secretary, whose gelled hair and French cuffs spoke of spending half his salary on what Karen calls "products," smiled up at me, said, "Gorgeous hair," and then asked what he could do for me.

"I'm the new owner of Tom Ford's house upstate, and he left something there that I'm sure he wants." I was winging it here, but I'd done enough improvisational business writing to trust that the right words would appear in my brain. The rule was that if you were going to stretch the truth, you needed to be specific but about something inconsequential. "It's a box of photographs, and some of them look like they go back to the sixties."

"Wow." His blue eyes crinkled in the corners. "That's so nice of you. Wait, let me check with my boss. I'll just be a minute."

Not a good idea. I took a deep breath. "Sure, fine, but I'm leaving in two minutes to catch a cab. You know how those airline security lines are these days. Hours. And for international flights . . ."

His left eyebrow arched. "Paris?"

I leaned forward. "Budapesht." I emphasized the *sht* on the end, hoping that would up the glamour factor even more. "Maybe you can give me the information. I have to —"

But he was already typing things into the computer, keys clicking as I held my breath. "Voila!" he said, grinning. He pressed another button and the printer whirred into action. As he handed me the sheet, he said, "You're not going to Budapesht. But I like your style. Now, scoot."

I saluted him and scooted, refraining from letting loose with a loud and exultant whoop. As soon as the elevator doors slid shut and I was alone, so to speak, with eleven other bored passengers, I read the printout with interest. The first address was a building in Tribeca that I knew to be the home of several film-and-fashionista personalities. The other address was in a town in Vermont called Shelburne.

I was much closer to Tribeca.

The doorman was so much more savvy than the hapless martinet dictator at the front desk of the law office. He looked to be in his mid twenties, with a pleasant smile, a noticeable Southern accent, and a practiced indignation when I tried to slip him ten dollars to let me upstairs to apartment five without being announced because I was an old girlfriend who wanted to surprise Tom Ford.

"Mr. Ford is not at home. Save your money for someone who needs it," he said, "and use it where it will do you good. You're not from around here, are you?"

And here I'd thought that my transformation had been only internal.

"Actually, I'm pretty far from home. Can you leave Mr. Ford a message for me?"

He reached for a paper and a pen, slid it across the counter, and read along, following the upside down words, as I put my thoughts on paper. Being a mediator and a writer didn't always give me the gift of clear communication in personal matters. I reminded myself that I had a goal here, and it wasn't simply to express my anger.

Please call me in Walden Corners, I wrote.

Not compelling enough.

I have some questions, and the answers might be important to you. Sincerely, Lili Marino.

That ought to do it. From the smirk on the doorman's face, Tom Ford had a fifty-fifty chance of ever seeing that piece of paper, but I couldn't do any more for the moment. Besides, I was ten minutes late for my lunch with Karen. I got her on her cell phone, told her I was on my way, and hustled the three blocks to the subway, muttering about how angry I was at Tom Ford as I dodged the scurrying pedestrians.

Why, I said to myself, should I just mutter? I grabbed the paper from my purse and punched out the number for the Vermont location. The phone rang three times, and then I heard his smooth, recorded baritone telling callers to leave a message, and a combination of relief and fury, pleasure and anger, battered me.

The familiar beep set loose a stream of words. I told him that I needed information, hoping that my tone conveyed a chilly disdain for the way he had treated Nora Johnson. Relieved, I ran down the steps into the dank, musty hole in the ground, where a brightly lit R train was waiting for me.

The car was empty, except for two muscled boys whose jeans looked in danger of falling off their nonexistent hipbones. They were punching each other, hooting, and practicing wrestling holds, and I tried to ignore them and concentrate on letting go of my anger. I fixed my gaze on the window across the wide aisle and counted to four as I inhaled, then to six as I let my breath out. Having one New Age friend had some advantages.

"I said, Hey, babe, you got any money?" From fifteen feet away, the voice startled me out of my meditation. I looked up in time to see both boys swaggering toward me, their eyes narrowing.

I was in no mood for this. I stood and grabbed onto the pole as the car hurtled ahead. We were going through the tunnel, the longest time between stops. Enough time for something very unpleasant to happen.

"You heard me. Give me your money, man." He tugged at the hood of his sweatshirt.

When I saw his face I realized that he was probably younger than Scooter, no more than fourteen at most. "You need to work on your self-respect, man. You think you want to tell your kids stories about how you robbed women on the subway? That's the future you want for yourself?"

The taller of the two boys came up and stood so close I could see the pores on his cheeks and smell the spicy cologne he'd practically bathed in. "Yo, I ain't got no kids. And I ain't got no money."

And I ain't got no patience, I thought.

"I'm sorry, but you know what? I work hard for my money." If I could keep talking for another ninety seconds, the train would reach Court Street and I might be safe. "I have a friend whose husband just died and she just found out that the money she thought he left for her was stolen by someone else. She discovered a piece of paper in a box in her basement, hidden behind a loose rock. Great way to find out you're broke, right? And so I'm trying to help her get it back, and I'm really not interested in your stuff. You think you're the only one with problems? Well, everyone's got their share, and they do the next thing, keep doing it, until something works out. My friend has a son your age, and she needs to figure out how to pay the bills. Me? My own problem is that my father has Parkinson's disease and my mother doesn't know how to handle the stress so she drinks too much and I don't know what I can do to help them. So don't whine to me, you hear? Go to school and become a man and vote and take care of the people you love and don't give me this bullshit."

My speech lasted long enough for the train to roll to a stop at Court Street. Shaking with anger, I got off and watched the two boys stare after me as the train pulled away. I gulped some air, stood as tall as I could, and stepped onto the next train that pulled in to the station.

"Wow, you look terrible." Karen wrinkled her nose and pressed me into a chair.

"Thanks. What are friends for, right? Awful feels like a compliment, compared to how I feel. I am sooo glad to see you." This was home, I thought, this friendship, this feeling of safety and comfort. Even her freckles seemed exactly right, the way they dotted her cheeks in happy, spontaneous splashes. I felt the tightness in my chest loosen a little as I told her about my subway adventure.

"No wonder those boys left you alone.

Anyone with that much righteous energy is like a hurricane that's been kept in a box of warm water." She laughed and waved away her own words. "So I'm not a scientist. But I do know you want to help your friend Nora and you can't do that without helping yourself first. I don't mean that we should sit here and analyze you and Nora. She probably needs someone to be with her, hear her. Be a reality check."

"Like you're doing for me." I laughed and leaned back in my chair. "Karen, listen to this. The man who gave me the cottage to pay for the work I did also took eighty thousand dollars of Nora's husband's money in some Swiss-cheesy investment."

Karen took my hand. "And unless you hit the lottery, it's unlikely you can get it back for her."

Right.

Reality again.

"What about finding the murderer?" she said. "The cops have any suspects?"

"Sure, the whole town." I shook my head. "Not anyone specific they're telling *me* about. They said they wanted to talk to everyone — people with grudges, you know, parents who thought he wasn't doing right by their kids. The town bigot. A guy who sued him and lost." But that wasn't the entire list, and I knew it. "Me."

"You? Because you found the body?" Indignation flashed in her eyes and I wanted to hug her in relief and gratitude.

"Maybe because I'm the new kid in town *and* I found the body. But they're overworked trying to keep the peace with these demonstrations against the Rickland cement plant. Every other day, it seems like. Demonstrators even sat on the train tracks and had to be hauled away when a bunch of Amtrak officials insisted that the police arrest them."

Karen waved away my words. "Enough about the high drama. What about the hard stuff? The everyday stuff? How's it going, living in the country? I still can't figure out what you do all the time. Without me around to call and tell you about the new movies and restaurants."

"Not exactly a lot of night life in Walden Corners." Karen would worry if I told her I didn't miss it, so I left out the editorial. "But it's not North Podunk either. Lots of movies, lots of restaurants, some good music, some decent amateur theater. A great bookstore. Mostly in Chatham, Hudson, and Rhinebeck, where you can pay as much for a silk blouse as you can at any

Fifth Avenue department store. So, see, this is not exactly deprivation. I manage to stay busy. And properly entertained. Which you would know if you would visit me."

"How about next Thursday? I'll stay the weekend." Karen grinned and leaned back in her chair. "I thought you'd never ask."

"You need an invitation?" Incredulous, I wondered whether we needed to have The Talk.

For years, she had agonized over relationships, over whether the guys she dated felt the same way she did. Sometimes, she was the one who wanted to keep a friendly distance. With Tony and then again with Christopher, she'd started to see the possibility of permanence, or at least years, of connection but she wanted to protect herself from disappointment and so she picked a time she thought would be good to have The Talk. And in most cases, within a week, what she got was The Walk instead.

Now I longed for an assurance from her that the friendship I'd made a bedrock of my life, a relationship I assumed could never be shaken, meant the same thing to her.

"That's great! How long can you stay? There's so much to show you. A path along the river. We can shop in Rhinebeck and go the secondhand store in Red Hook and stop for lunch at a terrific place I know in Hudson. We can see Olana, the great Moorish castle that Frederick Church built to escape the flu epidemic, and we can —"

"Hey, I can't stay for a month." Karen's relaxed grin assured me that my momentary worry had been groundless. "How about I'll e-mail you to tell you what train I'll be on? Thursday night, I guess, as close to five as I can make it. And then you can be my tour guide."

It wasn't until I was halfway up the Taconic Parkway heading for home that I remembered that Thursday was the night Seth Selinsky and I were supposed to go to the B.B. King concert. I dialed Karen's cell phone and said, "Oops, next Thursday won't work. Forgot about a previous, ahem, engagement. Translation: my first date in six months. Call you later and we'll pick another time."

The drive back to Walden Corners was uneventful, two hours on serpentine roads under a low, gray sky. The bare branches of the trees swayed in a chilly wind, and as dusk settled on the rolling hills and lights began to wink on in the few houses along the Taconic Parkway, my thoughts returned to Tom Ford. Finally, I realized that the word I'd been seeking to describe him was arrogant, a quality I detested. Its opposite, humility, certainly could be carried too far, and then become as unattractive as swaggering self-promotion, but in its purer form I preferred humility, infinitely, in politicians, friends, and lovers.

Why, I wondered, had that word popped into my head thinking about Tom Ford?

I dialed a country music station on the radio, turned up the volume, and let the simple melodies and basic emotions blow my complicated thoughts away. By the time I pulled up to the mailbox by the driveway and pulled out a sheaf of magazines and what appeared to be an equally thick stack of bills, I was ready for a bowl of soup and bed. I hauled my suitcase out of the car and stood for a moment in the silence of the starless night.

When you listen hard in the country, you hear the small sounds — tree limbs rubbing against each other, dry leaves rustling, the crunch of tiny footsteps as small nocturnal animals begin their evening jaunts. Friendly sounds to my ears, I realized, now that I knew what they were.

The house was cold, and I dumped all the papers on the table by the door and turned up the thermostat, relieved to hear the thunk and hiss of the furnace going to work. In my office, the telephone answering machine blinked invitingly. Eight messages. Not bad for a three-day absence. I wouldn't have to eat the worms of social isolation yet.

Two of the calls were from Elizabeth — the first friendly, the second annoyed, asking if I'd found out anything yet. Two calls were from prospective clients. Oh happy day for me and the bills I'd just carried in from the cold. Fred Benson told me that my lawnmower was fixed and I owed him fifty-six dollars even. Seth Selinsky, apologetic and funny, telling me that the B.B. King concert was sold out but that he'd like to take me to dinner instead. One call, a beseechingly lonely message from Ed Thorsen, asked me how I was doing and when might I be coming into the city because he wanted to talk to me. Glad that I hadn't phoned in to retrieve that particular message, which would have put me in the dilemma of choosing between the guilt of ignoring him or the discomfort of actually talking to him, I bustled about with the can opener and the soup pot, poured myself a glass of wine, and sat down to watch television.

The split pea soup smelled heavenly, my current version of comfort food. I raised the spoon to my mouth, savoring the rich, salty taste. Home. A good place. Maybe I really had found it at last. I dipped my spoon into the thick soup again, and jumped as the phone rang, banging my elbow as I tried to grab my glass before the red wine spilled onto the cream-colored placemat, and almost toppled the spider plant from its perch on the windowsill.

Could be a client, I reminded myself, and I found the cheery voice that lived inside me and said, "Hello?"

"I phoned in for my messages and couldn't believe it when I heard your voice. And a message from my doorman saying you'd been there. You agreed not to call me and just accept our deal. As is. That's how you got the house, so please abide by the agreement and just leave me alone. Whatever it is you want, I don't appreciate you snooping around and leaving messages all over creation. Please stop doing those things."

Tom Ford sounded so much in control I wanted to throttle him. Instead, I said, "My attempts to talk to you had nothing to do with our real estate transaction. I know the terms of our deal and I have honored them. Which is more than I can say for you as a businessman. You know you can't just go around —"

"What are you talking about? Now, listen, you have some kind of problem, then maybe you should see someone who can help you. I'm not joking. I thought we understood each other. The slate is clean. I paid you for the work you did by giving you the house, and you accepted. Don't go throwing up old —"

"Old?" I shouted. "You don't listen when other people talk, do you? This is not about me. I wasn't calling about the cottage. It's not even about you as a human being. If you think I spend any time at all thinking about you, after you played games being so mysterious, as though that would make me or any sane woman come looking for you, you have to be the most self-centered, and may I say, arrogant person in New England. If you hadn't lost all the money Coach invested with you . . . if Coach hadn't been murdered, I wouldn't give half a salami about you."

And before I could stop myself, I slammed down the receiver. Shaking with anger, I tried to finish my soup. But it was barely lukewarm, so I drained the last bit of wine from my glass and went into the living room to sulk about bad-mannered, arrogant men. I dialed *69 on my phone to see if I could find out how to call Mr. Ford back, but a message told me that the number was unavailable.

Canceling an eighty-thousand-dollar debt might, in some quarters, count as motive for murder. And spending years developing an elusive existence, never appearing in person, never showing your face to the small community where you were at the very least a property owner and taxpayer, never coming to a business meeting, was strange. No, I thought, totally weird was more apt. Or maybe downright nefarious came closest.

Chapter 11

The nice thing about gourds is that they make no demands, no accusations, show no disappointment or jealousy or selfishness. They are always available and responsive. I would never give up the company of people — not entirely anyway — but many days I take deep pleasure in losing myself in my work.

Not today.

Everything was going wrong, including another saw blade breaking and the discovery of a soft, rotted spot on the bottom of a gourd I'd been saving to make a bowl as a wedding gift for my friend Paula Gross. I started to heat up the woodburning unit so that I could finish a complicated Native American thunderbird design and then thought better of it. Whatever was distracting me was likely to ruin that too, and I hated the idea of tossing six hours of work out the window.

I should take a break. Maybe Nora

wanted to go for a walk, have a cup of coffee, something. But when I called, her answering machine picked up on the first ring. I left a message and then wandered the house, which didn't take very long. That left two choices: either I could make some cold calls on leads for new corporate clients or I could sulk. I stomped to the yard, but my bad humor didn't last long.

It was replaced by confusion.

One tree stump lay on its side, waving its tendrils in the breeze as though grasping for purchase in the soil that no longer supported it. Fine, good, just what I'd paid Bobby to do. But the other two were still solidly planted in the ground. A job half done is . . . a job unfinished. There should be some kind of saying about such sloppy workmanship, and maybe I'd figure one out, but for now I wanted to find out about Bobby's plan, if he had one, for finishing. He wasn't a craftsman and I wouldn't hold him to those standards, but the work ethic still mattered; and besides, I was worried about the boy.

Maybe, too, I was a tiny bit tense from the whole Tom Ford affair. He had violated my sense of fairness, but what was worse, he had disappointed me. I had created a Tom who was charismatic, compassionate, and clever and had scratched the surface to find an arrogant, self-serving crook. Boy, talk about the need to adjust to a new reality . . .

Before I could feel any sorrier for myself, I heard the sound of a car down the road, and was pleased to see Nora's Explorer pull into my drive.

"Yes," she said as she climbed out of the car. Her long fingers picked at invisible threads on her jacket sleeve and her eyes darted over my face.

I frowned in confusion, and then watched a small smile break on her face.

"You left a message, right? So, yes, I want to take a walk or something. I've been sitting around too much, thinking too much. And watching Alvin Akron."

"Alvin Akron?" I hated sounding like a parrot, but the words came out before I could take them back. "What do you mean, watching him?"

Nora's face clouded. "He's been marching up and down the field, the one he says Coach's grandfather stole from his father. Laying out strings. Measuring things, with a surveyor's thingamajig, I don't know what you call it. As though he's getting ready to pounce on me, now that Coach isn't around. I cannot believe the man is so cold, so stupid. If he thinks —" She stopped herself and inhaled deeply.

"You can always sic Elizabeth on him." Her cool tenacity would certainly be helpful in dealing with Alvin Akron.

"Not only Alvin's going crazy on me. I heard from the principal that the football team is in total disarray, half the kids not showing up, the rest of them just barely managing to get through a game without surrendering. They fight and bicker all the time. It's weird. They called a grief counselor in, but for all I can tell, they need anger counseling."

"Sounds like they miss Coach too." The thought of all those boys and how they used to keep their averages up because they wanted to please him made me sad. In their own ways, they needed to learn to accept the changes that violence had brought into their worlds too.

"Anyway," Nora said, shifting her weight at the same time she changed the subject, "I had to get out of the house, and I had a great idea. I don't know what this entails, but I want you to teach me how to make a gourd."

"Only God can make a gourd," I said, laughing. My heart fluttered — she was saying yes to something new and that was good. She was giving me a huge responsibility, and I hoped I was up to it. "But I can teach you how to work with one. Want to start now?"

Nora shook her head, her eyes widening. "I want to do some research first. I want to make gourds with African mudcloth designs. Don't worry, I won't compete for your market. I just want to do something . . . *black,* you know? Honor my heritage without denying the present. So this is how I can do that. Besides," she said, her voice lowering to a barely audible level, "I need to get out of the house."

"Sounds good, all of it." I didn't want to roll over those tender feelings she'd expressed, but I didn't want to wallow in them, either. "Research, huh?"

"Before she married Fred, Jane Benson was a nurse with one of those groups that goes into poor countries, Doctors Without Borders, and gives free medical help to people who never saw the inside of a doctor's office. Her last trip was three years ago. She brought back a suitcase full of fabric from Kenya, Botswana, Rhodesia — I mean, Zimbabwe — and a couple of other countries. I called her a while ago and asked her if we could stop by to take some photos. She told me she'd be home at four."

When Nora did something, it was never halfway. I was beginning to think that some of our concern about her was misplaced, and maybe we'd better be more concerned about whatever got in her way when she set her sights on something.

"Great, because I have to pick up my lawnmower and also find out if Bobby's run into some kind of problem with the other two tree stumps. Ground's going to freeze soon, and then the job will be impossible."

"Listen to the country girl." She linked her arm through mine and steered me to my car. "Purty soon you'll be hankering to plant by the full moon or something."

I laughed and almost skipped the last few steps to the car. "You plant by the *new* moon, silly. Let's take my car. Then you can just come back with me and go home whenever."

The drive to the Benson house took us on roads that still made me catch my breath. Not the spectacle of the Badlands or the rocky coast of New England or the Grand Tetons, these glorious vistas were gentler, rolling hills patchworked with the remnants of crops that had pushed up through the soil just months before. The trees by the side of the road seemed to be waiting in wintry austerity for the riotous surges of spring. I loved getting to know the seasons in southern Columbia County, loved the growing familiarity I felt with the byways that visitors seldom saw.

When we passed Seth Selinsky's house, I noticed his car in the driveway and I wondered at the warm anticipation that I felt. I had met the man for a total of ten minutes, and I knew hardly anything about him. Our upcoming date sometimes seemed like a bad idea. What was I getting myself into?

Nora, though, seemed manic again, chattering about gourds and her African ancestors a little too fast for my comfort. I'd been following her lead, talking about her grief and her worries when she needed that, distracting her with conversation about my work and stories about the button-down minds of the corporate world. Now, I made appropriate one-syllable comments when she stopped for a breath and wondered whether I should be concerned about these sudden shifts from withdrawn to bursting.

Before I could figure out how to frame a question, we'd pulled into the Bensons' crescent driveway. The trim white house was surrounded by holly bushes, an unexpected splash of green in the bleakness of the December landscape. A snowmobile rested upside down in front of Fred's shop, a metal toolbox beside it. A dented, faded orange Honda was parked next to a much newer sedan, cream-colored and sedate. As we got out of my car, a snarling dog sprang up like a snake uncoiling to attack.

I hadn't noticed him at first, had only seen the shadowed porch. Lean, straining at what looked like a tenuous leash, he reminded me of the cab driver who'd been cut off by a fish truck at Sixth Avenue and Thirty-fourth Street. Murderous, that was the look. I sat in the car trying to catch my breath, to slow my pounding heart.

When Nora swung her long legs down to the blacktop and started toward the house, I nearly fainted. The dog's white teeth — fangs, really — gleamed as he continued the snarl-and-howl routine. Nora kept walking at a deliberately steady pace, her voice soft as she approached the porch.

"Hey there, Buster, you're doing a good job, aren't you?"

Oh, sure, I thought, Buster. Now there was an aptly named animal. Rocky might have worked too. Or Don Corleone. Nora kept up the one-way conversation, the dog's head cocking to the side every once in a while as she approached.

"It's all right, Buster. We're here by invitation, you know, and we have nothing but good intentions. Sure, I know you don't see too many people who look like me every day, but it's really all right. Hey, Buster, we both know that protecting our families is our most important duty, right, and so we do what we have to. That's a good boy, sure, it's fine, you just keep —"

She had reached the bottom step of the porch. The dog leaped forward, the leash held, and Nora stood motionless looking up at the door, at the light that had flicked on in the living room. Jane Benson flung open the door and tapped Buster on the nose with a newspaper. As though by magic, the dog curled up in his spot and rested his head on his crossed paws, eyeing my car and sending shivers through me.

"It's all right, Lili. He won't hurt you. Not with me here." Gentle Jane, with her pink, round face, long braid, and soft voice, looked as though she might kick Buster if he so much as twitched.

But I wasn't convinced. "I'll just go around to the back, if that's all right with you."

Jane smiled as Nora stepped past Buster

and crossed the threshold into the house, leaving me alone outside with the potential attacker. With gingerly steps and my eye on the porch, I walked around to the side of the house, my chest expanding with relief when I cleared the corner and headed toward the door.

A sudden clank made me jump.

When I turned, I saw Bobby, wrench in hand, wiping his forehead with a crumpled blue bandana. He was glaring at a pile of metal and muttering, unaware of my presence and lost in his annoyance.

"Hi, Bobby. Looks like you're a mechanic too. How's it going?" I put on my most friendly smile; even after I saw the bruise on his cheek, an angry purple swelling below his right eye. I tried not to stare.

"Carburetor came loose and I can't get this bolt off to fix it. Might have to use the blowtorch." He seemed surprised that he had said so many words to me, and then a deep frown creased his brow. When he turned to set the wrench on the ground he winced, as though he'd forgotten about a tender spot somewhere near his beltline. "Sorry about those stumps. The tractor broke down. We're waiting on a part. Should be here in —"

I turned and followed Bobby's gaze and saw a small yellow car pull up beside my Subaru. Laura got out on the driver's side; someone else sat in the passenger seat, a familiar figure that I couldn't quite place. The back door of the house flew open and Jane stuck her head out. "Thought maybe Buster got you," she said, laughing. "You want to come in?"

"Talk to you later, Bobby. Hey, Laura, how's it going?" I said as I edged away toward the house.

"Fine." Laura smiled her cheerleader smile but her teeth seemed clenched and her body stiff.

That passenger, I realized, was one of the boys who had showed up at Coach's memorial, the one whose conversation with Bobby had made me wary and upset. Will Jackson: the feeling I'd gotten watching him talk to Bobby hadn't faded.

Jane Benson's kitchen smelled of dinner, and an uncovered pot on the stove bubbled gently with what appeared to be a rich tomato sauce. For a fleeting moment, I wondered what it would be like to have to cook for a family every single night, to take on the daily tasks of laundry and dusting and shopping, of seeing that everyone had properly matched socks and a stockpile of toothpaste and vitamins. I had enough trouble managing those things for myself, could barely imagine multiplying that by two or three.

"We're in here."

I followed Jane's voice to a small room off the hall leading from the kitchen. Nora and Jane stood beside a table piled high with the most wonderful and varied fabrics I had ever seen. The blues were rich, almost black, yellows glowed with the power of sunshine, reds, oranges, splashes of turquoise, and rich russet browns dazzled my eyes. And the patterns — stunning geometrics, little diamonds marching in rows alternating with X's in contrasting colors; spiral swirls enclosed in bordered boxes; dots in the center of tilted squares, repeated either all over or in stripes of alternating patterns. My eyes flitted from swatch to swatch, devouring the buffet of color and line.

Nora, too, seemed lost in a trance, her hands lifting and smoothing and rubbing the fabric, as though she might absorb Africa through her fingertips. "This one's from Zimbabwe. My grandmother made a sampler once, used a pattern like this. She drew it freehand, she said, from a memory of something her grandmother wore, maybe a headscarf."

"That's right." Jane reached over and held it to the light. "You can see a little bit of wax, still on one of the strips. They used a wax resist process when they were dyeing and then they boiled it to set the colors and melt the wax but sometimes little bits still clung to the fabric. The woman who made this was Anna Nwanne. She ran an AIDS orphanage. She was forty-one but she looked seventy."

Motherhood? Piece of cake compared to Anna Nwanne's lot in life. I'd made peace with my own choices, but every once in a while a story like Anna's stirred a wish that I had chosen a different path, one that would have made more of a difference in the world. You help others by setting an example, by being kind, by doing what you do with passion and honesty, I reminded myself, echoing the wisdom of a Zen teacher I'd studied with for about fifteen minutes when I was twenty-three.

I brought myself back to the present, to the discussion Nora and Jane were having about the significance of the different colors and patterns. Nora began taking pictures with her digital camera, adjusting the cloth so that light fell on each piece, arranging them so that overall design filled each frame.

"Wait a minute. Jane, is it all right if I make a turban out of this one?" The rich blue and startling white would look gorgeous against the cinnamon tones of Nora's skin, and I motioned for her to sit. Jane held up one finger as if to say she'd be right back, and disappeared into the hall.

"Where'd you learn to do a wrap?" Nora giggled and twisted around to catch a glimpse of her transformed self, but I wouldn't let her look in the mirror until I'd finished.

"Sit still. You think I lived in Brooklyn all my life for nothing? You can look when I'm done."

I began in the back, brought both pieces around and crossed them over a little to the left of the center of her forehead, then wound them back and repeated this once more, ending in the back. I tucked the ends under and examined the results, just as Jane popped back into the room.

"Oh, Nora. You look so . . . royal. All you need is a retinue of Nubians bearing fruit and playing drums." Jane salaamed and giggled.

"Let's make sure Denzel Washington and Derek Jeter are carrying my mangoes,"

Nora said, and we all started laughing so hard we couldn't stop.

Every time we looked at each other, new gusts of helpless laughter rolled through the room, and Nora hooted and I clapped and Jane clutched her sides. None of us heard footsteps, until a shadow appeared in the doorway.

"You done in here? I need some help out in the kitchen. Who's —" Fred Benson bit back his question as he scanned the room, his brown eyes shifting from Nora to Jane and back. He glanced at me, frowned, then said to Nora, "Sorry about your husband."

Nora swiped at her eyes. "Thanks, Fred."

"I didn't recognize the car." Fred Benson hesitated in the doorway, then said, "I'll bring your mower out, Miss Marino. Come to the kitchen, Jane."

Jane didn't even flip him a bird, as I would have.

Nora watched him disappear into the hall and then said, "I have to get back to Scooter. Thanks for showing us these wonderful fabrics, Jane. That must have been an amazing experience, going to all those countries. Helping all those people."

"Amazing." Her voice sounded wistful and she sighed and looked around the bright room.

What must it feel like to be Jane, to have had those experiences and then to spend the rest of your time in the small daily life of Fred Benson's small machinery repair shop? This must be my day for counting my own blessings, I thought, as I rose and followed Jane through the hall to the sunny living room with its slightly shabby sofa and two recliners all facing a giant television screen. As soon as I stepped out onto the porch, Buster growled deep in his throat.

I'd forgotten about the dog.

He raised his head and sniffed the air in my direction. Lazily, he stretched, then rose and pattered over to me, his nails clicking on the wood of the porch floor. Unable to move, I watched him as though he were my own personal and impending doom approaching. Nora and Jane had reached my car and stood with their backs to me, talking earnestly.

"Nice boy. Nice Buster." The choices were all unattractive. Run through the kitchen and face Fred Benson, tiptoe past a dog who looked like he was raised by Hannibal Lecter, or stand in the doorway until I was old and gray. *Don't show him fear.* That was the advice my Uncle Steve had given me when a dog cornered me against an iron fence when I was six. That was like the advice on dating that I used to get from my neighbor Teressa, older, wiser, and still unmarried. When you meet a man you like, don't think about the future. In both cases, I'm sure my emotions showed.

If only I had a bit of raw hamburger or a tiny rabbit to feed to him.

I started whistling, and Buster started growling. I stopped whistling, but Buster kept growling. I was about to shout to Jane for help when Bobby came around the corner of the house on the snowmobile, sailing across the grass and waving his wrench in the air like a victory flag. Laura and the yellow car were nowhere to be seen.

I took advantage of Buster's momentary amazement by skipping down the steps and out of the range of his leash. Nora and Jane hugged each other, Jane patted my shoulder like a good aunt — was there a counterpart for the word *avuncular*, I wondered — and then I drove Nora back to my house, never once mentioning the incident of the dog on the porch. Let everyone think I was brave. That was fine with me.

"Wonder what she's doing there." Nora inclined her head in the direction of the snug house surrounded by pine trees.

Michele Castro leaned against a sheriff's department cruiser in the driveway, Seth Selinsky standing by her side. It was hard to tell at forty-two miles an hour, but they appeared to be laughing.

"Maybe they're friends," I suggested, pushing aside the little bubble of jealousy that seemed impossible. But there it was. The undersheriff was pretty, she was smart, and she was local, all good reasons for her to have a relationship with the man who was supposed to be taking me to dinner on Thursday night.

"Or maybe she's talking to him about Coach. You know, his son is on the football team." Nora's sigh rattled through my car. "All those parents who disagreed with how my husband made decisions . . . I just don't know what to think."

"Hey, I meant to ask if you reminded the sheriff about Alvin Akron and the land dispute." I wanted to move the discussion away from Seth, away from having to tell her that I was going out with a man whose involvement in her husband's murder she'd just questioned.

She nodded. "And every parent on the football team who'd ever gone apoplectic on Coach, and that Jackson idiot who made remarks about a black man teaching his son. You know how it is. Surface is one thing. Trusting what's underneath is another."

We drove in silence the rest of the way to my driveway.

"Hey, who's that?" Nora pointed to a midnight-blue BMW parked beside her pickup. "Some rich patron of the gourd arts?"

Chapter 12

My heart sank. I had never returned his call, putting it off until I had wiped it from my memory entirely. I wasn't ready for a visit from Ed Thorsen, hated that he thought he could just drop in on my life whenever he pleased. When I broke off our engagement I'd said all the right things, and obviously he took me seriously about still wanting to be friends. I said softly, "It's the ex."

Nora giggled. She actually tittered, but I hate that word, and when I glared at her she clapped a hand over her mouth in mock dismay.

"Are you done snickering?"

She choked back her laughter. "No, don't think I'll come in right now. You're on your own with this one, Lili. Sorry. You're a good friend, but there are limits."

"I thought I was going to teach you how to work with gourds. Some student you are, fleeing at the first sign of a little domestic disturbance." I patted her hand. "I

213

can handle this. Call me tomorrow so we can figure out when to start your lessons. I've got to get rid of Mr. Ed."

Her giggle erupted again, and she slid from the car and hopped up into her truck, shoulders still shaking. At least she'd broken the laugh barrier twice in one day. It was worth having to put up with ten minutes with Ed Thorsen to see that. He unfolded himself from my front step, rising up to his full six feet four inches, and the smile that spread across his face as I approached seemed bright and true. He hadn't lost or gained weight, but some of it had shifted from his waist to his shoulders, and he wore his jeans and the black leather jacket well. I was suddenly aware of my own crumpled barn coat and frayed sleeves, of the sneakers splashed with stuff whose origins I'd long ago forgotten, and my hair, shoved behind my ears and in need of a cut.

"Lili! I was hoping I'd get to see you. I have to leave in ten minutes, but I was passing by, practically, and thought it would be all right. You look . . ." He grinned and nodded. "You look settled in."

Not *marvelous* or *smashing* or even *a sight for sore eyes.* Settled in. I stepped past him to open the door, tempted to hug him but annoyed enough to hold back. "Thanks," I said. "You look pretty good, Ed. Want to come in?"

"Remember how you used try to get me to the gym? Well, I've been going twice a week. With my schedule, I can't, you know, get away more than that."

He followed me inside, standing close enough for me to smell his soap. Ed Thorsen, principal of the Carl Sagan Middle School, never used cologne, he said, because some of his kids and several faculty members claimed allergies. I'd always heard that explanation as an apology to me, when I never expected him to smell anything but clean.

I tossed my keys on the table beside the door and turned on the lamp. A soft glow lit the room, and I looked around with satisfaction at the nest I'd created for myself. The living room, fireplace on one end, was now a deep burgundy with white trim, and the patterned rug my sister gave me brightened the floor. A small sofa, a single chair, a glass-topped coffee table, and a shelf full of Tom's books and the collected objects of my travels, and the travels of friends, had turned this room from Tom Ford's rather lifeless escape pod into my home.

"Nice," Ed said.

Not *Warm* or *Unique* or even *It's so you, Lili.*

"Thanks." Why did I feel so protective of my life choices in his presence? I had to get hold of myself. "Get you some coffee? A glass of wine?"

He shook his head. "I really do have to leave. I wanted to tell you in person. I'm engaged. I'm really very happy, Lili, and I wanted you to know that I think things are working out for the best. For both of us."

My stomach clenched with unexpected jealousy, and I prayed that my face didn't betray some of the shock and awe that I felt at his matter-of-fact pronouncement. I put on a smile and said, "Who is she?"

"Marion Fortune." He ducked his head boyishly and then took my hands in both of his. "I hope you wish us well."

I did well not to gasp. Marion Fortune used to sit around at school parties and talk about what a nerd my Ed was. Not in so many words, not to my face, but she'd make a comment about how hard it must be to be with a man who was so dedicated to his work that he didn't have time for fun and then look at me pityingly. And now she was marrying him.

"Of course I wish you well. I hope you're

happy, and that your future unfolds exactly the way you want it to." This time I did hug him, and I surprised myself by the tear that leaked from the corner of my eye. Unthinking, I responded when he lifted my chin and brought his lips to mine. They were warm and the kiss melted through me, rippling in soft, lapping waves as he lingered on my mouth.

He'd never kissed me like that before.

I pulled away and looked at him, then smiled. "Life's funny, huh? I'm glad you've found the person who can make you happy. Please don't be offended if I ask that you save the story of how you and Marion got together for another time. My friend Nora, the one whose truck was in the driveway, just lost her husband. Actually, he was murdered. And we're all a little lost and still in shock."

Ed rubbed my shoulder. "Wow, I'm sorry. I was so full of myself I didn't ask how things are for you. Murdered . . . how awful."

"I found the body," I said.

The jumble of emotions I'd been feeling for a month overwhelmed me, and with Ed Thorsen's arms firmly around me, I sobbed until I had no more sobs left in me. When he dried my eyes, kissed my forehead, and left, I was calmer, and totally exhausted.

For about five minutes.

Which was exactly how much time elapsed after Ed's car drove away before the phone rang. I waited through the sound of my own voice cheerily asking callers to leave a message, but when I heard Nora begin to speak, I grabbed the receiver.

"Hi, I'm here and I'm alone," I said.

"Lili, you'll never guess what happened." Nora sounded excited, almost the old Nora, without the sad edge to her voice. "Tom Ford sent me a letter. Overnight, no less. He was so kind, said he'd heard about Coach, that he's started a new company and is planning to pay back all his investors as quickly as he can."

Part of me wanted to shout that words were useless and no one could change the past. But she sounded so pleased that I just said, "That's nice."

"What's really nice," she said, her voice steady and soft, "is that there was a check for twenty thousand dollars along with the letter. I know you had something to do with this, Lili, and I wanted to say thank you."

It felt a little weird to take credit for my

anger, for the personal betrayal I felt when I found out that Tom Ford wasn't the person my imagination had created.

"I don't know what to say, Nora. All I did was vent a little at him over the phone. But I'm glad he's behaving decently. That gives you a little breathing room, right?"

Her sigh rattled over the telephone. "A little."

"Where'd the letter come from? What was the postmark?"

"Seattle." Her voice was soft, matter of fact. "Lili, I know how you felt about him. Before Coach died and then after we found the check. But this letter . . . it's not something a murderer would write. It's too sensitive."

I wanted to say that some people found Ted Bundy sensitive, but I held my tongue. "Listen, Nora, I think you should give his address to the sheriff. If he didn't have anything to do with it, then he'll be able to prove it. Anyway, I'm glad, that's all. Glad that you got that money. Want to come on Thursday morning to start the gourd lessons?"

"Ten thirty, if that's okay. See you then. Bye, Lili."

So, letting loose in a couple of telephone messages had borne good results. Maybe

I'd have to let myself lose it more often. I stood in front of the bookcase, scanning the titles of Tom's library, thinking of how happy I'd been to put together pieces of a puzzle to create so many different Toms. It was time to give up trying to figure out who or what he was. Such an exercise was bound to end badly.

"This one," Nora said, cradling a cannonball gourd in her palm. She stroked it, feeling the bumps, hefting its weight, smiling.

"Perfect. I told you one would call your name. You know what you want to make? A bowl, you said, but you have to show me where to cut it open."

Nora was already an enthusiastic student. She traced a line with her pencil about two-thirds of the way up the gourd, past its widest point. I made a starting cut with my Exacto knife, then inserted the miniature jigsaw and cut all the way around. The top pulled away easily.

"See? This is the stuff we have to clean out of the inside before we start work on the design."

Nora peered into the gourd and frowned. "How will we ever get rid of all that?"

"The magical power of water." I took the

gourd to the kitchen, let the water run to warm, and filled the little gourd. "Now we let it sit for the amount of time it takes to boil water, brew tea, and drink it. An hour, at least. Could be a day, but we'll check in an hour and see how things are going."

"I like this part." She filled the kettle, I reached for the mugs and the teapot, and she pointed to the Lapsang souchong, my favorite smoky tea. "This makes me feel good, Lili. Thank you."

"Feels good to me too." And it did, knowing that I could help her concentrate on only what was in front of her for a while.

"I just wish Scooter would open up more, you know?" She fiddled with the tray, rearranging spoons, setting the bamboo strainer beside the cups. Finally she said, "He's so confused. He doesn't know who or what to blame. Sometimes he glares at me as though I should be doing something to bring his father back and sometimes it feels like he's sending me waves of love to make me feel better. Yesterday I found him sitting in the bus shelter, you know that little shed by the road where he waits for the school bus when the weather is bad. He told me he didn't want to go to school anymore, that kids treated him like he was going to break. He hates the pity, he said. When he gets like that, all I want to do is hold him and tell him if we wait a few years those kids will grow up and maybe learn something. But he also needs to figure out how to get on with life. Meanwhile, it sucks."

"They probably don't know what to say. Kids sometimes get paralyzed when they see someone hurting so badly." My heart wrenched for Scooter, and for Nora, who had to help her child while dealing with her own sorrow.

I poured our tea and we sat in the pool of sunlight streaming through the living room window, turning our conversation to gourds and Africa and how such simple vegetables had been made into so many useful and beautiful things in cultures all over the world.

"Let's see if we can scrape those fibers out," I said when I realized I'd been staring at my tea dregs and wishing for the wisdom of an oracle to tell me what I could do to help my friend. Stick with what she wants, an inner voice reminded me, and I realized what an optimistic view of humanity that was, assuming that people really did know enough to find their way to a better place.

We finished prepping the gourds in about half an hour. "Now we have to let them dry completely before we start on the design."

Nora glanced at her watch. "That's all right. I have to go pick him up. I told Scooter that if he went to class today and it was still so awful we'd think about other possibilities. I guess I'm just hoping that Armel or some other good and sensitive kid will see what's going on and . . . and do what you're doing. Just hang out with him. I have to go home. Talk to you tomorrow."

I hugged her, set the damp gourds on a drying rack in the workroom, and spent the next twenty minutes working on the opening sentence for a corporate report I'd promised for January. It needed a concept, an idea that would pull it all together, and my mental cupboard was bare. The company was selling soaps, candles, Martha Stewart-y things, and I kept bumping up against the notion of "home."

Home is where the heart is.

Anywhere I hang my hat is home.

Home is where they have to take you in when you have no place to go. Was Walden Corners really my home, or was it just a stopping-off place on the way to some other destination?

I shoved those thoughts to the back of my mind and started some free association. Home, happy, kitchen, food, cook. Nope, try again. Home, comfort, haven, safety, danger.

Exasperated, I started to pull on my boots to go for a tromp in the woods when the phone rang.

"He's not here. He never went to class today. Nobody's seen him. I dropped him off at seven forty this morning and watched. At least I thought I saw him go into the main entrance of the school with about twenty kids from the Ancramdale bus route. But he never went to his first period class or any other class."

"Where are you, Nora?" I yanked the other boot up and glanced around for my car keys. "I'll meet you in ten minutes."

"I'm home. I figure he'll show up soon." Her voice cracked. "You can't use the same words anymore. You know what I was about to say?"

I could hardly speak because I did know.

"I was going to say that when I find him I'm going to kill him."

I got to see parts of Columbia and Dutchess counties that I never knew existed. We started at Armel's house and stopped at the homes of three other friends. We drove all the way to the river, to Clermont — a colonial estate that has been preserved as a beautiful park — and we walked until the path ended and then kept going over the railroad tracks to the river. "He used to love it here," Nora said, "and he'd run down the hill and wait for Coach to come find him and then they'd cross the tracks and skip stones on the water." We drove to the farmers market on Route 82, where Nora sometimes bought fruit for her pies and where one of Scooter's friends worked. We followed the ridge along the road outside of Hillsdale, so deep into the woods that blacktop became hard-packed dirt and eventually petered out into a deer trail.

Instead of betraying her nervousness in nonstop chatter, Nora was quiet and jumpy. At each stop, we got out and looked around, asking whoever we met if they'd seen Scooter. And every twenty seconds she dialed his cell phone number.

"It's dark," I said. "Maybe you should call the sheriff."

Nora shook her head, tears glittering in her eyes. "That would make him furious. He's not hurt, I know it. Nothing bad has happened. He's hiding. He's done this since he was four. He just disappears. For hours. He says he needs to be alone sometimes, but I think he wants to make sure someone is going to come look for him. It's his way of making sure someone's paying attention."

"So you could have stayed home, waited for him to come slinking back, and then said you'd looked everywhere and you were so glad he was home and he'd get the same feeling, right?"

She laughed. "You don't know by now that kids have a built-in bullcrap detector? He'd know. He's probably sitting in the garage or something, watching the house, timing me to see if I stayed out long enough to really look for him. What do you want to bet he'll be in the den, curled up in front of Monday Night Football?"

"Today's Thursday," I said, and then I realized what that meant. "Oh, no, I have an appointment in fifteen minutes. I'll call and cancel. Let me borrow your cell phone, would you? I left mine in the charger."

"Nuh uh. You go keep your appointment. Just drop me off at the house. I'm fine now. I really am." Nora's voice turned lighter. "Mr. Secret Admirer have a name?"

"Seth Selinsky," I said. "He's —"

"Oh, Lili."

I whipped my head around to check the expression that went with the note of lament in her voice. She had a pained look, as though her pet goldfish had just been found on the rug.

"Sorry, I didn't mean to sound that way. It's just . . . Watch out, okay? Someone said he borrowed money from a woman he dated and never paid it back, but that could be rumor. Still, Coach couldn't stand him. Got into a shouting match once over the same old stuff. Seth's son wanted to play but Coach took him out of rotation because he'd been late to practice three times. I don't usually have the pleasure of seeing these little duels, but I happened to be bringing some pies for a PTA fundraiser, and there they were, practically nose to nose. They both looked like they might explode. I mean, eyeballs popping and those veins in their necks standing out. Coach ended up walking away. Seth cursed him out good and then kicked the tires of his own truck. I think he might have broken a toe."

Anger management problems — just what I needed, to go from a man who never once in four years raised his voice or objected to anything to a man who broke his own bones kicking things when his frustration level got too high.

Or murdered someone who made him mad? I pushed the thought away and hoped it would stay out of the way. It didn't make sense, was likely just a way for me to sabotage myself.

"At least we know he's not going to never pay me back. No blood from this turnip, I can tell you that. Leave me a message when Scooter comes home, all right?"

Chapter 13

I was too tired and too worried about Scooter to be looking forward to dinner with Seth Selinsky. I almost called him to cancel, but I talked myself into thinking that a little first-date awkwardness was preferable to gnawing on the bone of Nora's problems for a couple of hours.

Slacks and a sweater, clean if not exactly the height of fashion, and a little mascara and lipstick were my only concessions to working on what Karen called "the presentation." Before I knew it, headlights flooded my driveway, and I watched from the darkened bedroom as Seth walked to the house.

I answered the peal of the doorbell, invited him in, offered him a drink.

He crinkled his eyes when he smiled, and his teeth gleamed white and straight. "Thanks, but we have about ten minutes if we're going to be on time for our reservation. I guess I should apologize for being late, but since you didn't notice until I mentioned it, maybe I'll skip that part."

We laughed together, and I found myself liking the ease I felt in his presence. "I'll just keep track of apologies owed," I said, and then I realized that that implied a long future and I wanted to take my words back. Instead I blushed and turned away to pretend to rummage in my purse. "I'll be right back. Forgot my . . . I'll be right back."

"Leaving me to wonder what you forgot. Take your time." He sat on the sofa, looking for all the world like the perfect accessory for a room that I'd always liked but felt was missing something I couldn't identify. His long legs stuck out under the glass table, and he reached for a magazine and started flipping pages. I noticed that his hands looked nicked and worn, as did most people's in this town, something I could appreciate and feel a personal connection with.

"Just my lipstick," I called over my shoulder, wanting to be clear that I wasn't making plans for what might happen after dinner. I grabbed the lipstick tube from my dresser and came back in to the living room in less than five seconds, but Seth was gone.

"Great kitchen," he shouted back. "Just getting a glass of water. Hope you don't mind."

I didn't, although the sudden familiarity with my domestic life seemed two or three dates too soon. But then maybe that was the way they did things up here. I followed his voice into the kitchen. "Sure I can't I offer you something else, a glass of wine, some soda?"

"Just water. Hope you don't think I'm a party pooper, but I don't drink. Not for five years."

"No problem for me. Shall we go?" I didn't tell him that my brother had just celebrated his sixth anniversary sober, that I understood the struggle, that I wouldn't ask more unless he brought it up again.

We drove to Rhinebeck in his truck, the black sky glittering with stars so dense they looked like an upside down carpet of light. We talked about the proposal for a new mall, and Seth sounded completely rational when he said that he thought it was inevitable and so the town should get concessions from the developers instead of turning it into a pitched battle. He asked about my work, and when I described my dual existence he said wistfully, "Good for you. It's not easy to find what you're good at and what you love, but it seems like you've found two of those things."

"What would you do if you could?"

"Cook."

"Wow! No hesitation, not for a second. Why don't you?"

Now he did hesitate. I could feel him pulling back, as though he'd just shown me his eleventh toe and quickly pulled his socks back on.

"I have a house to pay off, two kids to put through college, and another year of alimony to come up with. So I keep doing what I know how to do to make money. I arrange mortgages for other people and take a cut from the banks. Every time the interest rates go down, or threaten to go up, we do, as they say, land office business. I can't stop now, not for another eight, ten years."

"Pull over," I said. "Right here."

He glanced at me, frowned, and eased his truck onto the side of the road. "Something wrong?"

"Yes, what's wrong is that we're going out to dinner. Instead, I think you should cook for me. You know those shows where the celebrity chef comes to visit Jane and John Doe and makes the most spectacular meal from what's in the Doe fridge and cupboards? Well, that's what we're going to do tonight. But fair warning. It's going to a real challenge in my kitchen."

His laughter started in his belly and kept rolling out, the sheer pleasure in the sound infectious and happy-making. He nodded and squeezed my shoulder and said, "I love it. But we're about two minutes from town, and since I came unprepared, I would like to buy a bottle of wine for you to enjoy with dinner. Even though I don't drink, I don't expect other people to follow suit."

"That's a lovely idea but absolutely not necessary." As he pulled back onto the ribbon of road, I was grateful that I'd been through all this with my brother. I didn't want to patronize or insult him, didn't want to ignore him, and I certainly didn't want to lie to him.

We pulled into the crowded parking lot of Barton's Wine and Spirits and parked between a dusty pickup truck and a ten-year-old Honda that I recognized as Bobby Benson's car. Another car, yellow and gleaming as though it had been freshly waxed, idled on the other side of the Honda. When I glanced over I thought I recognized the boy. Will Jackson sat in the car with a scowl pasted on his handsome face.

Inside, the store was warm, bright, and crowded. People meandered through the aisles, chattering, the cash register merrily chinging with each sale. I looked around for Bobby, didn't see him, then turned my attention to the riojas, my current favorite. Spanish red wine made me think of savory tapas and flamenco dancing, not bad images to have in your head when a good-looking man was in your kitchen cooking for you.

"How about this one?" I said, picking up the bottle and showing it to Seth. "I mean . . . never mind. Let's try that again. I think this one would be nice."

"Great. I love labels with chateaus on them. What do they call chateaus in Spain?" He shrugged and smiled and set the bottle on the counter. "Butter?"

I nodded.

"Mushrooms? Eggs? Ham? Cheese? Broccoli?" He handed a twenty to the young woman behind the counter, scooped up his change.

"Salami and spinach. No ham. No broccoli." I followed him out the door.

"Mmmm, great. I can smell it now."

But I barely registered his words, because as we approached the car angry voices shouted words that made me cringe.

"I didn't, I swear I didn't. Now let go of me."

Bobby. I'd recognized his voice anywhere. I didn't know what to do. Seth cocked his head and listened.

"Don't give me that crap! I know what you did. You better not forget that." This voice was one I didn't recognize, one I'd rather not hear ever again. It was so filled with hostility, so cold, so threatening.

"Just leave me alone," Bobby pleaded.

Before I knew what was happening, Seth thrust the foil bag into my hand and strode to the corner of the building. I hung back, not wanting Bobby to know that I had witnessed another of his embarrassing moments — the tractor pull debacle was bad enough, but this would surely be something he'd rather no one knew about, especially a woman he was working for.

"Hey, Bobby, Will, how you guys doing? What's up?" Seth's voice boomed out as he approached the dark corner of the parking lot. His long stride carried him to within a couple of feet of the tense figures.

Neither boy offered an audible answer, and Seth kept moving closer. "It's me, Seth Selinsky. I heard voices, came to see what's up. Everything okay here?"

"No problem," Bobby mumbled, and he stepped sideways, out of the reach of the other boy and headed for his car, casting a glance over his shoulder when he was halfway there. He didn't look in my direction at all, just walked right past me without seeing me. Or without wanting to; maybe that was more like.

Seth's voice had dropped in volume and I couldn't hear what he was saying to Will, but the boy kept looking past him to follow Bobby with his eyes.

In Walden Corners, it appeared, even an angry teenage football player didn't cross the line of disrespecting his elders, in this case the parent of one of his teammates. I wasn't sure how this scene would have played out in Brooklyn, but I was happy see Seth amble back to where I stood in the shadows.

"You should be a mediator," I said. "You defused that without a problem."

He smiled and shrugged and tugged at the collar of his leather jacket. "They're good boys. I don't know what the particular problem is, but this happens. All that testosterone and nowhere to go. They should learn to sublimate a little. Transform some of that energy into something useful."

"Like making dinner for a hungry woman," I said as I climbed into the truck.

It was too early in our relationship for me to say that I hoped he didn't use all that energy at the stove. I could think of a couple things it would be fun to heat up with Seth Selinsky.

My kitchen was awash in delicious aromas of onions and garlic sautéing in olive oil. The mushrooms and salami were diced and ready to go into the pan, the spinach was washed and the cheese grated. After registering his astonishment that I had no flour in the house, Seth buttered three crustless slices of nine-grain bread and pressed them into a pie pan while he regaled me with stories of how people tried to make themselves look financially better than they are so that they might qualify for a loan.

He was a good storyteller, tuned to the quirky subtleties of human behavior. He spun the tale of a doctor who claimed to be an anesthesiologist making $250,000 a year but was really only an on-call substitute for a large medical practice in Poughkeepsie and was lucky to clear $60,000. He described the woman's solemn face when she described how she'd never lost a patient and that was why she was in such high demand.

"It's amazing that people think they won't get caught in lies like that. It always turns out to be more trouble than it's worth. I mean, hasn't she ever heard of pay stubs?"

"Haven't you ever lied and thought you'd get away with it?" If I was going to get to know this man, he'd have to put up with Ms. Blurt, who let the occasional thought slip right past my internal censor and land in the conversation.

"Of course." He grinned. "I lied when I told you I could make a soufflé with salami in it. Too dense. It pulls the whole thing down until it's nothing more than quiche."

"But I love quiche. Really, Seth, everyone lies, don't they?"

He wiped his hands on the red checked dish towel he'd stuck into a belt loop and leaned back against the counter. "I'd be lying if I said otherwise. What's all this about?"

Good question. What did I think would happen? He'd just fess up to murdering Coach and I'd phone the sheriff and be a hero? Scooter and Nora were never far from the front of my mind, but I didn't want to share my worries about them with

Seth. It was none of his business, not his to mention casually to his son or anyone else.

"I guess I'm a little tense tonight. Every once in a while, I just can't get Coach's murder out of my mind. Sorry, it's not you, it's totally me."

He folded his arms in front of his chest and studied my face with those searching, sober, beautiful eyes.

"I'm sorry too, but I do understand. You want me to go?" He glanced over at the pan sizzling on the stove, at the neat little glass bowls filled with their bright, pretty ingredients.

"No. But give me five minutes. You keep doing what you're doing and I'll try to rewind and start this evening over from about half an hour ago, okay?"

"This will be ready in twenty minutes. I'll holler if you're not back by then."

I laughed. "It's a small house. No shouting necessary. Thanks for understanding, Seth."

Behind the closed door of my bedroom, I dialed Nora's number. She answered on the first ring, not a good sign.

"Nora, it's me. Is Scooter back?"

"No. I'm going nuts. I just drove all around again and nobody's seen him. If I don't hear from him by eleven, I've decided I have to call the sheriff. Oh, damn, Lili, I should have seen this coming. I thought I was paying attention, but I missed something. I can't stand this."

"I'm coming over."

"Thanks, but Elizabeth is here with me. I'll call you if I hear anything."

A little spark of jealousy flared in me and then died away. I splashed water on my face, ran a brush through my hair, and went back out to the kitchen, where Seth stood with his back to the door and his attention on a salad he'd managed to put together with half a cucumber, three carrots, some mint, and what appeared to be a can of black olives.

"Olives? Where did you find them? And what are you doing with the bananas and apples?" I asked, pointing to the artfully arranged fruit bowl on the butcher block counter.

He turned slowly and grinned. "I like this evening better than the one I'd planned. Olives were tucked away behind a large can of tomatoes, and you should never keep apples in the refrigerator. They lose their taste. Dinner will be served in ten minutes, Madame. The wine is breathing, and so am I, but just barely. I've never cooked for someone that I've known only"

— he glanced at his watch — "three hours."

And for the next ninety minutes, we ate and talked about movies and laughed at how much I didn't know about winter in the country. It was easy and warm, and I forgot for a while about Scooter, and about my concern that Seth might have had something to do with Coach's murder.

When he pushed back his chair to clear the table, I stopped him. "You cooked. If I let you clean up too then I'd have to tip you, and I can't calculate twenty percent of the bill."

He grinned. "I'll collect another time. My mama taught me to leave a party when I was having fun, so I'm going to head on down the road. Whoa, there I go slipping into Cowboy Mode. Ron warned me not to do that, that women just think it's silly."

I nodded and smiled back. "Smart boy you raised. Thanks for cooking, Seth. It was a great meal."

"Thanks for practically forcing me into it. I had a terrific time." He walked behind my chair, kissed the top of my head, and pulled his coat from the hook on the wall as he passed by on his way to the door. "See you soon."

I waited until I could no longer see his

headlights on the road and then cleared the table. One of the nice things about living alone was that I could leave the dishes sitting in the sink until I felt like doing them. I wrapped up the piece of quiche, stuck it in the fridge, and stopped myself just in time when my hand reached for the fruit bowl with its banana and two apples. I left it on the counter, reaching instead for the phone. But it was eleven thirty, too late to call Nora. I could hardly imagine her sleeping until Scooter turned up, and something told me that he would. I was more worried about Nora than I was about a bereaved fifteen-year-old boy who had run away from home for a night or two to be alone with his pain.

Chapter 14

Armel Noonan slumped in the front seat of his car. He avoided my eyes, looking instead at the steering wheel, at his fingers, at the scuffed dashboard.

"So, you haven't seen Scooter at all? You know Nora is really worried about him. It's supposed to storm tomorrow, maybe eight, ten inches of snow. Where is he, Armel? I promise I won't say who told me."

His head whipped around, sandy hair flopping into his eyes. "I'm not going to tell you, so you can just quit the guilt stuff. He's okay. He needs to take care of something, that's all. He's mixed up and angry but he's okay. He doesn't stay in the same place all the time, but he's fine. Please don't ask me any more questions."

Take care of something? That sounded too much like vigilante justice, too much like a sure bet for someone, probably Scooter, ending up in trouble or hurt or both. Armel had obviously had contact with him, didn't seem worried about the impending snowstorm or anything else, which made me glance over to the tool shed next to the big, fenced garden plot.

Armel followed my gaze and smiled. "He's not there. You want to see?"

I felt foolish. I wanted to prove that he could trust me, so that if something really important came up, he would know that he could come to me.

"No, that's okay, I believe you. But, Armel, if you can convince him to call his mother, just even leave her a message, that would be a good thing. And if there's anything I can do to help . . ." I scribbled my telephone number and my e-mail address on the back of an old Walgreens receipt and handed it to him. "You take care. Of yourself, and of Scooter."

Armel's beautiful smile flashed a dimple at me before he pushed open the car door and got out. "You too," he said, the relief noticeable in his voice.

As I got into my car and backed down the Noonan driveway, I saw that Armel was leaning against the rear fender of his car, watching me. Wondering whether I was wrong not to take him up on that offer to check the shed, I drove to town, glancing at the brush and the woods on the sides of the road, checking the fields and the doorways of houses and barns. Scooter did not miraculously appear. I had the feeling that all attempts to find him would be futile, that he would emerge from his hiding place when he was ready and not because I'd traced him to a tiny garden shed at his friend's house. But that didn't mean it was possible to stop looking. As long as I was out and doing errands, I'd keep my eyes peeled.

The Agway parking lot looked like Times Square just before curtain time, cars jammed at odd angles, some trying to park, others attempting to find or create by force a lane big enough for shoppers to carry their snow shovels, sand, portable heaters, and snow blowers home with them. At a time when I was sure everyone would be busy stocking up on groceries, they'd all had exactly the same thought that I did. After what felt like an hour, I finally slid my car into an empty spot and made my way into the store.

The smells, of machine oil and birdseed and metal, reminded me of the hardware store on Fifth Avenue in Bay Ridge near my parents' house. More relaxed now, I realized that I might not know what to do with Nitro-Max, but I could make my way around this store and find what I needed.

A wire shopping cart waited at the door, just for me, it seemed, and I rolled it down the aisle, the melody of "O Holy Night" running through my head.

If he was smart and Nora was lucky, Scooter would have the good sense to return home well before Christmas, a week away.

The bag of birdseed fit easily into my cart. I maneuvered down the aisles between other shoppers until I came to the shovels. I picked one up, hefting it for feel, smugly triumphant that I'd beaten the crowd who might have cleaned out the shelves.

"You planting a garden?"

When I turned to see who was talking to me I nearly bumped into a familiar face, pinched and scrubbed. Alvin Akron sported a red and white canvas apron over his checked shirt and pressed jeans and wore a smirk on his narrow face. It was clear that I wasn't going to enjoy anything about this conversation except the end of it.

"As a matter of fact, I am. But not until spring. I'm just getting ready for the snow. Can you tell me where I can get a bag of sand?"

Snorting, Alvin grabbed the shovel out of my cart, startling me. But before I could say anything, he snickered and ran his finger along the point at the end. "This is for digging dirt. The point cuts through the soil. You try this on snow it'll all just fall off the sides. Here."

He held out another shovel with a rectangular blade curved so that it could scoop snow. I tried not to blush, but the warmth crept up my cheeks. "Thanks," I said. "My first winter here. I should have asked someone. I guess that's my lesson for today."

I reached out for the shovel, but he kept it away from me, looked down the aisle, and then said, "Since you're new here, I'll just tell you something that will help you get along. We don't much care for outsiders coming around and getting into our business. Especially women who go looking for trouble and then find it. So, you stop nosing around my property, you hear me? You — I know you're a friend of the Johnson family, and I don't want to see you on my property. You look smart enough to figure out that you should pay attention when someone tells you something important." He held out the shovel, his mouth turning up at one corner, then he snatched it back out of my grasp.

I was tempted to walk away, but it

looked like the last snow shovel around, and besides, I didn't want him to think he could play games with me, although he was doing a pretty good job of getting away with it.

"Please let me have that snow shovel," I said evenly. I looked down at the badge on his apron. There went my next statement. Calling the manager would do me no good. He *was* the manager. "I was looking for someone. And I wasn't on your property. That's Nora Johnson's field. Now, is there something else you want to tell me?"

Alvin Akron snorted and shook his head. "I'm not going to debate property lines with you. Just stay away from my land, that's all."

I grabbed the shovel, resisting the impulse to swing it at his pointy, shiny little head. Even the nine minutes of standing on line waiting to be checked out didn't make me feel one bit more charitable toward the man. He was petty, mean, angry — someone I would cross the street to avoid. What if Coach hadn't been able to avoid Alvin Akron?

Bobby Benson's tractor chugged into sight at four the next afternoon. The sun was low behind the trees, but the last glints caught the gold in Laura Miller's hair as she sat behind him on the tractor, her hands gripping the seat by her sides. As instructed, I'd been soaking the stumps for hours, and now, with the sky heavy with impending snow, he was sure he'd be able to finish the job in about an hour.

Laura hopped down and ran over to me as though I was her best friend, and although I smiled, I wondered what was on her mind. Girls can be hard to read, changing with each breeze and hormone surge. Whatever Laura wanted from me, I hoped I could give it to her. In under fifteen minutes. I had a ton of work to do.

Bobby marched over to the stumps, his round face looking as severe as I'd ever seen it, reminding me that girls had no corner on the strong-feelings market.

"Hey, Ms. Marino, how's it going today?" Laura's bright voice and bouncy good cheer felt forced.

"Fine, Laura. What about you?"

She smiled, showing a mouthful of perfect teeth. "Great. Everything's great."

"Have you seen, uh, Scooter Johnson lately? How's he doing?" That sounded innocent enough, I hoped.

"Gee, you know, he's not in any of my classes. I know if it was me, if my father . . ." Her blue eyes glistened and she patted the dampness away with a tissue she pulled from her pocket. "Sorry. That reminds me. Can I tell you something?"

I waited for what I knew was the real reason for her sudden interest in me.

"I, uh, just wanted to let you know not to worry about Bobby. He's having some trouble at home, so he's a little bent out of shape, you know? His father . . ."

I almost didn't want to hear any more but she leaned closer and then looked over her shoulder at Bobby, who had climbed back into the high tractor seat, and then she whispered to me, "His father drinks. And then he yells at Bobby, you know? And Bobby doesn't know how to handle it so he gets all mad inside and, well, I didn't want you to take it personally. You know what I mean?"

"Thanks for telling me, Laura." She shivered slightly, and I wondered whether I should invite her to wait inside. I had to get back to my gourds and not babysit a teenage girl who seemed to be attached to her boyfriend if not at the hip then at least by an unseen force that kept them within shouting distance of each other. But I could let her wait inside, couldn't I? "It's pretty cold. I can't stay around and chat, but if you want to watch television or something while Bobby's finishing up, that's fine with me."

Her wistful smile turned to a delighted grin and she said, "Thanks. I guess I could do that for a couple of minutes. It's really freezing out here. I'm gonna tell him and then I'll come in. If you're sure it's okay."

She trotted away to the corner of the yard, where Bobby was adjusting the blade on the tractor. I couldn't hear what either of them was saying, but something in Bobby's face still seemed more angry than loving. I felt sad that poor Bobby never seemed comfortable, never seemed happy, except for that one moment when he'd taken the snowmobile victory ride after finishing the repairs.

Laura pivoted and loped back to the porch, breathless, her cheeks glowing and her hair flying out behind her. "Brrrr, I need to get warm."

I opened the door and she followed me inside, plopping down on the couch and huddling into a heat-conserving ball. Her plaid skirt barely covered her knees, and she rubbed at them and then leaned back as if exhausted. I clicked on the television, handed her the remote control, and said, "I'll be in my studio if you need anything."

"Well, uh, maybe you could . . . oh, never mind." Her expression suddenly was that of a confused six-year-old. She stared at Oscar the Grouch and the letter M doing some kind of dance — a mambo, I guessed, or a mazurka — and scrunched her legs up tighter.

I had no interest in teasing out her question, whatever it was. The part of me that wasn't sympathetic to this child's general hesitancy felt bad, but that part of me that had to get the gourds ready for the show felt even worse about all the interruptions. I mumbled something about getting to work and headed for my studio.

Just being in that small room, surrounded by my gourds, my tools, shelves filled with leather dyes and gilder's paste, long pine needles in a galvanized bucket, acrylic paints, brushes, and cans of spray paint, brought me peace. I picked up the round bushel gourd. The wheat design that I'd burned onto its side really needed to be free of color, but the expanse around it would look good in a mahogany leather dye wash. I picked up the sponge and applied a thin film, my mind slipping into a quiet place. But not for long.

A tremendous wrenching sound drew me to the window and I watched in amazement as Bobby strained, his body tense and his hands clenched on the steering wheel, to push the tractor forward one more time. I couldn't decide which comparison was more apt, that of a newborn baby being dragged from its mother's body or Neil's vision of a tooth being pushed rather than pulled out of the mouth of a dental patient.

The tractor engine sputtered, coughed, and died. Bobby slammed his hand on the wheel, pushed his cap back on his head, and hopped down. I half expected to see another outburst, but instead he knelt and tightened a screw on the back of the blade. When he climbed back to the seat his grim determination seemed to have won out over his anger.

The engine started on the first try. Bobby slammed the gear shift lever, and the tractor pressed against the half-uprooted tree stump, pressing, pressing, until the thing seemed to pop out of the earth.

Bobby's loud hoot of triumph made me smile. He deserved that moment of victory. I ran out to the yard, excited and happy for both of us.

"That was amazing, Bobby. You really did it. That's so great." I must have looked like an idiot, practically bouncing up and down with my excitement, but I didn't care.

His smile transformed his face and made him almost handsome. "I just had to get the angle right. It's all the angle. If you get it wrong, then you can't budge these old stumps, so you have to hit it in the right place. No big deal. Any jerk can do it."

"Well, I couldn't. I honestly don't know anyone else who could." My heart squeezed a little at the notion that he thought of himself as a jerk. "You want to come in and have some hot chocolate before you ride home? Laura was pretty cold, maybe she wants some too."

At the girl's name, his smile disappeared. "No. I mean, thanks, but I have to get home."

"You sure? It's really good. Or some lemonade, if you're thirsty."

"Yeah, the lemonade sounds good. I do have to get home pretty soon. My dad promised to take me to town for some stuff." His features softened and the smile returned to the corner of his mouth. "We're getting new rifles. There's a big sale over to Honiker's, and I'm getting a twelve gauge. I'll just wait on the porch. Don't want to get mud on your floors."

"Listen, step inside and stand on the mat. That's what it's for. Your boots won't hurt anything."

I dropped my own boots at the front door, passing through the empty living room on my way to the kitchen. Assuming that Laura was in the bathroom, I poured lemonade into two glasses. Bobby didn't sound like a boy disturbed by his father's behavior, but more like someone who looked forward to every opportunity to spend time with his dad. I was thoroughly confused until I thought back to my own teen years, to my ambivalence toward my parents, my siblings, anyone who still carried around memories of me as a child and refused to treat me as the fully formed adult I considered myself to be.

"Here's the lemonade," I said. "I'll let Laura know you're done for the day here. Thanks, Bobby."

I know I didn't imagine the flicker of annoyance that returned to his face at the mention of her name. Lovers' quarrels at sixteen are high drama, I recalled. A wistful wish snuck up on me, that Ed and I had had a fight, ever, in the four years we were seeing each other. That would have been good for us. For me, anyway. But he was so good at deflecting or absorbing potential conflict, at conciliation, that I could never tell what he wanted. How he managed to run a school and make decisions I never understood.

The television's cold blue light was still flickering in the living room, but Laura was nowhere to be seen. I checked the bathroom, but the door was open and the room empty. Alarmed, I looked in my bedroom, in the gourd workroom, and then the kitchen. No Laura.

Then I heard a voice from outside, and I glanced out the kitchen window to see Laura sitting on the back steps, hunched over a cell phone, her free hand clutching her forehead as though her head ached. Her voice rose and I heard her say, ". . . but I don't think he's told her anything. I can't stay with him every second, you know."

Fascinated, I remained motionless at my spot at the window. Maybe it wasn't eavesdropping if it was your own house.

"No, I didn't. Listen, I have to go. Love you," she said, and slipped the cell phone into her jacket pocket.

I pushed open the back door and Laura whipped her head around, a smile rising to her mouth when she saw me.

"Hey, Ms. Marino, just talking to my

mother. She wanted to know when I'd be home. Bobby done for the day?"

She said it so brightly, I instantly regretted the suspicions that had nibbled at the edge of my mind.

"Yes, that's what I was coming to tell you. He's ready to go."

"Thanks," she said, jumping up and brushing off the seat of her plaid skirt. "Thanks for letting me wait inside."

She walked to the side of the house and headed for the tractor, which was idling in the driveway. I watched Laura climb up onto the seat behind Bobby and wave to me, and then they rumbled out of the driveway.

Those two left me feeling uneasy, but then these days that seemed to be my natural state.

An owl hooted in the dark, and I was glad for the company. The quiet night felt lonely, and I thought about Scooter out there in the cold, alone, possibly afraid, likely angry and confused.

Without really deciding anything, I realized that I was pulling on my jacket, jamming a knitted cap onto my head, and heading out the door with my car keys and a flashlight in my hands. The air stung my warm face and made my eyes water, but I got used to it quickly and my eyes adjusted easily to the moonlit shapes and shadows. At the end of the yard, near the stumps that Bobby was nearly finished removing, six glints of light shone in the night, and then I saw three white tails twitch as a family of deer bounded away silently into the woods.

Sorry to have disturbed them, I pulled out onto the road, not sure where I was going. If my goal was to find Scooter, one spot was as good as another — he could be anywhere and probably would be smart enough not to hide in places that Nora already knew about.

At midnight, Walden Corners looked constricted, worn, not at all picturesque. The convenience store seemed like a shabby, overgrown Lego set in need of painting, and the gas pumps stood thick and graceless under the sickly glare of the fluorescent lights. Liberti's Pizza, The Creamery, and Hogan's Country Properties lined the road forlornly. I saw no huddled shapes, no sign of Scooter, only one gray and white cat, belly hanging, patrolling the window box of the pizza place.

I headed for the high school and then thought better of it. My headlights were sure to attract the attention of a state trooper or the sheriff's deputy. In four hours, the dairy farmers would trudge to their barns to start morning milking, milk trucks would start their rounds to collect milk and bring it to the processing plants, and the county would wake to another day. Where was Scooter?

Not in the Agway parking lot. Not behind the Safeway store or anywhere near the Rhinebeck fairgrounds. Not walking along Route 9A, not tramping on Kerley Corners Road, not resting against a tree in the church yard at the intersection just before my turn to go back to Iron Mill Road. The black sky covered the fields like a soft blanket, and I headed home.

The living room light drew me like a beacon, and I hurried through the crunchy frost that rimed the lawn and was relieved to be back in the warmth of my house. No blinking light on my answering machine — if Nora had heard anything she wouldn't call until morning anyway. I went into the kitchen to put on the kettle for tea, slinging my backpack onto a chair and eyeing an unwashed pot.

Hungry, I decided that for once I'd be good. An apple would be enough, at least until I could have breakfast without wondering whether to count a snack as the fourth meal of the day before or the first of the day to come.

But when I turned and reached into the basket, all I found was air.

Had I automatically put the fruit basket in the refrigerator, despite Seth Selinsky's warning? I yanked the refrigerator open. No apples. Certainly no banana, the horror of refrigerating bananas long ago instilled in me by my grandmother.

Someone had been in my house — a creepy feeling. My little haven suddenly became a scene in a horror movie, with the heroine tiptoeing through her home and the shot cutting back to the man lurking in the closet.

So, I thought, I'll just skip the tiptoeing part and sit down and wait for the lurker to burst out. I grabbed a kitchen knife, turned off the lights, and sat down on the sofa, vowing to stay awake until the sun rose, if necessary.

Ten minutes ticked by, and then an hour. I fell asleep once, only to be startled into wakefulness by a sleety rain, its icy patter on the windows annoying, ominous.

This was silly. The clock said nearly five. I'd been sitting on the sofa for too long, my legs cramped and stiff. I was about to get up and make coffee when I saw a blur streak by at the far end of the yard, crouched low and running from tree to tree.

My heart raced and I squinted at the shape crouched behind the tallest of the two apple trees.

Scooter.

I jumped up and ran to the porch, nearly slipping on a thin sheet of ice that had formed in the cold. "Scooter, it's all right. You can come in. It's so cold and wet."

His hunched shape was still visible behind the tree. I wasn't wearing shoes, and I feared that if I went back for boots, he'd take advantage of my absence and disappear. On the other hand, if I went after him, I'd probably scare him away or slip and break my foolish neck or give myself frostbite. He started to run again and I shouted, "I promise, I won't tell anyone you're here. Come inside and get dry. I'll leave the door open. I won't ask you any questions."

It was risky, but it was the only thing I could do. I turned, walked into the kitchen, and started heating water for coffee. My attention was focused on listening for sounds from the front of the house, but I heard none. Please, I begged silently, trust me.

It was enough to make me believe in the immediate power of prayer. The door closed, quietly, but I heard it, heard what sounded like a boot being pulled off, then another. Footsteps sounded in the hall.

"You won't call my mother?"

When I turned around, I couldn't stop the tears in my eyes as I hugged him. Scooter stiffened and I let go and looked into his eyes.

"I won't call her. But I think you should. She's so worried about you."

He sat shivering on the stool, his eyebrows white with frost. The collar of his knitted shirt was damp and his jeans were dark and wet all the way past his knees. He watched as I grabbed two mugs, his puffed, red eyes following my movements. "I know. But I can't call her yet. I have to figure something out first. Maybe later . . ."

Obviously, the boy hadn't slept and probably hadn't eaten, and whatever he was wrestling with, hunger, cold, and exhaustion wouldn't help him.

"Tell you what. I'll go get some dry sweats and socks so you're not sitting in my kitchen and dripping ice water onto the floor. While you're changing I'll heat up this quiche and then you can figure out what you want to do next." I kept my voice soft, determined not to singsong as I sometimes do when I'm nervous.

He shook his head. "You'll call her when you get the clothes."

"Scooter, come with me into my bedroom. And then we'll come back to the kitchen and I'll turn my head and work on breakfast while you change behind the counter. I told you that I wouldn't call."

I took his shrug as consent and started for the bedroom, glad to hear his steps behind me. My house is clean, but I'm not always the world's most organized person, and I had to rummage through several drawers to find the sweats. "Voila! They may be a little short on you, but I think they're one-size-fits-all, kind of medium. And they're not pink or anything. Want to go to the basement and toss your wet jeans and socks in the dryer?"

He accepted the folded garments I handed him, shrugged again, said, "You come with me."

"Fine." I wouldn't call Nora until he said it was all right, or until he left, but I was aching to phone her. A million questions flooded my head, about where he'd been and why he'd left and how he managed to end up at my house, but I wanted to give him some recovery time, at least until he was dry and warm and fed.

I turned my back while he changed, then followed him down the stairs to the cellar, tossed his wet things into the dryer, and headed back to the kitchen. On the way to the stairs I noticed that the sweatshirt I'd given him still had a little heart-shaped American flag pin stuck onto the chest, which meant that I probably hadn't worn it since some time in the winter of 2001 when everyone in New York City was sporting some declaration of patriotism. He wouldn't care — his own clothes would be dry in about half an hour, anyway.

The coffee aroma filled the kitchen, and I poured each of us a cup. Neither of us said a word as I pointed to the bread for him to make toast, and in a few minutes we were sitting at the table, where a couple of nights earlier I'd shared quiche and conversation with Seth Selinsky.

This meal was proving to be considerably less fun.

"Did something happen? I mean, that made you run away?" I asked when he'd finished his third piece of toast and most of the quiche. Little crumbs clung to the corners of his mouth, but I resisted the impulse to reach up and wipe them away.

His eyes blinked rapidly and he stared at his plate.

"Sorry," I said softly. "I want to help, you know, but I'm not sure how I can. I'm not trying to pry."

His jaw tightened, and he wrapped his hands around the warm mug. He took a deep breath in, opened his mouth, and said . . . nothing.

I started clearing the table, thinking that I'd given him the opening and he hadn't moved into it. I could neither drag nor push him, like a stubborn tree stump, against his will. I rinsed the plates, hoping that Scooter would still be in the living room when I finished wiping the counters and scraping a pale yellow spot of melted butter from the stove.

Just as Laura Miller had the day before, he huddled on the sofa, knees drawn up and arms wrapped around his waist. I breathed a sigh of relief.

"Listen, you can rest here for a while, if that's what you want, while I finish washing the dishes. You want a blanket?"

"I know who killed my father," he said.

Chapter 15

I really thought my heart had stopped beating.

When I could speak, I said, "What do you mean?"

He frowned. The question was too open-ended, the words he'd said not really in need of explanation. For once, I wished my mediator training hadn't become such an ingrained part of my communication.

"Sorry. I know what you mean. But who? And how did you find out?"

Without hesitation, he said, "I can't tell you. That's what's so hard about this: I can't tell anyone. I have to figure this out on my own. What to do. How much to say. That, or I can just take care of it myself."

He thrummed with rage, and I was almost afraid to try to comfort him. My mind raced, falling into empty voids at every turn. I had no idea what to do.

It's all right to sit with the silence, my mediation mentor used to say. And it was true that sometimes the tension of the quiet in the room caused a key idea to bubble up, something that one of the parties had been holding back with a wall of chatter.

I counted to one hundred, then kept going. When I'd counted off another thirty-six seconds, Scooter said, "What if I know but I can't prove it?"

"Then maybe it's not true. Maybe you want an answer so much you might do something that would jeopardize getting the proof that's needed to make the case stick. It's not for you to prove, Scooter. That's the job of the police."

His eyes fell closed, and his head tilted forward until his chin touched his chest. He looked the very picture of defeat, and as I watched his face I saw only impassive resignation.

His head lifted slowly. "If I tell you what I know will you promise not to say anything to anyone?"

Now it was my turn to close my eyes. He'd put me on the horns of a dilemma, a classic no-win situation. Clearly he needed to talk to an adult, and whether by reason of circumstance or of choice, I was the one he was auditioning for the job. But if he told me something important, how could I join him in withholding information from the police? On the other hand, if he didn't tell me then he'd be dangling out there alone.

I didn't reach across the table and take his hand and tell him it was all right to unburden himself, nor did I withdraw into righteous huffiness at the position he'd put me in. I said, "Scooter, I just can't promise you that. If you want to tell me, I can listen without making up my mind until I've heard the whole story. But I can't promise what I will or won't do in the end."

He smiled a little then and looked me in the eye. "I thought you'd say something like that. Okay, Lili, this isn't gonna stay secret for too much longer anyway. Too many kids are talking about it, and eventually one of them is going to go to their parents or a teacher or even the cops, so I'll tell you."

My turn to show my relief. "I'm glad you decided to talk to me."

But he didn't seem to hear me, lost again to his own thoughts and his own anger. His fingers gripped a teaspoon so tightly I thought he'd snap the handle in two. "Every year the football team has a night when the varsity guys get to make the new players do whatever. If they can't take it, then they're not tough enough to play for the Bobcats."

He was taking me into unfamiliar territory. Growing up in Brooklyn, I'd dealt with turf battles and intramural baseball and basketball competitions but not football hazings.

"Usually they do things like make you steal the goal posts of the opposing team or paint the side of their school with fingerpaints, you know, so that it washes off but everyone knows you got them. My dad didn't exactly encourage it. But he didn't stop it either. If anyone ever wanted to tell on the guys who did it, my dad would pretend he hadn't heard a thing. So they kinda got the picture that he was saying it was okay to prank on the other school."

An artifact of the local culture, part of the rites of passage. Instead of having to mug an old lady on a subway train to earn your stripes, all you had to do was some innocent fingerpainting. Clearly, though, this build-up was leading to something a little less innocent than the previous years' activities.

"This year Will Jackson was in charge."

The boy with the sneer, the boy who had made Bobby so uncomfortable. I felt myself getting ready to strangle him with my own hands, not wanting to share that pleasure with Scooter or anyone else.

"He had it in for Bobby Benson from second grade. From the time Bobby tripped him when he was walking to the front of the class to write an answer on the board in math. It was the only class that Will was any good at and he always had his hand up. He was a bully and didn't care beans about school; but math, that was a different story.

"After that, Will used to steal Bobby's books and pinch him and punch him on the school bus and make it seem like it was Bobby who started it. So the stuff between them has been going on a long time. Will was looking for his chance to really finally get Bobby. The rest of the team tried to talk him out of it, but Will was captain and what he said they had to do."

As accustomed as I was to sitting in a mediation room and listening without judgment, even when people spoke about marital infidelities or drug use or stealing from their parents, I couldn't stop myself from leaping ahead. Scooter rubbed his hands over his eyes, as though he could make the images behind them vanish, as though he wished he could wipe away the whole story. He pushed his fork around on his plate, moving a crumb from the rim to the center and then back again.

I watched his face, waiting.

"Aw, shit, I can't do this. I'm going to take a shower and warm up." He was out of his chair in a flash, and he fled into the bathroom.

The only sound from behind the door was the water running in the shower.

I cleared the table, wiped the counters with a soapy sponge, scrubbed the stove, and sprayed it with glass cleaner to remove the soap so that I didn't have to run the water in the middle of Scooter's shower. Will Jackson had nurtured his anger and planned a final revenge on Bobby, and somehow it all connected to Coach's death. According to Scooter, anyway.

Walden Corners hardly seemed like a good place to harbor hatred. After all, these were kids who grew up with the relative good luck of living in a beautiful spot in America, and they had bright futures. Had Coach uncovered something terrible about a member of the football team? Although he hadn't said that outright, Scooter had come right up to the edge, gotten scared, and then retreated.

The shower stopped, and I heard the rustling sounds of the boy getting dressed. His own clothes were still tumbling in the dryer, although they probably would be ready in the next couple of minutes.

"Hey, Scooter, you want me to get your clothes? I think they're dry," I said to the closed door.

He didn't answer. He continued to move about in the bathroom, but he said nothing.

"You hear me, Scooter? You want your clothes?"

Finally he said, "Yeah, that's great, Lili. Thanks."

Relieved to hear him speak, I told him I'd be right back and headed for the cellar stairs. Just as I reached the bottom step, the dryer's buzzer, set loud enough for me to hear it from my studio at the back of the house, went off.

Good timing, I thought, and I opened the door, reached in for the warm jeans, being careful to avoid the hot rivets, shook them, folded them in half, then did the same with Scooter's long-sleeved T-shirt and the cotton sweater and his mismatched socks. The warmth would feel nice to him, I knew, and I bounded up the steps.

As soon as I got to the landing, I felt the chill breeze and I knew I'd been tricked.

The back door stood ajar, and a cold wind poured into my house. Scooter was gone.

I drove slowly to Nora's, my eyes scanning the woods for signs of movement. He'd taken his jacket and my red knit watch cap and mittens, which I'd left hanging on a peg by the back door, and they would make him easier to spot . . . if he'd actually put them on and not stuffed them into his pocket until he was far away from my house.

When I pulled into Nora's driveway, my stomach knotted. I had to tell her, had to betray Scooter's confidence. He was a confused young man, and as much as I valued his trust and friendship, I was more concerned with getting him home and getting him help in navigating this second crisis in a month.

I knocked on the kitchen door, then pushed it open and called Nora's name into the stillness. She answered from upstairs, and her shuffling footsteps told me that she was probably still in her nightclothes. When she appeared I had to keep myself from gasping.

Her hair stuck out at odd angles and her eyes were swollen. I hadn't realized how much weight she'd lost, but it was enough to make her sweatpants hang loosely on her body and her face look drawn. Her skin looked ashy instead of shining with its usual gleaming luster, and her mouth was a thin, tense line that pulled in toward the center with a forbidding pucker.

"Lili. I must have fallen asleep about an hour ago, sitting in the chair in Scooter's room. My neck hurts." She shuffled to the sink to fill the kettle, and when she'd set it on the stove and lit the gas, she turned to me. "Sorry for the scary sight. Nobody sees me like this, ever."

"Scooter was at my house this morning." I couldn't wait for a good time to say it. "He's all right, but he's very upset. He wouldn't tell me where he'd been, but he was freezing and his clothes were practically stiff with ice."

Nora's eyes fell shut and a single tear slid down her cheek. "Thank you," she said, and I couldn't tell if she was talking to me or to the power to which she addressed her prayers. She looked over my shoulder, a big grin starting to form on her face.

"He's not here. He ran away again. I

should have known. He said he had to do something. He took a shower and I went down to the cellar to get his clothes out of the dryer and when I came back he was gone. I'm sorry, Nora. I'm so sorry."

I hugged her, unable to bear the sight of disappointment on her face so soon after the relief. Even if the rational part of her knew it wasn't my fault that her son hadn't returned in the car with me, I knew that some sliver of blame must be lodged in her heart. I knew it with a certainty, because I felt it too.

"It's not your fault, Lili." Her voice was soft, her tone even. "It's Scooter, not you or me. He's a good boy, but as Coach liked to say, he's our stone-headed child. When he gets an idea in his head, it's hard for him to let go. He kind of has to be dragged back down to earth. So what's the idea that has him going on this way?"

"He said he knows who killed Coach." I recounted the story of Will Jackson and Bobby Benson, in as much detail as I remembered, and said, "When he got to the part where he was talking about how the boys on the team had to listen to Will and do whatever he told them to, he freaked out and ran into the bathroom. I felt like he needed time to calm down, so I left him alone in there. He probably wasn't thinking of running away until I gave him the opening by suggesting that I go get his clothes out of the dryer. Anyway, that's as far as he ever got."

"He never said what Will told them to do? Never said any other names?" She poured each of us coffee and gulped hers eagerly.

"No. No plans, no names. Just what I've told you. I think we should tell the sheriff and let him sort this out."

Nora pulled her hair back, secured it with a couple of combs, and shook her head. "Oh, Lord, this is awful. So confusing. I can't stand it. You know what my first thought was?"

She really didn't want an answer, so I waited for her to go on.

"What if things were the other way around, if Fred Benson was murdered and Bobby had run away and then named Scooter and Will in half a story? Would I want the sheriff to put my child through the trauma of being questioned, being a suspect, based on that little bit of a story?"

I would never have thought of that, had only considered that the sheriff was the person who would best find out if Will and

Bobby and the football team had anything to do with Coach's death.

"Fair enough," I said, "but what about Scooter? He's out there trying to gather evidence to back up what he believes."

Nora looked calm, calmer than she'd been in weeks. "Maybe," she said, "we need to let my child go through this hard time and come to his senses on his own. He's got the foundation: he knows what's right and what's not. Maybe he needs to do this thing for his father."

"Do you think that's what Coach would have wanted?" I asked softly. "If a kid came to him and said the things Scooter said to me, would he say, 'Let's wait and see'? Think about it, Nora."

From the dark hall, the fat orange tabby pattered across the living room floor and jumped up onto Nora's lap, settling into a furry, purring ball. Absently, Nora's hand drifted to the cat's head and she stroked it gently, her fingers automatic and graceful. We sat that way, I in my chair wondering about my responsibility, and Nora and the cat giving and receiving comfort to each other, until my friend looked up and said, "If we don't tell the sheriff, we may be protecting Coach's killer. If we don't say anything, Scooter may feel he has to even the score. Telling the sheriff may end up protecting him from himself. I guess it's time for me to stop pretending that Scooter is going to come waltzing back home after a good sulk. It's time to get Murph and his people involved."

Relieved that she'd agreed to call the sheriff, I squeezed her hand. "I'm glad. For lots of reasons, I'm sure it's the right thing to do."

"Don't say anything to anyone else, okay? Don't mention those boys' names." The cat leaped from Nora's lap and she stood up, squaring her shoulders and preparing for whatever lay ahead.

Chapter 16

Melissa Paul stood in the middle of the inn's elegantly luxurious dining room, in her elegantly understated suit, and surveyed the scene. "Norma Tozin, you forgot what I told you. The flowers are too tall. People won't be able to talk across the tables. They need to be about half the height."

A young woman who looked as though she'd rather cut off all her gorgeous raven hair than displease Melissa blushed crimson and scurried away behind the swinging doors with two of the floral arrangements in her hands.

"The room looks beautiful," I said.

"Lili? What are you doing here?"

Confused, I checked my watch. "Didn't your phone message ask if I could come by at four?"

She rolled her green eyes. "Oh, dear. *Tomorrow*. By the time I phoned you I must have forgotten to say tomorrow."

"So, you mean all these preparations

aren't a surprise party for me? I'm crushed." Laughing, I pointed to the large gold bells topping a lovely, five-foot-tall Norwegian spruce decorated with red ornaments and gold bows. "Wedding party?"

"Nope, fiftieth anniversary. Hence the gold accessories. We have two hours to make sure everything is perfect."

"You look so calm." And she did — her face relaxed, her hair perfectly silken.

"And they call David Copperfield an illusionist. I guess I'm better than I used to be. I know at least some of the things that can wrong by now. So I can —"

A loud crash of breaking glass in the kitchen made both of us jump. Melissa paled and then ran through the swinging doors. I had visions of glass in the caviar or all the wine goblets shattered to smithereens. Curious, I followed.

Before I reached the doors, though, the sound of laughter came rolling from the kitchen. By the time I'd pushed open the doors, the laughter had subsided to giggles. The two women stood with their backs to me, pointing at the top shelf.

A big black bird stared down at us as though delivering a warning about what might befall the person who even tried to get near him.

On the floor below the shelf, big pieces of broken glass glinted in the light from the window and the open door. A vase, judging by the shapes on the floor, had been a casualty on the crow's way to its landing pad.

"Okay, Mr. Nevermore, you have to leave now," Mclissa said, and the bird cocked his head and then thrust his beak forward, talons clinging to the wood. Her invitation didn't seem to interest him.

"A broom," I said. "If you can push him toward the door with a broom, I bet he'd be much happier to be out there than in here."

Melissa's assistant looked lost in thought. Finally she said, "You know, in my psyche class we learned about how people respond to stimuli. You know, approach and avoidance. Well, this guy has an approach thing going with the smoked salmon, which is where I found him when I came in. So maybe if we put most of it back in the fridge and take a piece outside and then help him get the idea with the broom, we'd have, you know, an approach-avoidance solution going that should work."

Melissa nodded. "Sounds like a plan, Norma."

The girl scurried to put the platter in the

walk-in refrigerator, and then started for the door with what looked like a quarter pound of lox.

"Hey, we don't have to give him enough for a bagel. Just a little, half that, ought to do it." Arms folded across her chest, Melissa waited for her assistant to return some of the fish to the cooler, and then nodded as a flame-cheeked Norma carried the remaining portion out the door.

I might have been intimidated by a barking dog with sharp teeth, but this bird didn't scare me one bit. With gingerly movements, I picked up the straw broom from the rack in the utility closet and approached the shelf. Melissa's frown was deep enough to draw her eyebrows together in a single line. The bird was engaged in a staring contest with her, which kept my creeping little steps from his attention. Two more steps and I'd be in striking distance. Melissa glanced my way, and so did the bird, and his squawk split the air. He flapped his wings but stayed on his perch, and I felt the broom connect with his surprisingly resistant bird body.

I pushed with a slow, even pressure, and Mr. Nevermore squawked louder, but I kept pushing him forward. He scuttled away from the broom, until he was at the edge of the shelf, and then he looked down in alarm.

"You can fly, you know," I said soothingly, and the big black bird swooped with widespread wings right toward my head.

I ducked, batted at him with the broom, and he flew out the door, landing five feet from where Norma had set the smoked salmon. Melissa hugged me.

"Very brave. Thanks." She turned to look at Norma, who was busy sweeping glass into a dustpan. "Now I have to find out how he got in here. I don't want him going around telling his birdie buddies that Melissa Paul's inn is easy pickings."

"I swear, the door was closed when I came into the dining room, and then it was open when I carried those flowers inside. I didn't see him on the counter at first, and when I did I tried to shoo him out, but he flew to the top shelf and knocked over that giant glass vase." She looked pale and worried. From her kneeling position, she seemed to be a supplicant asking for Melissa's forgiveness.

Melissa knelt beside the girl, took the dustpan from her hands, and said, "I'm not blaming you, Norma. I just want to know what happened. Was the door locked?"

Norma's eyes scanned the room, as though she were mentally running a movie in reverse. Finally, she shrugged. "I don't remember. I thought I locked it, but I might not have."

Patting the girl's shoulder, Melissa rose and dumped the glass into the trash with a clatter. She pulled open a drawer, unlocked a metal box, seemed relieved at what she saw, and then she began a slow, careful circuit around the room. I watched in silence, not wanting to interrupt her concentration as she went through her mental inventory. Halfway around the room, she picked something small from the counter, whirled around, and said, "Where did this come from?"

Between two fingers, she held up a pin. A heart-shaped American flag pin.

"Scooter," I whispered before I could stop myself. I didn't want Norma to hear the story, so I said, "Scooter gave me one like that. Everyone in New York City was wearing these after 9/11. Could have come from anywhere."

I motioned with a jerk of my head for Melissa to come with me into the dining room. Frowning, she followed a couple of steps behind.

"What's this about?" Depositing the pin

in my outstretched hand, she picked up what looked to me like a perfectly folded napkin, shook it open, did some magic that turned it into a pleated swan-like shape, and stuffed it back into the goblet. "I have to get to work. The guests are going to start arriving in an hour and a half, and I still have two hours worth of things to accomplish."

"What I wanted to say was that I'm sure the person who left your kitchen door open was Scooter. He came to my house last night and he started to say that he knows who killed his father, but he got scared and ran away again. I gave him some dry clothes, and this pin was on my sweatshirt. I have to call Nora and let her know."

"Poor Nora," Melissa said, hugging herself. "Now she's got to worry about her son too. I think we should call Elizabeth and Susan and see if we can move that meeting from tomorrow to tonight. Maybe together we can figure something out."

"But you have a party tonight."

Melissa straightened the edge of a red tablecloth and headed toward the kitchen. "These Golden Anniversary parties sometimes last longer than weddings. People trying to prove that they're not done having fun quite yet, thank you very much.

Could go until midnight, one. But I don't have to be on the floor the whole time. If we all meet here in the kitchen at nine, we should be able to get some good talking time in."

The suggestion sounded good to me, but the prospect of driving fifteen miles down the road to the cottage and then driving back another fifteen miles was about as appealing as cleaning the bathrooms in a college fraternity house. "Good idea. I might as well hang out, so if you need help with anything, put me to work."

"Okay. Just remember, you asked for it. First, why don't you call Nora and tell her you think Scooter was here? Then you can call Susan and Elizabeth and see if they can come tonight instead of tomorrow." Melissa looked at me appraisingly, tossed me an apron, and pointed to a mountain of spinach. "And then, if you really want something to do, you can wash this. Three changes of cold water."

Phoning Elizabeth Conklin, followed by my least favorite kitchen job. But I'd offered and it was too late to back out now. Nora was the easy call — she said almost nothing except that she was tired and not really into conversation, that she was glad I'd called, that she'd talk to me in the morning. I phoned Susan and Elizabeth and, happily, left messages on their machines. I started humming a Lucinda Williams song and pretty soon the time was flying by as the kitchen began to fill up with more helpers and more activity.

If you've never been in the well-run kitchen of a busy caterer in the middle of a major event, then you've never seen controlled chaos. Servers grabbed plates from the trays of other servers and scurried out the door; the prep cook sliced, diced, and wielded sharp objects while the head chef oversaw oven thermometers and flaming pans, managing to snatch her fingers out of harm's way without spilling the sauces she stirred. Amazing aromas filled the kitchen, and then were replaced by even more amazing aromas. From butternut-squash-and-shrimp bisque to spinach salad with goat cheese and walnuts to rack of lamb, horseradish mashed potatoes, and haricots verts all the way to pistachio and white chocolate cake, I was astonished at the skill and the art of the production. Nothing spilled, nothing was forgotten, and a fabulous dinner for one hundred went off without a hitch.

I loved being part of that machinery too, garnishing plates with chopped parsley or pistachio nuts, handing off trays to the servers, being alert to whatever needed doing. And when I held the door open for a young woman struggling back to the kitchen with a load of dirty dishes and looked out into the dining room at the beautiful flowers and the flickering candlelight, the hum of happy conversation and the harp music, my chest swelled with the pleasure of having helped so many people have a good time.

"This is fun," I said to Melissa just before the dessert plates were taken down from the cupboard shelves.

She put hands on hips and smiled. "Want a job? My assistant is leaving to have a baby."

"Whoaa," I said, laughing. "It's fun *once*. You need someone who likes playing with food for that job."

"Holy arugula, Lili, you're brilliant! Maybe if I got Nora to run the restaurant, I might even be able to open a new B and B. I am totally in love with a beautiful Victorian in Chatham, and she needs a job and . . ." She shook her head, smiled, and headed for the swinging doors. Over her shoulder she said, "I better focus on tonight first."

The head chef, finished for the evening,

sat on a stool working on a crossword puzzle and nibbling at some salad. I was about to sit down at the small table near the back door when a voice behind me said, "You don't need no job here."

I wheeled around and found myself looking into Ira Jackson's eerily pale, watery eyes. Adrenaline coursed through me, the fight instinct much stronger than any thought of flight.

"What I don't need is you sneaking up behind me and threatening me." I glared, hoping that my face looked fierce, resolute, determined not to blink first. Ira Jackson's smirk made me want to punch his weasily face, but I kept my fists at my sides.

"Hey, Ira, give me a hand with these," one of the servers said, pointing to three bulging black plastic bags.

Without a word, Ira snorted once, then turned to help the boy. The encounter left me thrumming with restless energy, and I was glad to see first Elizabeth and then Susan arrive a few minutes after nine. Both settled down at the table with slivers of cake. When Melissa joined us ten minutes later, she looked tired and triumphant.

"This is about Scooter, right?" Elizabeth wiped the corner of her mouth with her napkin. "Fantastic cake, Melissa."

Everyone murmured assent, and Susan said, "I thought I saw him yesterday in the woods behind the school parking lot. And then again walking down Main Street in Rhinebeck. I hate thinking about him out there alone. If I'm so worried, I don't know how Nora can stand it."

Then it was my turn to tell them about my early morning visit, about what we thought was another drop-in at the inn. "He's okay, at least so far. But he's very upset. First he said that he thinks he knows who killed his dad, then he ran away again before he could tell me the whole story." To honor Nora's wish, I wouldn't mention names or even say that the football team was involved.

"So, with no more information than that, we can't do a single thing. Nothing. If we have any suspicions," Elizabeth said, making lingering eye contact with each of us around the circle, ending finally with me, "they'd better have some substance to back them up. The sheriff isn't going to take kindly to frivolous accusations. I know because Michele Castro told me."

Susan looked startled. "You mean, you went to her with . . . a name?"

"Yes. And I still think they're not checking out the right people, or at least not in enough depth." Elizabeth sighed and cleared her throat. "Frankly, I have heard Ira Jackson express animosity toward Coach and Nora and even Scooter enough times to make me thoroughly sick. He's such a throwback, rednecked son of a —"

"Ira killed Coach because he's black? Is that what you're saying?" Melissa's skeptical question seemed like a challenge, but she didn't wait for an answer. "He's a bitter, spiteful, racist jerk who I hire once in a while because sometimes my bleeding liberal heart feels that everyone, if given a chance, can be redeemed; and Ira's the hardest case I know, so I get to feel virtuous. But I don't see him acting on his resentment. It would take too much energy."

I glanced at Elizabeth, who seemed miles away. "I was sure you were going to say you told her about Alvin Akron. About the land dispute and the threats. Now, there's a man I can see making a plan and carrying it out and feeling as though justice was finally done. Or some such warped thing. I only saw him a couple of times, but boy, he gives me the creeps."

"And all those parents." Susan shook her head. "The kids on the second string football team who sat on the bench a game or three last season, maybe didn't get scholarships to colleges because Coach wouldn't let them play unless they maintained a C average. And the parents who think Coach was too tough on the kids — Charles Cohen, Seth Selinsky, Bert Smothers. I could probably name four or five more who've been known to try to harass Coach into lowering his standards."

This was not where I wanted the conversation to go, but it had managed to get there without anyone directing traffic. The mention of Seth Selinsky's name made me want to shout that it wasn't fair, that I'd had dinner with him only once, that the tiny little dating pool in Walden Corners couldn't stand being reduced by one.

I had misgivings about staying silent about Tom Ford and the lost investment and the angry exchange of letters and the partial repayment, but that particular piece of business wasn't mine to divulge, even to Nora's childhood friends. If she wanted to tell them, then we could talk about it; but if no one brought it up, then I would assume it wasn't public knowledge.

"I think we've gotten a little off track here." I waited for everyone to look up so that we could be in synch. "We're supposed to be trying to figure out how to find Scooter and get him to go back home. This will be the second night he's been away. Nora goes in and out of trusting that he'll come back when he's ready and being terrified about what it means that he's so shaken by Coach's death. I'm wondering if you know about his friends, who he'd turn to for help, where he might stay."

Suddenly, new energy sparked the group and the brainstorming began in earnest.

"He might end up at Peggy Navarette's house. He had a crush on her right before school started. Or Armel's, of course."

"I bet he'll hang around somewhere near school. Where he can see his friends and maybe meet with them in secret."

"There's Armel Noonan, Indhira Wilson, Ron Selinsky, Rene Schnall, Bobby Benson, Joey McAllister. I mean, everyone liked Scooter, so we might as well name the entire high school student body."

"Yes," I said, aware that Will Jackson's name hadn't been mentioned, "but did Scooter like everyone? That's really the question. Who would he trust with his troubles, with the questions that his father's death brought up in him?"

"Scooter and Armel have been practically each others' shadows since second grade. Armel. That's where I'd start. I know Nora has spoken to his parents, but they both say they've asked Armel, and he swears he doesn't know a thing."

I might not know the Noonan family, but I did know that teenage loyalty was thicker than blood in a situation like this. "Maybe we should get a message to Armel to give to Scooter."

"He already knows Nora is worried about him," Elizabeth said quietly.

"But it can't hurt anything to try," Susan said.

Melissa nodded.

"Susan, you're the logical person to do it. You see Armel in school. The rest of us might scare him off. What should we say?"

After laboring over the wording of the note we'd give Armel, we finally settled on the simplest message: *Your mother is very worried about you and wants you to come home. If you need to talk about anything, you can call one of us.* I fought to include that last sentence, arguing that if he was staying away because of some moral or emotional dilemma, he needed to know he had places to turn besides his mother and the police.

We each went our separate ways into the

cold December night. I thought about Scooter still out there and prayed that he had the good sense to find a warm place to spend the night.

Chapter 17

He was curled up on my sofa, my clothing neatly folded on the chair beside him, his boots standing like little sentries on the doormat just inside the back door. A plate with a few crumbs and a glass with tracings of the milk he'd drunk sat on the coffee table.

My first impulse was to kiss his cheek and cover him with a blanket, turn out the light, and tiptoe up to my own bedroom to sleep. But of course I couldn't do that, no matter how exhausted the child might be. This time, I had to make sure that he got home to Nora. I tapped his shoulder gently and Scooter jerked awake, looked around as though he didn't recognize where he was, and then smiled at me.

"Hey, Lili. Thanks for keeping my clothes. I was afraid maybe you brought them back to my house." He sat up and stretched, young muscles rippling through the thin shirt. "I guess I was tired."

I sat at the other end of the sofa. "Listen,

Scooter, you're putting me in a terrible position here. I want you to trust me, but I need you to let your mother know what's going on. She'll talk things through with you and you two can work out whatever it is together. She told me that she trusted you to do the right thing, but that doesn't mean she's not worried. She wants to help, you know that."

"I'll call her in a minute." His brow furrowed with a frown and his eyes glittered. "She's having such a hard time, I don't want to drag her into this. I mean, she's gonna have to know about it eventually, but I guess I was trying to, I don't know, protect her."

My heart wrenched with pride and sadness at his situation. "She's stronger than you think. You have to be honest with her."

He blinked back tears, then swiped at his face with the back of his hand. The furnace kicked in, startling us both. We smiled in sheepish admission of how thick the tension had become in the room.

"I'll tell her. But can I tell you first? My brain is a total zoo, a complete wacko mess. I've thought about this so much in the past three days I thought my head would crack open. I don't know if it's something or nothing. I can't tell. You're the mediator, you know a lot of stuff about people. I don't know beans, not anymore." His sigh rattled through the room, and he closed his eyes to calm himself.

"I'd say you know plenty. But go ahead. And then I'll drive you home."

He nodded. "Football practice. That's where this all started, like I told you the other day before I got all scared and ran away. Will Jackson, he told the kids to do things to Bobby Benson. Horrible things. Most of them left, just walked out when he said he was serious, that Bobby needed to know his place and he was gonna learn his lesson once and for all. Three guys, his little *slaves,* he counted on them to do everything he told them to." The contempt in his voice and his anger had transformed him into a rigid caricature of himself, eyes slitted, fists and jaw tight.

I wanted him to keep going, but I couldn't rush this. I said, "Can you tell me more about what happened?"

He blinked himself back to the room. "I heard this from three separate kids. The ones who left, you know? One of the guys who stayed thought it was cool, what they did, and he bragged about it. Sick. What they did? They took Bobby out to the woods not too far from here after football practice one night. You know, no Coach, no teachers, no parents. Just the football team. There's a big, flat rock about thirty feet into the woods near where the stream bends. The kids always call it the table rock, because when we were in sixth grade we used to come out here and have picnics. Anyway, they . . ." His voice dropped, and he seemed to swallow back bitter bile that had risen to his throat. "They did terrible things to him. Pine cones. I don't know. I can't even think about it without wanting to barf."

My stomach grabbed, and I closed my eyes and forced myself to breathe. How could human beings act that way? I'd never understand. I felt my own anger rising, and my eyes flew open. Poor Bobby.

"When did this happen, Scooter?" I knew the answer, and the ache in my chest grew sharper, the pain deeper.

"Couple of days before Ag Day. Monday, it had to be that Monday. It's like Nazi Germany or something, you know? Kids going along with some demented idea because someone told them to. I don't get it." He pushed the crumbs around on the plate, pulled up his socks, sank into the corner of the sofa. "So the thing is, Bobby was freaking furious at my dad because he told him he'd heard rumors that Will was gonna do something gross for hazing. And Dad told him to stay away from Will, asked Bobby if he wanted a lift home from practice, and that's all he did. I mean, it's like those rules we learned about in American Studies. You can't arrest someone until they do something, right, even if you're sure in your gut that they will. So what could my dad do? What could he do? What could he do?"

His voice had risen to a shout, and then he slammed his hand against the back of the sofa and started to sob, great, hoarse gulping cries that wrenched my heart. I sat beside him and rubbed his back for a few seconds, then I waited while he cried himself out. This was too much for a sixteen-year-old boy to carry around with him. Too much ugliness and too much pain.

"That's really terrible. Your dad did what he could. And poor Bobby suffered so much. But the part I didn't hear is who you think killed your dad."

Scooter stared out the window into the dark night. "It was Bobby. That's what everyone is saying. They're saying that his hunting rifle is missing. Bobby won't talk to anyone, and they're definitely not talking to him."

I was still trying wrap my mind around the fact that he was talking about the same boy who had come into my house and shared a glass of lemonade with me, who I'd seen on that victory ride when he fixed the snowmobile. I could imagine Bobby being the victim of a hazing that went too far. But then going after Coach in blind fury? Why not kill Will Jackson instead? It didn't make sense. Still, from what I'd seen and what I remembered of my own adolescence, reason could be a rare commodity.

"You know, Scooter, you just said it yourself. You heard this story, maybe from a couple of friends, bits and pieces. And that's all it is right now."

"I know. That's why I tried to sneak up to Bobby's house and to Will's. I had my tape recorder, right? And I thought I'd be able to catch them saying something." Scooter's laugh was bitter. "All I heard was Will telling Laura that she was doing a good job keeping Bobby quiet."

Now it was my turn to blink and frown. Scooter had just added the puzzle piece that made my confusion about that relationship fall away. *Of course* that perky blonde cheerleader-type wasn't Bobby Benson's girlfriend. She was sticking close to him on orders from Will Jackson, making sure that Bobby didn't tell his story to anyone because Will's kingdom would fall apart under the glaring light of an investigation.

I hated the meanness of it all, hated that I'd allowed myself to be fooled and, in a weird way, to become part of this terrible cover-up.

"So, what's next?" Whatever the truth, lives would be changed forever. Some because they'd taken part in those horrible activities, Bobby because his humiliation would become public knowledge. For the Johnson family, questions of how Coach handled the situation would be the subject of public debate in which there could be no victory. If Scooter had even a slight inkling of the mess that was about to blow open, it was no wonder that he'd run away and tried to fix it before it came to light.

His shoulders sagged with the burden of his knowledge. "I'm ready. I hate it that I have to tell this to my mother. I hate it that she has to go through what I went through these past three days."

"You'll be going through it together," I said, squeezing his hand and rising. "That won't make it easy, but it usually feels better to share the burden. And next time, just knock on my door and ask. I'll give you apples and dry socks anytime."

He didn't respond to my feeble attempt to lighten the moment, and I realized that it was my own discomfort I was trying to allay. He had the right to the full impact of his complicated, even contradictory, feelings.

"Ready?" I shrugged into my coat, afraid that if I waited around he might decide to take off again.

We drove the seven miles to his house without saying much. I bit back a stream of advice, confident, as Nora had been, that he would come to appropriate conclusions on his own. Nora and Coach had raised this child to be thoughtful, caring, and perceptive, but it was going to take a lot of energy to see him through to the end of this crisis.

When I glanced over at the shape huddled against the passenger door, his eyes were closed. I tried to empty my mind for the rest of the trip, paying attention only to the road.

"Okay, Scooter, we're here," I said gently, and his eyes snapped open.

"Thanks, Lili. I *do* feel better. I mean, I hate that I have to go to the sheriff now

303

and tell him everything. But I do, I have to do it." He started to open the car door and then turned to me again. "What happened to Bobby . . . it wasn't my father's fault. Will Jackson's the one. I don't know if other people will see that, but I do."

"It is going to be hard, what you have to do next. I agree, it's Will who hurt Bobby." I couldn't quite make myself say that I thought Coach was blameless. It was his watch, after all, and he was responsible for more than just winning football games. But I said nothing more as I got out and walked to the back door. Scooter followed me into the brightly lit house, its familiar odors of spices and fruit still warm and welcoming. I expected to find Nora in the kitchen, but as we walked through the dining room we nearly tripped over her outstretched legs.

At midnight, she was sitting on the floor, cleaning out the cabinet where she kept serving pieces, candles, linen napkins, birthday candle holders, and fancy spoons and forks.

She looked first at me, blinked, then looked at Scooter and said, "Oh!" She pushed herself to a standing position in a single motion and grabbed her son into an embrace, rocking back and forth as though they were about to break into a lopsided waltz.

I backed out of the dining room and headed for my car. They didn't need me to be there, and I was exhausted.

Sleet rattled against the bedroom windows and I groaned when my eyes focused on the clock. Nothing. No bright green digital display to tell me what time it was, but the light, or rather the lack of it, outside indicated that either I'd slept away an entire day or I'd gotten up at a time fit for only farmers and insomniacs. My watch said ten minutes to five.

The air was cold when I tossed back the covers and the floor even colder.

No power. Ice storms do that at least once a year, I'd been told by Tom Ford when he was listing all the reasons I might not want to live in the country. No-see-ums every June — but not as bad as Maine, he'd said — and the occasional lightning storm in the summer that made it clear that Thor and Odin and Zeus and Jehovah had all gotten together and decided that the mortals could do with a little scare to make them straighten up and fly right. And ice storms in winter.

Shivering, I pulled on several layers of

clothing and headed to the living room to build a fire. In a few minutes, the flames were roaring and I went inside to make coffee. Not in the electric coffee maker, I remembered. Hopefully, the propane stove would come to my rescue. I turned the knob. Nothing — no clicks to light the pilot. Matches. I was beginning to feel like a pioneer being tested by the elements.

Finally I found some matches and lit the burner, realizing that no power also meant that my water pump wouldn't work, that I should avoid opening the refrigerator too many times because who knew when the power would return. Glad for the pitcher of water that I kept on the counter, I opened the fridge, took out coffee, eggs, butter, cheese, and juice. Anything that I didn't eat or drink could be put on the porch and it would fare just fine. Humming, I made scrambled eggs and coffee and carried them into the living room to sit in front of the fire.

Outside, the rising sun cast an orange glow on the sparkling diamonds crusting the trees and the lawn. The world looked like a scene from a fairy tale, and I wondered where all the rabbits and the deer were right now, what they made of the slippery surfaces, how they would survive. A cardinal swooped down from the woods, tried to land on the bird feeder but couldn't grab hold and flew away. Everyone was having a morning of discovery, it seemed.

I was curious to know how things went with Nora and Scooter, but my phone was out, there was no television, no computer, nothing. I couldn't send John Stacy the article I'd written for his Web site on the upcoming Gourd Gathering in Cherokee, North Carolina. I couldn't use the electric jigsaw to cut gourds, couldn't heat the pyrography tool, and the leather dyes would take forever to dry in such cold temperatures. I wouldn't venture out on the roads, which looked like mirrors of thick, opaque glass, certainly nothing I wanted to experience from behind the wheel of my car. Which left reading or taking a walk.

I'd do both. First the walk, to get my circulation going and my head clear, and then I'd settle in with one of Tom Ford's books, to be determined by whatever came up during my excursion. It was exhilarating, this mandatory spontaneity, and I remembered childhood snow days, building forts or playing spy with my brothers, waiting for my sister to ask me if I would help her bake cookies. Those days felt like treats, and this one did too.

Dressed for a Siberian blizzard, I opened the door and was struck by the total stillness of the morning. The air was warmer than I expected; little drips plinked onto the ice-crusted lawn from the smallest branches as the sun's weak rays grew stronger. I grabbed the walking stick I kept in the corner of the porch and headed for the woods, curious to see if I might find signs of animals that had ventured out in the aftermath of the ice storm. I jabbed the stick into the ice until I got the feel for sliding along in short steps. *Look, Ma, I'm skating!* I wanted to shout.

The crunch of my footsteps and the thunk of the walking stick were magnified in the frosty silence. I stopped to see if I could hear bird calls or animal rustlings, but nothing seemed to be moving except me and those occasional drips of melting ice. A younger me would have shouted into the quiet morning, for fun or to relieve the tension, but I felt enveloped by it and didn't want to break the spell.

When I reached the edge of the woods, I realized that I had walked in the direction of the screams I'd heard that night, the ones that had awakened me, that had made me think of bobcats and mountain lions. That was Bobby. My stomach lurched again, and I leaned against a tree to force the sourness back down. The thought of what those boys did to him made me dizzy, and I told myself that I had to think about something else.

Even as I was struggling with these thoughts, I was drawn another ten feet forward, and then ten feet more until I found the bend in the stream. Ice slicked the banks, and the water that usually rushed by was reduced to a slow trickle between the icy channels. I stepped into the stream, the title of the Zen book on Tom's shelf flashing into my mind and confusing me for a second. And then I was across, weaving between the trees, going forward as though I were hypnotized, until I was standing beside the rock that Scooter had described.

The rock itself was bigger than an ordinary table and rose about three feet out of the ground, as though someone had jammed it into the middle of the woods to provide an interesting contrast to the thin birches and needley pines nearby. I made a slow circuit around it, then circled the rock again, my eyes fixed on the ground under the ice. At first, I didn't see anything but old leaves and twigs, could barely make out smaller pebbles that lay scattered near the rock.

But then I began to notice other things. A pale, cloudy mass that looked like a wadded-up tissue. Something round and silvery, a quarter, probably. I widened the circle, swerving to avoid a bent birch that seemed to have grown up out of the ice when I wasn't looking. A comb that was missing several teeth. A button, black, with four holes, that looked like it came from a navy pea coat. I chopped at the ice with my walking stick, broke through the surface, and managed to pry the button loose with my gloved fingers and drop it into my pocket.

Making three expanding concentric circles around the big flat rock, I uncovered an empty rifle shell, a chewed-up pencil stub, and two bottle caps from Saranac Christmas beer. None of the items meant anything to me; none of them seemed to have a connection to anyone. And then, on the last circuit, I spotted a glint of green and white, and even before I saw what it was, I knew that if I'd found anything that might have significance, this would be it. I had discovered a key ring, with five keys, including a key to a Dodge, still attached.

Who drove a Dodge? Not Coach, not Bobby. What was Will Jackson's vehicle of choice?

Even if those keys confirmed that the hazing incident had happened, that wouldn't mean much in proving who had murdered Coach. But if Bobby was charged with the crime, some clever attorney might be able to use that history during sentencing to establish Bobby's emotional state. And besides, the community needed to know that some of its traditions had gotten out of hand, and the boys who had participated needed to know that they couldn't get away with such abuse.

Chapter 18

Michele Castro looked up from the computer screen on her very neat desk and gestured me into a chair, holding up one finger to tell me to wait.

"They don't have a permit for speeches." She leaned forward and looked at the speaker phone sternly, as though it were a camera that could transmit her picture to whoever was on the other end. "You can tell them that I don't want to interfere with their rights to peaceful protest, but they need a permit to set up a sound system and have speeches. They can gather, they can wave signs, they can pray together in the freezing rain, but they can't make speeches."

The male voice on the other end said, "What if they keep doing it?"

Color rose to her cheeks and she held her breath. I could practically hear her counting to ten. Finally she said, "Politely . . . arrest . . . them. *Politely*." She jabbed the button to break the connection and then looked up at me.

I passed a plastic bag containing the button, the spent shell, and the pencil across her desk to her. On impulse, I held back the car keys, waiting to see her reaction. If I was going to be dismissed out of hand, I didn't want her sweeping what might be the key to the case, so to speak, into a drawer, to be ignored and then forgotten. I felt the hard ridges of the keys through the pocket of my wool coat, wondered about the owner of the key chain with a miniature New York Jets football helmet and two Dodge keys, plus two more that looked like house keys and a smaller one, probably from some kind of small padlock.

"And?" she said.

"I found these things in the woods beside my house. I have reason to believe that some kids on the football team engaged in a particularly nasty form of hazing about a week before Coach Johnson was murdered. There's been some talk that one of the kids might have been so upset that Coach didn't stop this from happening that he . . . well, you know."

I still didn't know whether Nora and Scooter had spoken to anyone in the sheriff's department, but my hope was that they had.

Her face was impassive, but I could have sworn she winced when I said the words *football team*. She poked at the items in the package, pursed her mouth, said, "Who told you this?"

"I can't remember." I wasn't ready to put Scooter on the hot seat and didn't mind if she thought I was hiding something.

She smiled with the left side of her mouth. "You hang out with so many high school–age kids that you don't remember who told you? Come on, Miss Marino, you think about it a minute, I'm sure you can do better than that."

"Maybe it will come to me." I shrugged, feeling a little buzz of excitement about this game of wits. Not a game, I reminded myself. This is about finding Coach's killer.

"All right, let's try another question. What names did you hear?" Both hands splayed on the table, she leaned forward, then looked down at her hip, where a pager hung amid her other paraphernalia. "Damn. Excuse me."

I nodded, glancing around the room while she stepped into the hall and shouted for the deputy. In seconds he was standing in front of her, his head cocked as she spoke, her words too low for me to hear. Her tall, lithe body looked almost slight beside his considerable paunch, but he responded to her as though she were the one with the weight advantage, backing up when she stepped into his space, flinching when a cross expression flitted over her face. Clearly, Michele Castro didn't think much of the velvet glove and instead relied on her iron fist to get things done.

I respected her, but I didn't like her very much.

She watched the deputy walk away, then returned to her seat behind the desk. "Has your memory sharpened any? About where you heard this talk or about the kids who were involved?"

"I heard three names but there were more. Will Jackson, Freddie Koster, and Bobby Benson. Bobby was the victim and Will was the ringleader."

Her eyelids fluttered a couple of times and a frown creased her forehead. "Will Jackson? Who told you this, Miss Marino? I want an answer, a real one."

My hand pressed against the keys again, and I rose and grabbed my backpack from the floor. "I'm sorry but I don't remember. I thought you'd be interested in the information and in the things I found, that's all.

Now, if you'll excuse me, I have an appointment and I'm already late."

"Miss Marino, have you told anyone else about what you heard?"

I shook my head.

"Have you told anyone about these things?" She inclined her head toward the plastic bag on her desk.

I shook my head again. Not yet, anyway, I thought as I broke her gaze and reached into the backpack for my own car keys.

"Do me a favor. Don't start rumors. Don't say anything until I've had a chance to investigate," she said sternly. "I want to get to the bottom of this. And please stop tampering with evidence, Miss Marino. Next time, call me. Don't just go picking things up that might be of some forensic value. You might contaminate them."

Cooties, I thought petulantly. You're the one with the cooties.

For me, a sense of achievement comes from mastering some skill I want to learn — gourd crafting, mediating, cutting the back of my own hair with a mirror in one hand and sharpened scissors in the other. But driving on icy roads felt like something people were born with, and I was woefully lacking that particular gene. I crept along, my heart hammering and my white-knuckled grip on the steering wheel so tight I was sure I'd have to holler for someone to come and pry my fingers off.

I could make my way back to the cottage, and for the first time in days, relax about Scooter and be happy in my little nest. As long as Scooter wasn't home where he belonged, I could hardly think of anything else. Now that he was with Nora, I could let down my vigilance, at least for a while.

What about the keys? a little voice piped up.

I was withholding evidence that might eventually place someone at the scene on the night of the hazing. But something about Michele Castro's reaction had made me wary. That little flicker when I mentioned the football team gave away something more than the normal concern and distaste that any sane, civilized human being would feel. I couldn't hold out for too long, but when my warning lights flashed, however briefly, I paid attention.

I needed help figuring out how to proceed. Moral advice. Legal advice. Practical advice.

Elizabeth Conklin's laugh was tinged with bitterness. "Of course she stonewalled you. Her brother is the mastermind, the quarterback, the about-to-be-infamous Will Jackson."

"Her brother . . . No wonder she reacted that way when I said his name. What do I do now?" I stirred my coffee and looked around Elizabeth's kitchen, cherry wood cabinets and granite counters gleaming in the afternoon sun. Baskets of all sizes and shapes lined the top of a hutch that displayed three white pitchers that ranged in size from huge to normal. It was like sitting in an *Architectural Digest* layout, but curiously the paintings of fruit, four of them close together on the wall beside the hutch, and the basket of real bananas and oranges, made the room homey instead of intimidating.

"You turn over the keys. You can't go around trying these in every Dodge you see in Dutchess and Columbia counties. First of all, you'd get arrested for attempted car theft."

"Well, I know a good lawyer . . ."

She smiled and said, "Special prices for people who put me in ethical dilemmas. Anyway, there's nothing to be gained from holding onto them. Put them back exactly where you found them and then call Castro, tell her you spotted some keys in the woods, picked them up, and then re-membered what she'd said about calling her if you found anything else that might be suspicious. She'll grumble, but she should send someone out right away. *If* she doesn't come out herself."

"Ira Jackson is her father, then?" My mind was still trying to grab hold of the notion that the undersheriff was the sister of the boy who had brutalized Bobby. *Allegedly* brutalized, I reminded myself. It didn't take much imagination to link Will with the small-minded Ira Jackson, but something about Michele seemed more humane, more rational.

"No, Ira married Michele's mother. Actually, Will is a half-brother. Same mother." Elizabeth sat back in her chair and seemed to be gathering facts to present them, as she would if she were liti-gating a case. "Ira was a batterer. I think I told you how I was assigned to take Florrie's case. His approach to problem solving must have spilled over to Will. Great role model, huh? To learn what it means to be a real man from Ira Jackson. Susan has her own stuff to add about the family from gossip in the teachers' lounge at school. Melissa too, of course."

Ira and Will Jackson, related to Michele

Castro — it wasn't really so surprising when I thought about it. In a town as small as Walden Corners, some kind of connection among people whose families had lived there for generations was surely the rule. For most people, it probably provided a familiarity that they found comforting. But at the sheriff's department, it might mean that maintaining objectivity in this case would be more difficult.

"What if the story about the hazing were true, if there hadn't been a murder, if Coach were alive right now? What would happen when it became public knowledge? Aside from ruining lives, I mean." I wanted desperately for Bobby to be innocent, but even as I thought that, I feared hearing the truth.

"*Lives ruined* is right. Coach would probably have taken some heat, even if he was cleared of any kind of direct knowledge or complicity. He knew that hazings were ritualized tests of new kids. He should have exposed the practice, gotten kids and parents together, spoken about it openly. That's what the righteously indignant would say."

My heart sank at the confirmation of my fears. "Won't they say it anyway? And without Coach to defend himself, his name will be tarnished forever."

"Maybe not." Elizabeth looked directly into my eyes. "It all depends on what Bobby says."

"But if Bobby is the one who shot Coach . . . wouldn't he say every terrible thing he could think of to justify his act?"

My question hung in the air, clouding my ability to think clearly. The weight of what lay ahead pressed on my chest like a heavy stone. I wished I hadn't found the keys or gone to the sheriff.

Too late, I thought. This runaway train can't be stopped by me.

Elizabeth read my mind — or my dismayed expression. "Look, this was all going to come out eventually."

"Yes, and it's going to put Nora and Scooter in an awful position. My best hope is that this can be kept quiet until the cops finish their job."

"I'm not going to be the one to phone everyone I know and spread gossip. But you have to understand: kids who do these things brag about them. Sometimes they're even asking to be punished. I've seen it, read about it. They can't live with what they've done, can't figure out how to confess and ask for forgiveness, so they brag. And they get caught because, thank God, someone they've told is so troubled by what they heard that they turn them in. If Scooter heard those stories, then so did fifty other kids."

I wondered how they were sleeping tonight.

I didn't have to wonder for long.

The next day, two hours after I phoned Undersheriff Castro and told her that I'd found a set of car keys near the table rock, Susan phoned.

"There's an emergency school board meeting tomorrow night, closed session, and I've heard that it has to do with Coach's death and with some scandal involving the football team. When I called Nora to give her a heads up, she told me that she already knew and that she was too exhausted to talk about it so I should call you." Her words had tumbled out in breathless rush. "This sounds like it's going to be awful. What's happening, Lili?"

So Elizabeth hadn't said anything, after all. Not even to one of the Gang of Four. But Nora had said that I would explain, and I couldn't lie to Susan.

"It has to do with a football hazing gone terribly bad. A brutal one. And there's been talk floating around that the victim

322

may have been so angry at Coach that he killed him."

"Bobby," she whispered. "He's been practically a zombie in school for months. He always looks as though he wishes he could just disappear or something. I've seen kids behave that way before, and too many times we've learned that they're victims of some kind of abuse. Fred Benson has growled a lot through the years, but as far a I know, he's never hit Bobby. I know Jane too well. She'd never stand for violence at home. The violence happened somewhere else."

I remembered the warmth I felt from Jane Benson, and I agreed with Susan's assessment. If her churlish husband was beating Bobby, she would leave in an instant. And judging from Susan's assessment, Laura's whispered revelation about Fred Benson's drinking was probably another lie, meant to explain away Bobby's stony silence.

"Listen, Susan, have you ever seen or heard anything that would lead you to believe that Bobby was capable of losing it so completely he could . . ." I couldn't say the words.

"No way." Her voice was barely audible. "I don't think so."

But I wasn't so sure. Thinking about the hazing, I had come to believe that the humiliation Bobby suffered could push him, any boy, over the line.

"How did Nora sound today?" I asked.

"Terribly sad. I think she wants to just stay in her little cocoon with her son for as long as she can. But she was grateful to you for helping Scooter get back home, and glad that I warned her about the ugly stuff that's about to be visited upon us. Maybe she'd welcome a phone call. If she's answering the phone."

"I'll wait until tomorrow. She knows we're all here for her. God, I wish this were over."

"Hey," Susan said, "if you're gonna wish for impossible things, then at least wish it never happened. Talk to you soon. Bye."

I looked out the window, in the direction of the woods where the hazing had occurred. The bare branches formed a lacy pattern that let me see a glint of gray that was the rock. All the ice had melted in an overnight thaw, and the runoff trickled down the lawn in the direction of the one remaining tree stump, which stood like a lonely afterthought, the muddy earth around it testament to the effectiveness of Bobby's work.

But I couldn't let myself dwell on unknowables because that would keep me from doing the known long — and getting longer — list of things I had to do. Work on the gourds for the show — I'd learned early on that you can never have enough gourds for a high-traffic show. Complete the report, due in a week. Pay bills. Wash the dishes that had piled up in my sink. Start with the thing you'd least like to do, I told myself, and then you'll be feel like you've earned the fun stuff.

This was the first time I'd thought of washing dishes as fun. It was the corporate report that I wanted to get out of the way, and I sat at the computer and tapped out three pages that sounded about as interesting as the list of side effects on an antibiotic prescription. I could fix them later. The important thing was to get the ideas down in first draft form. I was finishing the last paragraph on page three when I heard a familiar rumble and looked up to see Bobby chugging into my driveway on his tractor. His shadow, pretty Laura, was right behind him in the seat.

An instant headache gripped me, wrapping itself around my temples as though I were being squeezed in a vise.

Laura jumped down and walked toward

the house, and I nearly locked the door and told her to stay out in the cold for all I cared. But then I thought I could make better use of her presence. What I really wanted was to talk to Bobby alone, to see if I could find out something that sounded like the truth. First, though, I wanted to hear what sweet, innocent Laura had to say.

"Hi, Miss Marino. I mean, hi, Lili." She smiled brightly and rubbed her hands together, shivering dramatically for my benefit.

"Hello, Laura. Do you want to wait inside?" *Said the spider to the fly.* This visit would not be all cocoa and soap operas.

She nodded and followed me inside, pulling off her boots, her gloves, unzipping her white down jacket. Her cheeks glowed with healthy color and her blue eyes sparkled. The very picture of robust health. I wanted to throttle her.

"So how's school?" I needed to ease into the real questions, and I watched her smile grow wide, her pearly whites gleaming in my kitchen light.

"Great. One more week to Christmas vacation. My family is going to Cancun. I've never been out of the country before, but my dad got a bonus at work and he says he wants to give us a special treat. I can't believe it."

Cancun. Beautiful beaches, hotels that were much too American for my taste. Unlike Cozumel, where I'd found a very Mexican hotel sandwiched between a Hilton and a Marriott on a gorgeous stretch of the Caribbean. If I wanted to stay at an American hotel, I'd go to Ft. Lauderdale.

"That's wonderful. How's the football team doing? I haven't kept up with the games." I tilted my head, smiled, waiting for her to answer.

The skin around her mouth developed tiny little lines as she pursed her lips, and I got a flash of how she would look as a seventy-year-old. Not unattractive, but creased by life.

Finally she said, "They lost the last four games. Last in their division."

"How does Will feel about that?"

She blanched. "Will? I . . . uh, I guess he's bummed. Is that cocoa ready?"

"Oops, I forgot to turn the flame on." A part of me was enjoying the good cop/bad cop dance, and I kept my back to her when I asked, "How long have you been going together?"

I turned around in time to see her eyes widen. She had the good grace to blush

327

and hang her head. I actually felt a little sorry for her, but not sorry enough to let up now.

"Laura, tell me the truth. Why do you go everywhere that Bobby goes? Will is making you do that, isn't he? What are you supposed to do, keep Bobby company?" I drummed my fingers on the counter, unable to stop the motion. "Or keep him quiet?"

Tears leaked out of the inner corners of her eyes, and soon the floodgates opened. She blinked back her tears when I handed her a paper towel, and she hiccupped her way through half the glass of water I passed to her. It has always been difficult for me to watch another person cry without wanting to fold them into my arms and offer comfort, but I felt no such impulse now.

"Why are you babysitting Bobby?" I asked softly.

"Will said I had to. To keep him from talking to other people." Her brows knitted together in a frown. "But I don't understand what's the big deal, really. It was just a prank. Will says they'd get suspended for it but I told him I didn't think so. But he said I had to stay with Bobby so he wouldn't say anything."

My mind reeled with what she was saying. *Just a prank?*

"I hate it." Her voice was barely audible, and fresh tears rolled out of her eyes and down toward the corners of her mouth.

"Hate what Will did?" I held my breath, hoping that my faith in humanity was about to be restored.

"Hate being with Bobby all the time. He smells like an old engine and his fingernails are so dirty. He's a retard mechanic, that's all, and I can't stand it anymore."

"You can't stand it?" My own shrill voice careened off the kitchen walls. "What about Bobby? What about what they did to Bobby? That was despicable. It crossed a boundary. Don't you have any conscience at all? You're a very sad excuse for a human being. You —"

I clapped my hand over my own mouth. This was a child I was berating. I needed to put the brakes on, needed to get her out of my kitchen before I said things I would regret.

Laura drew herself straight and tall and looked at me as though I were a worm. "If you think that pouring honey in someone's hair is such a bad thing, I feel sorry for you. That's what they did. That's just a prank. And I won't stand here and be yelled at like that. I'm getting out of here. Thanks for nothing."

"Honey?" I felt doubly foolish repeating her words, but I couldn't stop myself. "In his hair? That's all?"

She frowned and stared at me. "That's all. That's what Will did, but if he got caught he'd be suspended and then he wouldn't get a scholarship to Alabama and his whole life would be ruined. You ask them. Ask any of the kids."

And she turned, grabbed her things from the coat hooks by the door, and stomped outside. She didn't walk to the tractor, but instead kept marching down the driveway and out onto the road. I followed her progress through the window, watching her white jacket bob along until she disappeared around the curve in the road.

Bobby's tractor groaned and revved higher, and the last remaining stump popped out of the ground. He sat back and wiped his forehead with his bandana, then swung the tractor around so that it was pointed toward the road. When he hopped down and headed for the house, my heart pounded in my chest. For all my experience reframing potentially explosive statements into neutral language as a volunteer mediator, I had no idea how to ask him about what happened that night in the woods.

Or that morning when I found Coach face down in the pond.

Chapter 19

"She just left. She seemed a little upset." Stick to the truth, I reminded myself. Tricking this boy into saying something would be a bad move for a lot of reasons, not the least of which was how it might affect my conscience. "We got to talking about football, and she mentioned that the new varsity players usually get a hazing from the kids who've been on the team a while. And that you were —"

His cry told me everything I needed to know about that night.

Bobby Benson started shaking, and he ran into the bathroom and retched into the toilet. He flushed, spat into the toilet, flushed again.

I stood in the hall, uncertain about what I should do next. In the end, my paralysis gave Bobby enough time to rinse his mouth, splash water on his face, and then come out, paler and unable to meet my gaze. By that time, I knew what I had to do.

"Bobby, she thinks they poured honey in your hair. That's what she thinks. But your reaction was so strong, I think something much worse must have happened. I don't know exactly what it was, but I think you need to talk to someone — a guidance counselor, a priest, some adult you trust. I have a feeling that whatever secret you've been carrying for two months is not going to be secret much longer. I'll help you however I can."

His contorted face relaxed a little. He was pressed against the wall, his body tense and his shoulders drawn in as though he were protecting his chest from a blow he knew was coming. Finally he said, "I know what they're saying about what happened that night. I don't care. We're moving to Florida next week. My father's sister lives down there. I don't care."

My head spun with his revelation. Moving to Florida would give him the chance to make a clean start with classmates who weren't snickering behind his back, going over the details of his humiliation in the school cafeteria. And it would conveniently remove Bobby from the investigation into Coach's death.

"You have anything else you want to tell me, Bobby?"

His gaze still focused on his shoes, and he shook his head slowly, sandy brown hair falling into his eyes. But when he finally did look at me, his confused expression spoke volumes. "What else? What do you mean?"

Either Bobby Benson was a very good actor, or the thought that he murdered Coach needed some serious revision. Did I have an obligation to this child, or to his parents, to report the rumors that were circulating, or should I simply let the school board process unfold? Whether he was called in to tell his side of the story or not, Bobby was going to be the hot topic in the halls of the high school for weeks.

"No, I . . . I was just asking, that's all."

Before I could say anything else, he was out the door, sliding his way over the muddy lawn to the tractor. I could have run out and caught up with him and told him how confusing everything was for me, and that I was just trying to find out the truth, but that would have been more comfort to me than it would be to him.

In my family, the holidays traditionally have been celebrated in one long hopscotching party that begins on Thanksgiving and has been known to go as late as

Valentine's Day, at least once when my parents were vacationing in the Caribbean and my brother Neil had to report for try-outs for the Mets in January. Celebrating Chanukah with latkes and dreidls, taught to us by the cousins on my mother's side of the family, and then celebrating Christmas with stockings and the traditional and endless Italian dinner of soup, lasagna, veal, broccoli rabe, salad, and my aunt's homemade cassata, takes so long that I still have a hard time thinking of December and January as real months, when real work and other real life events go on.

This year, we were to gather in two days at the family compound in Brooklyn, a three-story row house in Bay Ridge, for the last night of Chanukah. Again by tradition, Chanukah was the time for each person to receive eight small gifts. The big gifts were exchanged on Christmas. Since the family had grown, we each drew a name and bought eight gifts totaling no more than forty dollars for that person, instead of eight gifts for each of the thirteen of us, including my parents, my two brothers, my sister, their spouses, and their combined output of offspring. I hadn't gotten very far with my shopping, and even though this one would be relatively easy because I knew my brother Neil's tastes, likes, and dislikes, I'd been putting it off until I was in a cheerier mood. I'd found three old postcards of Ebbets Field that were hidden in the four-for-a-dollar box in the second-hand store in Red Hook, so I needed seven more items.

A little retail therapy, even as modest as this, might be just thing to distract me for a while and help establish that good cheer.

I grabbed my jacket and purse and headed for Rhinebeck. At five in the after-noon, with dusk descending, the holiday lights twinkled merrily. I found a parking spot right away, and headed for the book-store first, then continued on down the street. By the time I rounded up the paper-back of *The Old Man and the Sea*, acid-free photo corners for his scrapbook, a tube of tangerine-flavored lip balm, a two-inch potted ivy, a purple bungee cord for his motorcycle, and a crystal to hang in his window, I was humming Christmas carols and feeling a little lighter.

As I made my way back to the car, I heard my name from the other side of the street, and when I turned I saw Seth Selinsky standing there, a big, gaily wrapped box in the crook of one arm, as though it were a precious child he was singing to sleep. I waved and was about to keep walking when I realized he was crossing the street.

"Hey, I'm glad I ran into you." His smile widened and his brown eyes crinkled. "Can you spare half an hour for a cup of coffee?"

I couldn't decide whether I was pleased that he wanted to spend time with me or annoyed that he'd waited until he bumped into me instead of making the effort to phone and set up a date.

"Half a cup," I said, not surprising myself. I liked this man and his smart, warm style. He took my elbow with his free hand and guided us between parked cars and then down the street to the coffee shop, whose windows were fogged with steam, making it feel like its own separate universe.

Vivaldi played softly from the speakers on the shelves high up in the small room. Half of the eight tables were occupied, mostly with Bard College students talking quietly, reading, playing backgammon. The soft colors, pale peach and dove gray, and the gauzy half-curtains in the windows made the place soothing and inviting.

I followed Seth to a table in the back, told the waiter that I wanted a mint tea, and unbuttoned my coat.

"You look like you're ready to bolt. Relax. Life's too short to live in the future." Seth had tossed his jacket over the back of the chair, and his body language, loose and slow, was that of a man taking his own advice. "I wanted to ask you about how Nora and Scooter are doing."

"They're holding up. It's a hard time for them." I'm sure I frowned over his question. It wasn't exactly what I wanted to be talking about with him, but everything that touched on Coach's death — the football team, the Johnson family, and what the local police were and weren't doing — were major topics of conversation all over two counties.

"I hear there's something going on at the school tomorrow night, some top secret school board meeting. I just wish this would all get resolved so we could go back to living our normal lives." He sighed and sipped his coffee.

"Nora and Scooter won't ever have that chance," I said, more harshly than I intended.

"Sorry. You're right, of course you are." He stared at the table. "I guess there's no such thing anymore. Normal — that's for other people."

The little bell tinkled and a chill draft curled around my ankles. I looked up to see Fred Benson, bearing down on our table like a charging bull. My first thought was that he and Seth had some old Hatfield and McCoy thing going on, but he stood right in front of me and glared, his face red and the cords on his neck standing out as he gritted his teeth.

"Stop saying things about my boy. That's all I'm here to say. Just quit it. He doesn't need you to hold his hand or tell stories about him. I'm telling you, leave him be."

Seth pushed his chair back, totally alert now and rising slowly to a full standing position. "Hey, Fred, there's no need to come in here and talk that way. Whatever has you so upset, you better think a little before you come into a public place and start making threats. Now, maybe you should go cool off somewhere else."

I wanted to tug on his sleeve and tell him that I could have said the same thing, but then I realized that maybe I couldn't have. Perhaps if I'd lived here all my life . . . or if I'd been a man. I understood Fred's concern for his family, for the well-being of a son who might have been victimized, either in a physical way or by a story that other kids had circulated. I understood his anger too. But directing it at me didn't seem rational.

There I went again, expecting sanity in the middle of a slightly insane situation.

"Mr. Benson, I know your family is —"

"You don't know anything about my family. And I intend to keep it that way." He wheeled and stomped to the door, letting it fall shut behind him.

Through the window, I watched him climb into his truck, and I felt sad all over again. This was not how I wanted to get to know the neighbors in my new town, not how I wanted to start this country life.

"Fred's not always this way," Seth said. He covered my hand with his for a moment, then leaned back in his chair. "He's been under a lot of strain lately, with his business going bad and all. He shouldn't have taken it out on you, though, and I'm sorry I let him do that."

"Thanks for saying that. Listen, can we talk about anything else for a while? Like, what's in that box? It looks very important." I had little heart for flirting, but a shift in topic might change that. Sitting so close to Seth Selinsky, smelling his warm skin that reminded me of cedar shavings, I remembered how nice it was to touch a man, and be touched. My exile had been self-imposed, but the stirrings I felt were comforting reminders of the possibilities.

"That," he said triumphantly, "is a new set of shoulder pads for Ron. He's been getting more play time in the past couple of weeks, and he's been complaining that his old ones aren't really doing the job. I think the problem is that he must have gained about twenty pounds and grown three inches since last year, and he's just plain too broad for the old ones."

Getting more play time since Coach wasn't around to enforce the rules about maintaining passing grades? Seth didn't seem to be aware of the implications of his statement.

"That's great. A great gift." Suddenly, I wasn't sure I wanted to get any closer to Seth Selinsky, no matter how good he smelled. "Listen, I have to get going. Have a nice holiday."

Seth tilted his head questioningly, his eyes searching mine through his long lashes. "That sounds a little like you'll be too busy to see me until January or February. I hope that's not true. I was thinking of getting tickets for *The Nutcracker* in Albany for Boxing Day. Can you join me?"

"Thanks, but I'll be in Brooklyn. Enjoy the ballet, Seth. Bye." With my jacket zipped and my purse slung over my shoulder, I strode to the door without looking back. Brooklyn felt like the quietest, safest place in the world right now, and I thought wistfully about what I would be doing if I still lived in Carroll Gardens.

As soon as I got home, I called my mother.

"Just wanted to say hello, nothing special," I said when she asked if everything was all right.

"Well, I'm glad then. I've been missing you. Things are nuts here. I've had two parties for visiting Iranians, a gathering of parent coordinators being honored by the Department of Education, three luncheons of various Arab, Israeli, and of all things New Zealand special interest groups, and the big City Hall holiday party. I have not had a single second to put my feet up and just chat with any of my children, never mind my friends and far-flung relations."

"Mom, you're wearing me out just talking about it." As one of three special events coordinators for the mayor's office, my mother's work was especially demanding during the holidays, and I'd gotten used to what her litany really meant — that she was overworked, and overjoyed to be doing it all. "How's Dad?"

"Holding steady, as he likes to say."

"Oh, no, not another Parkinson's joke! He's too much." Dad was in good humor, Mom was in her element, and I was in a mess of confusion that was best kept to myself. "Well, just checking in. I know you're busy and —"

"Oh no. You don't phone me for no reason, unless it's Saturday and time for your weekly duty call. What's up with you, honey child?"

"You'd think by now I'd know I can't slip one by you. I guess I'm feeling a little blue. Things have gotten out of hand. Not just Coach's murder, but now there's a chance that one of the kids I've gotten to know may be responsible. Because of a horrible football hazing."

"And you're feeling like the shiny veneer of your new country life has worn off and you don't like what you see underneath. That's what I hear, sweetie."

I should have known it would take Ruth Marino about thirteen seconds to nail me and make me face facts.

343

"Something like that," I said. "I thought I was going to come up here and simplify my life, grow a garden, work on my gourds. Instead I'm caught up in this mess and I don't know how to untangle it all."

"Sweet Lili, you do know, though. You know it's not up to you to untangle it, but only to understand yourself. First you need to accept what *is* and not try to force your life into the shape you wish it would be. And second, life is life. City or country. Complicated and messy. And gloriously rich." She laughed. "You've turned me into a philosopher today. You know you can come down here any time you want a little advice and exotic leftovers."

Even at thirty-four, it was comforting to have such a standing offer. "Thanks, Mom, I'll be there for the holiday dinner. Give Dad a big kiss for me. Love you."

"Love you, too, sweetie," my mother said before she hung up.

I understood why my sister used to say that she had to move to California to get away from Mom's all-knowingness and Dad's hot-and-cold inscrutability, but that was her. She needed to protect herself from them because she didn't feel strong enough to move forward on her own and didn't want to have to justify herself to them. For me, it was both easier and harder. I liked them a lot, my parents, enjoyed spending time with them, and wondered what I'd ever do when they were no longer around.

But they were still here, and still important to me as teachers, friends, and supporters, and although I was grateful for that, my conversation with my mother hadn't changed anything. Except now I had to admit to myself that perfection was only an idea and moving to the country wasn't some magical panacea that would cure whatever ailed me.

The thought actually made me feel better. It was my life, that's what it came down to. With a tiny backward glance at my old fantasy, it was time to make this reality work a little better. I longed to be in my studio. My gourds had been calling me for days, and I was feeling snappish, itchy to get my hands on the smooth little cannonball that was crying to be a Japanese rice bowl. First, though, I had to finally finish the corporate report that was due in two days. I had five pages left to rewrite, and then an index to pull together, and I brewed myself a pot of coffee and carried a cup over to my desk, turned on the computer, and began to work.

★ ★ ★

An hour later, when the light from the half-risen moon spilled into my yard and turned the bare trees into lacy, graceful fingers reaching for the sky, I stretched and looked around, satisfied and maybe even a little smug. A phrase that had been eluding me for days had finally worked its way to my consciousness, and the five pages had then flowed easily.

I was about to turn off the computer for the night when the bright headlights of a car pulling into my driveway drew my attention. Ten o'clock — too late for a social call or a delivery. My heart pounded. Something I was sure I didn't want was about to be dropped on my doorstep. I flipped on the porch light and stepped into the cold, watching my breath make white puffs in the clear, cold night air.

Susan Clemants headed up the walk.

"Hey, Susan, come in. I'll make some tea." I stood aside to let her go in first, then shut the door behind me.

"Not tea. I need a drink." Her face looked stony, with an anger I'd never seen from her before. "I just got word about what's going to happen at the school board meeting. Apparently Will Jackson was questioned this morning by Jonathan

Kirschbaum — you know, the principal — about the hazing. He gave some cock-and-bull story about honey and was oh so surprised at the accusation that he'd taken part in some kind of sexual humiliation. Three other members of the team backed him up. And that is likely to be that. The estimable members of the board, the superintendent, and, of course, the sheriff, all have good reason to go along with that story."

My indignation rose like a tsunami threatening to wash over everything. "This is outrageous. I heard those cries. That had nothing to do with a little honey being smeared on someone's hair. That was pain. That was the howl of someone being violated. I am certain of that."

Susan took a big gulp of the red wine I handed her and nodded her agreement. "I'm sure you're right. I know how Bobby's been behaving since then."

"So, what happens now?" I joined her by taking a healthy slug of wine myself, and we sat in silence on my sofa.

"Will and the three boys who said they participated might be put on probation for a week or two. Which means nothing happens. If they cut someone's heart out in the middle of math class and ate it in front of everyone, then maybe they'd be considered in violation of the probation." Half-empty glass in hand, Susan paced the length of my living room. "I heard someone say that Scooter's name was on the record as the person who blew the whistle on Will. That's not going to make things any easier for him."

By now I understood that such information in the hands of at least one person in Walden Corners probably meant that it would soon reach the ears of anyone not deaf or unconscious.

"What about the talk of Bobby and Coach? Do you think that will come up at the meeting?"

"That's the six-hundred-dollar question." Susan stopped pacing long enough to pour us each another glass of wine. "Inflation, you know. I can't drink any more than this, unfortunately. Or fortunately. I have a husband who expects me home or I'd get roaring, blasted drunk with you and sleep on your sofa. No, nobody mentioned that. Still, there's no telling who's going to show up and what they'll say. What a mess."

Chapter 20

I couldn't even buy bread and milk without being reminded of the trouble Bobby and Nora and Scooter faced. Even on the fifteen-items-or-less line in the supermarket the next morning, the talk was all about the upcoming school board meeting.

"You know that Will Jackson. He's the one who goes out with the pretty Miller girl, the middle one. He's a good boy. Always a smile. I don't believe he'd do such a thing." A plump woman with a cart full of Sugar Pops, Captain Crunch, house brand orange soda and root beer, and, in a concession to health, a bottle of multivitamins, passed the checker a loaf of white bread from her cart.

"I don't know, Alice." The checker looked old enough to be Alice's grandmother, her flawless skin rouged and her hair permed. "He's got a temper. I saw him kick a dog once. Honest to God, I almost kicked that boy myself. Poor animal, just lying there in front of the door. Right out

349

here, happened last year. He's got a mean streak."

Alice swiped her credit card and tut-tutted. "My daughter says that even Bobby Benson says it was just a joke. Honey, they poured honey in his hair, that's all. He's going to that school board meeting tonight and that's exactly what he's going to say. That's what my daughter told me."

I could hardly believe what I was hearing. Would he do that? Would Bobby lie to avoid the humiliation of exposing his ordeal for all the community to see? I knew that what had happened in the woods was no innocent joke, and my heart ached anew at the thought that Bobby would go along with that phony story so that he could put the horrible incident to rest. That Will Jackson would go free. That nothing would change, and that Nora and Scooter would be no closer to knowing who killed Coach.

Maybe it really had happened that way — honey in Bobby's hair. Maybe what Scooter had heard was the phony story, concocted by kids bored with stealing goal posts. Bobby's reaction the other day seemed to be real and visceral, but now I wondered if I was reading too much into it.

"My son is on the school board," Alice sniffed, "and he tells me that based on what he's heard already, the whole hullabaloo is about nothing and they're going to let it drop. They'll have that meeting tonight, but he's sure that the football team will get a little lecture about treating each other with respect and that's the end of that."

Indignant, the checker slammed the cash register drawer shut. She glared, her bosom quivering. I was worried for her health.

"Well, your son never did know what he was talking about. I have good information that says Will Jackson and two of his friends did really terrible things to that Benson boy, and they're going to be severely punished. As well they should be."

Alice snorted, tossed her bags into her cart, and stomped to the door, in such a hurry that the electric eye barely had time to open the door before she ran into the glass. I handed over the money to pay for my own groceries, hefted the bag, and walked to my car. Despite his sister's warnings, I had to find out for myself about Will Jackson. Talking to the boy wasn't tampering with evidence — she wouldn't like it anyway, but that was too bad.

★ ★ ★

An old red Dodge pickup that looked as though it had been the loser in decades of demolition derbies was parked in front of the Jackson house. Perfectly at home in the debris-strewn yard, the truck smelled hot and oily, and the sharp pinging of the engine told me that someone had driven it recently.

This doesn't prove anything, I reminded myself. But it sure looked like the shoe fit Will Jackson, and the key that I'd found in the woods probably fit his truck.

I approached the two-story house, picking my way past two old tires, a rusted fifty-five-gallon drum, and a small rocking horse that was missing one runner and had the words *School Sucks* painted in childish letters across the horse's hindquarters. Charming, I thought — just the atmosphere for growing up sensitive to other people's feelings. The whole place had an air of brutality about it, and for a second I actually felt sorry for Will Jackson. In another environment, he might have turned out differently.

But I wasn't about to excuse his behavior and give him a pass, the way some members of the school board apparently planned to.

The thumping, angry beat of a recorded bass pulsed from somewhere deep inside.

I knocked on the door, stepped back, waited. Nothing, no footsteps, no call to come in. I knocked again, and then decided to walk around to the back of the house. If someone was in the kitchen they might not hear my knocks. The hard-packed dirt was littered with nails, rusting cans, a mitten of indeterminate color. A car passed by on the road a couple of yards away, startling me. At least there was traffic nearby, the isolation not as daunting as it felt at first.

The music, louder and angrier, wasn't coming from the house at all, I realized, but from a garage about forty feet away. By the time I reached the open doorway, the sound was nearly deafening. When I peered inside, I was surprised to see Will Jackson, stripped to the waist and rhythmically working hand weights from his position on a bench. Even in the dim light, the sweat on his well-muscled chest and arms glistened as he lifted the weights, brought them down, lifted them again.

On the garage walls, pictures of professional football players, most of whom I couldn't name, shared space with photographs of a girl who might have been

Laura Miller, but I wasn't about to get close enough to confirm that. I stood in the doorway, knowing that he wouldn't hear me, wondering whether I should approach him, when his arms dropped to his sides and he let the weights fall to the dirt floor on either side of the bench.

When the song — it was a kindness to call that noise a song — ended, I said, "Hi. Can I speak to you for a minute?"

At the sound of my voice, he jerked into a sitting position and frowned, reaching for a grimy towel. He wiped his face and neck, then pointed a remote control at the CD player and the music stopped. "Who are you?"

"My name is Lili Marino. I live on Iron Mill Road in the yellow house with the three apple trees out front." Which didn't tell him anything about my mission, but I wanted to take it slow with this boy, even though I wasn't quite sure where I was going with my questions. "I'm the one who found your car keys over by the big rock in the woods."

In the dim light, I smelled his sweat, and I began to wonder whether I'd truly lost my mind in coming here. He sat staring at me, his eyes narrowed, his chest still heaving with the exertion of his workout.

"I found this near my driveway," I said, holding up an inexpensive old watch that one of my brothers had left behind at my apartment at least six years earlier, "and I wondered if it was yours too."

His first reaction was to glance at his own bare wrist, and then he looked back at me and rose from the bench. "Lemme see it," he said, looming too close to me for comfort.

I handed him the watch and stepped back into the cold air, examining his face for any clue to the truth of that night. Impassive, he didn't meet my gaze when he handed me the watch. "Not mine. Sorry, but I have to get back to work here."

I nodded. "Know who it might belong to?"

"Nope. You really came here to ask me about a watch?" The challenge in the words and in his posture was almost scornful, as though he'd caught the city girl trying to pull a fast one and had shown her just how sharp the country boy really was.

"Yes." His arrogance brought out my own stubborn streak. Maybe I should have listened to the voice that had told me this would be a waste of time, but I was here, and I wasn't leaving until I had at least a crumb of information. "I do have something else to ask you. I want to know why you thought it was necessary to have Laura stick like glue to Bobby Benson. Doesn't seem like the behavior of someone who only took part in a harmless hazing prank."

His laugh was harsh. "Lady, I don't have to explain anything I do to you. Bobby Benson — he's the one you should go see. Go ahead. Ask him about how Coach told him he was going to have to cut him from the team if he showed up late to practice one more time. Ask him where he was when Coach Johnson was killed. And ask him where his hunting rifle is."

Bobby's hunting rifle? "What do you mean? Where *is* his rifle?"

Sneering, Will said, "Missing. Ask Laura. She looked and it's not in the gun rack. Bobby Benson — that's who you should be talking to. Maybe you better think twice before you come asking me any more questions."

My mouth opened but nothing came out. Whatever Will Jackson was saying to me, surely he'd already told his sister the same story.

"I heard Bobby's screams that night," I said softly.

Before I lost it completely, I strode back to my car and pulled away, glad that I was heading into the sunlight and away from the darkness of the Jackson property. I drove straight to Susan's house and rapped loudly on the kitchen door. When she appeared, she looked a little disheveled, her eyes heavy and her mouth pulled down at the corners.

"Sorry, I guess I must have dozed off. Five in the morning is not a civilized time to get up. By the time I get home from school, I'm ready for a nap." Her face brightened as I watched, and she seemed to come fully awake. "Come in, it's cold out there. I have some water on for tea. It'll be ready in a few minutes."

Her living room was warm and welcoming, soft fabrics and heathery colors making for a restful haven, but I couldn't sit still. I paced the perimeter of the room, following her into the kitchen while she peppered me with questions about my visit to Will.

"No, his father wasn't there. Nor was Laura. He was out in the garage, pumping iron and sweating. All that was missing to complete the whole Spartan gig was a fox chewing on his entrails."

"But something *has* been eating at

him," she said, smiling at her own joke. "Seriously. He's been sullen instead of arrogant. Big difference. Much easier to ignore him in the halls. Maybe he's just waiting for that hearing to be over. I don't know."

"Susan, do you remember whether Bobby was in school the day Coach was murdered?"

She knitted her brow in concentration, then laughed. "Of course he wasn't. At least half of the boys were out of school that day. First day of hunting season, I always show a great movie, *Platoon* or *The Patriot* or something, hoping it will make some of those guys come in to school. Turns out to be a reward for the kids who do show up, but it never changes attendance. Nope. Bobby wasn't in class."

"And Will?"

Susan shrugged. "He's not in any of my classes. Was last year, but not this year. Can't say I miss him either. Since his mother died, that family has been one big mess. Not that anyone could ever really turn Ira Jackson into a civil human being. But first Florence divorced him and then she died, and suddenly Ira had two teenaged boys to take care of, and the whole place fell apart. Not that she was any great shakes herself. Until she left him, that woman used to drink all the time. Once she even came to Open School Night reeking, I mean positively reeking, of alcohol. And once Will —"

The peal of the phone interrupted her, and Susan jumped up and answered with a cheery greeting. I stirred my tea, curious to hear the rest of the story, but as Susan's expression went from sunny to concerned, I knew that something was wrong. She shook her head, as though she were saying no to whatever she was hearing, then said, "We'll be right over. Lili's here with me. Just don't do anything and stay away from the windows."

"What! Stay away from the windows? What's going on?" My heart pounded as I followed her to the hall. She grabbed a jacket and pulled on her boots and headed for the door.

"Isn't that what you're supposed to say when someone's being threatened?" she asked. "Someone left a dead mouse in Nora's mailbox. A dead, frozen mouse with a note under it. The only thing the note said was Scooter's name. She's freaking out. He's been moping around the house all day. She hasn't told him about it yet. She was going to do that as soon as she got off the phone." Susan was running now, heading for my car. "You drive. I'm too nervous."

If I'd been on blacktop, I would have burned rubber, but in Susan's gravel driveway, I backed up slowly, turned left onto the road, and then drove fast enough to send my rear wheels fishtailing twice on the still-slick road. Susan babbled the whole time, whether in an attempt to calm me, herself, or as a nervous and uncontrollable reaction I couldn't tell. I didn't hear half of what she said, and she didn't seem to require a response, so the arrangement worked for both of us.

Every light was on in Nora's house, and we ran up the steps to the back porch, knocked, and pushed open the door. Nora and Scooter were seated on stools at the counter, their eyes glued to the small kitchen television set, the laughter from an old episode of *Seinfeld* the only sound in the room.

"You okay?" I gulped out as Nora hugged Susan and then me.

Nora nodded. "We're fine. Scooter thinks it's some kind of sick joke. I called Michele Castro. She's on her way out here. You want anything?"

"Not me, thanks." Susan smiled and sat

down next to Scooter, who looked as though he wanted to be anywhere but in this kitchen with his mother and two of her friends.

But I understood why Nora wouldn't want to let him out of her sight, at least for a while. She'd lost her husband, and now someone was sending cryptic messages to her son. Before Nora could offer us anything else, the sound of another car pulling into the driveway announced Michele Castro's arrival.

"You call Elizabeth?" I asked, surprising myself with the thought that it would be nice to have her cool appraisal of the situation, and especially her presence when the undersheriff's antagonistic bluster pushed its way into Nora's kitchen.

"She's in Family Court, petitioning for a change in a client's custody arrangement. She won't be out for another twenty minutes. Scooter," Nora said, turning to her son and fixing her gaze on his pouting face, "just answer the sheriff's questions. Truthfully. You hear me?"

He blinked his curly lashes and mumbled, "Yes. Mom. What do you think, I'm going to lie to her?"

I couldn't tell whether he was genuinely hurt or just needed to say something to

361

save face for the sake of the onlookers. Michele Castro's knock, two firm raps on the door, stirred Nora from Scooter's side, and she opened the door.

Even in the bulky jacket, and with all her paraphernalia dangling from her belt, the undersheriff managed to look more like a schoolgirl than someone who could sling a three-hundred-pound attacker over her shoulder and then slap cuffs on him in twenty seconds.

"By the way, I just heard about Tom Ford. He's still in Seattle," she said. "The Seattle PD says they have proof that he was there the morning Coach was murdered. In business meetings from seven in the morning until eight that evening. Just thought you should know that."

So, when he'd sent that check to Nora and when he'd phoned me to protest my tracking him down, he'd been too far away from Columbia County to have any connection to the murder.

Relieved, I watched Nora's face for a reaction but she only frowned and said, "Fine. That's good."

"So, what's this about a dead mouse?" Michele Castro's tone was different now, impatient and skeptical, a this-better-be-good edge to it that made me angry. She unbuttoned the top of her jacket and leaned against the refrigerator.

"It's out on the front porch. I didn't want it defrosting in my house," Nora said.

We all trooped to the front of the house, Scooter bringing up the rear. Nora knelt and picked up a plastic bag and handed it to Castro while Susan, Scooter, and I leaned closer to see the sad creature whose long, stiff tail poked at the plastic. The paper, which covered the mouse's belly like a blanket some thoughtful soul had placed there, looked like it had been torn from a school notebook. The single word, *Severn,* had been pasted onto the page from letters cut from magazines.

"Severn?" Michele Castro looked at Scooter questioningly.

His cocoa face flushed with pink and he tsked, shook his head, then said, "That's my real name."

"Who knows it?" The sheriff took out a small pad and clicked a ballpoint pen impatiently.

"Everyone." The corner of Scooter's mouth screwed up. "At least everyone who was in third grade with me. Mr. Smith said he didn't like nicknames and he called me Severn the whole year. I hated him for that."

Sighing, Michele Castro rolled her eyes. "Well, who calls you that name?"

"No one. That first week of third grade, I beat up Arnie Levenger on the school bus for saying it, and even though I got grounded for two weeks, it was worth it. No one calls me that." He frowned. "At least, not to my face."

"You get into a fight with anyone lately? Anyone have a grudge against you?"

Nora stepped between Castro and Scooter, her dark eyes flashing with anger. "You should know. I'd imagine Will is pretty mad that Scooter came forward about the football hazing. I'd imagine that he might decide that the school board is giving him license to continue being a bully, to keep making life miserable for anyone who doesn't kowtow to his whims. I don't know if you can be objective about this situation, Michele, but if you can't, I'm not going to sit around and let this town sabotage justice. If I have to go to Albany to make sure my husband's death and the threats to my son are being handled properly, believe me, I will."

I nearly applauded. Instead, when Nora put her arm around her son's shoulder and hugged him to her, I stepped forward and said, "It's cold out here. Nora and Scooter have answered your questions. If there's nothing else, I want to take them inside."

"You're making this personal, you know that?" Michele Castro ignored me and looked directly at Nora. Her expression said that too many things were happening at once and she was annoyed that she wasn't in control of any of them.

"It *is* personal. It's my husband and my son we're talking about. That's all I care about." Nora's voice was low and controlled as she wheeled and headed for the door.

"Listen, I'm sorry if you think I . . . We *are* doing everything we can to investigate Coach's murder. If you have any information that I need to know, I want to hear it. And I'll have Murph talk to Will and, if necessary, run fingerprints on this paper." Michele Castro didn't follow Nora into the house, but instead looked at me, then at Susan, and finally shook her head and walked down the steps, heading for her cruiser.

"You think she'll really get the sheriff to talk to Will?" I asked as Susan and I headed into the house.

"Would you if you were his sister?"

Chapter 21

I hadn't said anything, not to Castro or Susan or Nora, about Will's jeering suggestion that Bobby's hunting rifle was missing or about the inferences I was supposed to draw from that supposed fact. But he got me thinking — if the rifle was where it belonged, or even somewhere else but if it could be produced by Bobby, it might be the very thing that would exonerate him, prove that the shot that had entered the back of Coach's head had come from a different weapon.

If I continued to stay silent, I might be helping Coach's killer get away. If I said something, I might be helping someone set up Bobby to take the blame for something I couldn't imagine him doing. Somehow, I needed more than Will's word before I would pass his creepy accusation on.

And the way to find out more would be to talk to Bobby, a difficult task even when he wasn't being confronted with questions that might determine whether he'd spend the rest of his life in jail. I'd learned a bit of patience, of opening myself to see the less obvious possibilities, from working with gourds and in all those hours of mediation. I've practiced waiting, until a gourd — or a person in distress — gave up secrets. Maybe Bobby would do the same.

With all my heart, I didn't want this odd-duck, likeably self-effacing kid to have to live with the double trauma of abuse and guilt. It troubled me to think I might learn that he had done it. If he wasn't Coach's murderer, then the names on the original list — racist Ira Jackson, disgruntled Alvin Akron, all the football players and all their parents including Seth Selinsky — were back to swimming in the Suspect Soup. If Castro's information was reliable, at least Tom Ford was high, dry, and of no interest to the police.

Paying Bobby for the work he'd done would give me a good excuse to drive over there. I waited until nearly five, when I knew the school buses were finished with their routes, and drove over to the Benson house. As soon as I got out of the car, I remembered why I'd put off coming here. It wasn't Bobby, wasn't Fred Benson's dour looks and protective posturing. It was that monster animal, barking and scratching at the porch screen, creating the perfect barrier between me and my goal: the doorbell of the Benson house.

As I did on the last visit, I went around to the back entrance to avoid another face-to-fang encounter with Buster. And there, his jacket tossed carelessly on the ground, was Bobby, an axe raised over his head as he approached a log. He swung in one powerful, swift stroke, the log split in two, and then looked up at me. He didn't say a word, but neither did he pick up another log. Fleetingly, I wondered why Bobby was bothering to split firewood if the family was moving to Florida the next day.

"Hi, Bobby. How's it going?"

He let the axe dangle at his side and said, "Fine."

A boy of few words, at least in my presence. "I wanted to thank you for doing a good job with those stumps. It's going to be a great gourd garden."

Bobby Benson became a boy of even fewer words; he nodded and then looked away.

"I came by to pay you. How much, exactly, do I owe you? I think I paid you a hundred already."

"I don't remember." He wrinkled his nose, appeared to be thinking. "Was it fifty more? I don't know. But a hundred fifty total, that's a little less than twenty dollars an hour. That's about right."

All I could recall about the price was that Nora's eyebrows had risen nearly to her hairline at my offer, so it must have been more than what Bobby would consider right.

"I think I said I'd pay more than that. I'm pretty sure I did, in fact. But since neither of us remembers, I'm going to write a check for one hundred fifty more." I took my checkbook from my purse, started writing the date. When I got to payee's name, I asked him how he wanted the check to be made out.

"I guess to . . . can you do it without my name? And I can't take more than a hundred. It wouldn't be right." His scowl, which looked more like confusion about how to be polite while telling me I was off my rocker, softened a little when he said, "I didn't think for sure the tractor could do it. She's still got a little juice left."

I wrote the check for one hundred dollars to cash, tore it out, passed it to him. He had just said more to me than I'd expected, and I wanted to take advantage of his apparent good mood.

"So, is hunting season over? I don't see

anyone with deer on the tops of their cars anymore." I looked back into the woods and jumped when Buster barked from the front of the house. When he stopped, I heard the pinging sound of an engine cooling. Someone must have pulled into the Benson driveway; vaguely, I hoped they weren't blocking my car.

"Been over for a while," Bobby said. "Got my deer that first day. Four pointer, he was. You like venison?"

I smiled and shrugged. "I don't know. Never tasted it. I hear it's pretty good, though. So you were out hunting on opening day? You go alone?"

A dark mask came down over Bobby's face, and he looked at me with questions in his brown eyes and then said, "I gotta finish this. Thanks for the check."

I'd blown it. As I was trying to think of what to say to get back on track, to find out about the rumor of the missing rifle, a voice called from the back porch.

"Lili! This is a nice surprise. You want to come in for coffee?" Jane Benson stood beside the open door, her sunny smile lighting the quickly dimming afternoon.

What a cheerful person she was. Her gloomy stepson seemed to owe more to the genetic material he'd inherited from his father than to the kind and loving atmosphere Jane had created in that house.

"Sure, thanks, Jane, but I can only stay for a minute. Lots of gourds waiting for me." I glanced over at Bobby, who was already hefting another piece of wood, then bending to pick up the axe. Regretful that I hadn't found out more from him, but with a smile on my face, I ran up the steps and followed Jane into her warm kitchen, which was piled high with moving cartons. The walls were bare, the curtains down, all the signs of real people carefully packed away and ready to be loaded onto a truck.

Buster greeted me with a snarl and prowled around my feet, even when Jane commanded him to sit. With a disdainful snuffle, he disappeared into the living room.

Jane poured two cups of coffee from a carafe, stuck them in the microwave, and then turned around, her face suddenly serious.

"I know what the kids are saying about Bobby. But it's a smokescreen, I'm sure of it. It's Will Jackson, he's the one who started the rumors. He's been a problem for years, and his sister doesn't know how to control him and his father doesn't think it's necessary." Her voice was colored with pain, suffered on her stepson's. "I don't really know what to do, Lili. I'm just glad my new family is going to make a fresh start."

I took her hand in mine, hoping that my gesture would mean to her what I intended — simple human consolation. "I hope the move works out the way you want it to," I said finally, "for you and Fred and Bobby."

Jane covered my hand with her own. "Thanks. It's been hard lately, but it seemed like we had to keep trying. Now, all these rumors keep cropping up and pretty soon, you know how it is, if you've heard something from three different people, most people start believing it. I don't want that boy living with that hanging over him. I didn't bear him and I didn't raise him, but I can see how hard this has been on him and it truly pains me."

As gently as I could, I said, "One of the reasons the kids are talking about Bobby is because he was angry at Coach. And he was out hunting that day. You might clear his name by insisting that the sheriff take his rifle and run a ballistics test on it to see if it matches up with the bullet they found embedded in . . . with the bullet they found."

Jane's face brightened. "Lili, that's a

great idea. If they don't match, then people won't be able to say that Bobby had anything to do with the murder. Why didn't Michele Castro ask for it in the first place? And why didn't we think of this before? I'll have to check with Fred, of course, but I think he'll agree that we can get this over with. Oh, Lili, thank you so much. I'll be right back. The gun rack is in the basement, in Fred's den. That's the last room, we're not finished packing there yet." She jumped off her stool, grabbed me in a hug, and disappeared into the hallway.

I waited in the warm kitchen, listening to the not-quite-comforting sound of Buster snoring in the other room, just feet away from where I sat. Bobby's rhythmic thunk and thwack — log hitting stump, ripping in half — nearly lulled me into forgetting that I had sent Jane on a mission that might end up pointing to her stepson's guilt.

When Jane returned, she was pale and frowning. "There're only two rifles in the case. Should be three. I wonder what happened to the other —" And she clapped a hand over her mouth as the realization of the possibilities struck her with full force. She shook her head, leaned against the butcher block island with both hands, and took a deep breath.

"Don't jump to conclusions," I said quietly. "There could be lots of explanations."

Jane peered out the window at her son. "He's a good boy. He's been quiet lately, subdued, kind of, but he's a *good* boy."

Feeling awkward and intrusive, I murmured my agreement. The ticking clock on the wall sounded very loud in the quiet room, and finally I said, "Jane, is there anything I can do to help?"

Her blue eyes seemed to flash with sudden conviction, and she straightened and said, "Thanks, Lili. I'll figure it out."

"Call me if you need anything," I said as I slipped my arms into my jacket and headed for the back door. I meant it, but I hoped she didn't have to take me up on my offer.

All I wanted was to get back home and find a way to turn my mind from the troubles that had plagued Walden Corners, Bobby Benson, and my friend Nora and her family for the past two months. Guiltily, I thought again that Nora couldn't turn her mind away from the situation, but I had hit a wall, unable to figure out how to help and unwilling to run in circles.

By the time I got back to the cottage, it was full dark, and I looked forward to a soak in the tub, a bowl of soup, a glass of wine, and a night of sitting on the sofa with the phone unplugged, my feet propped up, and a parade of silly television shows that would make me laugh. Amazingly, the answering machine wasn't blinking, no urgent e-mails had arrived, and no brothers, former lovers, or friends whose kid had run away were camped out on my doorstep.

I ran hot water and splashed the ginger-grapefruit bubble bath into the tub, stripped off my clothes, and sank into the luxurious bubbles. Each muscle in my body ached from tension, and I leaned back against the towel I'd folded under my neck, closed my eyes, and let the damp heat go to work. As I scrubbed my arms and legs and my back with the luffa, that gourd sponge reminded me that I hadn't done any real work in my studio for days. But after a while, even my anxiety about finishing the gourds for the Rhinebeck show melted away as I said an old mantra, repeating the sound over and over as Karen had taught me to do. Before I knew it I was twitching awake in a tub of luke-warm water.

In my cotton nightgown and chenille robe, I prepared to execute the rest of the plan by opening a can of split pea soup and pouring a glass of cabernet, but I was so relaxed that wine seemed unnecessary. I took my heated soup into the livingroom, sat down with my legs under me, and clicked on the television. By the time fifteen minutes had passed, I remembered why I didn't do this more often — I wasn't interested.

I wandered around the room, flipping magazine pages, moving a stack of paper from one corner of the desk to another. This wasn't relaxation, it was . . . boredom. Unfocusedhood. I drifted over to the bookshelves and pulled down the first thing my hand touched. *Wuthering Heights*.

Was Tom Ford a fan of Emily Brontë? Of her brooding countryside and romantic love, and death to those who defy it? It seemed a strange choice for a man who had apparently made a career of stealing other people's money under the guise of starting a business. As harsh as that sounded, I couldn't help the feeling of betrayal that arose every time I thought about the man. His real sin was to destroy my fantasy of him. The stealing part was just business gone bad; his repentant act of returning at least part of the money spoke of his good faith.

With Castro's report that he had been in Seattle that day in November, his name fell off the list of suspects, but that didn't mean that I was ready to think of him kindly, fondly, with happy curiosity, the way I used to. He'd still taken a huge chunk of money, other people's money, and turned it into ashes. Tom Ford might think that repaying Nora twenty thousand dollars would permit him to pretend to be one of the good guys, but I wasn't letting him off the hook so easily. I pictured him on a sailboat in Puget Sound, the wind blowing his golden hair away from his face as he watched the green hills race by. The picture filled my head for a short time, until I drifted off to an uncomfortable sleep on the sofa.

Susan's voice on my answering machine woke me, and I rushed to the phone and picked it up.

"Start over," I said. "I fell asleep, and I didn't register what you said."

"I was calling to tell you about the school board meeting. The closed door session. It was amazing. Totally and wonderfully amazing."

Even without the details, I felt better.

"You would have been proud. Ron Selinsky changed everything. He stepped up, said he was one of the kids who refused to go along with Will and his plan for Bobby, but that he knew two of the boys who had participated along with Will. And they caved in. One by one. They admitted what they'd done. And the board had no choice. They suspended Will and the other two, pending criminal investigation."

I felt almost as proud as I might if it were my own son who had dug deep and found the courage to do the right thing, and very relieved that Seth's son had raised the father's stature in my eyes. But that still left a lot of questions unanswered.

"Was Bobby there?"

"No." Susan sounded as relieved as I felt. "He'll probably have to tell the story to the sheriff and even in court, but the school board members didn't want to put him through that, especially since Will didn't hold out too long, thanks, I hear, to pressure put on him by Michele Castro."

"What about Coach? What did they say about his part in the hazing?"

I heard Susan's breathing, but she said nothing.

"Susan?"

"The kids all said that he wasn't there that night. That he didn't know anything about what they were planning, that none of the parents or teachers knew anything. But they did say Coach was the responsible adult, that he should have paid more attention, should have warned the kids to stop any kind of hazing activities."

"That's kind of closing the barn door a little late, isn't it?"

"Well, they also acknowledged that Coach's attitude was shared by most people, that hazing was a part of a tradition that had been going on for years, that everyone else knew about it and accepted it as the way things were. So, they stopped short of actually blaming him. They plan to have some kind of task force look into it, and it sounded as though they might actually make some changes. We'll see." She sighed into the phone. "I think, all in all, that it's an outcome that Nora and Scooter can live with."

"That's good. But we still don't know who killed Coach, do we?"

Susan's voice was soft when she said, "No. We know a lot of other things, but not that. Not yet."

The snow really did make everything look like a postcard, clinging to the pine trees, sitting atop fence posts, and creating a hush that made the boiling water in the teakettle sound harsh. I stretched and stood in front of the window, watching the fat flakes drift lazily through the air. The rising sun painted the snow with pink streaks and fell across the prints of what I thought must be a pair of rabbits that had crossed the lawn to get to the woods.

Before I could finish my first cup of coffee, though, the blare of the telephone warned me that this wasn't going to be a peaceful day.

"Hello?"

"They got him." Susan's breathless voice announced. "Sorry to call so early, but I have to be in school in forty minutes and I still have to shower and get dressed. But I knew you'd want to know. Gotta go now. Talk to you later."

"Wait!" I shouted. "Who? They got who?"

Susan snorted, and said, "Sorry. Alvin Akron. They found his prints on the Dremel bit in that parking area where your car and Coach's Taurus were parked that day. They also found some stuff on his computer, plans for what he was going to do when the land was his. And his only alibi for that day is that he was out hunting in some spot ten miles away. Alone. Like half the male residents of Columbia County."

Relief flooded through me, and I laughed nervously. "So Bobby's off the hook. And Tom Ford. And Seth Selinsky. I can go back to my fantasies in peace now."

"Fantasies about Bobby? That could make you notorious, if you acted on them."

I giggled. "And rich, if we sell the movie rights. No, that wasn't exactly what I had in mind. Thanks for letting me know, Susan."

I couldn't have asked for a better resolution. Ira Jackson might be the meanest, most hateful player in the whole story, but Alvin Akron and his petulant, self-righteous campaign to change the boundary lines that separated his land from the Johnsons' would finally get his just desserts. Nora and Scooter could get on with the rest of their lives, and Bobby and his family could start over knowing that the past wouldn't come up and bite them just when they thought they were sailing on calm seas.

My glad heart wanted to share the good feelings, and I decided it would make me and the Benson family feel good if I gave them a gourd as a going-away present. I chose one of the new geometric designs, covered it in bubble wrap, set it in a cardboard box, and put it on the table by the door. The snow plows, which hit the main roads first and worked their way to my country road by mid morning, would have my way cleared by the time I showered, dressed, and put on all the layers it looked like I would need for a morning of errands. Errands that included a stop at the bank to deposit the check for completion of my last writing job, a visit to the hardware store for some fine-grit sandpaper, and a pass through the market for something to stave off scurvy. I could drop the gourd off on my way into town, wish the family good luck, and then take care of the rest of my business.

Buster was more agitated than usual, probably a reaction to the chaos that surrounds any household leading up to moving day. He barked and snarled, nipping at the feet of the moving men, three ordinary-looking men with the extraordinary ability to toss heavy pieces of furniture around as though they were tennis balls. At least that meant that I was of little interest to him, for a while, anyway.

Cartons teetered in every corner, and

the gray, stained padding that had been wrapped around all the furniture left the place looking anonymous and vague. Gone were the fabrics and the ebony statues, the cross-stitched samplers, and the intricate baskets. The bare walls and floors were reduced to barriers separating the interior from the elements. Jane waved to me and then veered off to supervise the loading of her grandmother's oak hutch as two of the movers tried to wrestle it out the front door.

"Go around to the back. That door's wider. And don't damage it." Fred Benson pointed to the kitchen and then frowned when he saw me. "You need something?"

I held up the box. "I brought something for your family. A going-away memento. Oh, and I thought you might want to know that they've got Alvin Akron in jail and are charging him with Coach's murder."

Fred Benson's face was stoic, not a flicker of emotion visible, except for the twitch in the corner of his eye. "I heard that. Thanks for the gift. You can set that box on the counter too." He looked as though he was trying not to growl at me, and barely succeeding.

Having lived through my own moving day at least six times since college graduation, I knew how even the most positive and hopeful of moves ups the stress level to skyscraper heights, so I just nodded and smiled, looking around as though I were saying good-bye to a familiar sight. In the midst of the commotion, Fred stared back at me, arms folded across his barrel chest impatiently. He was waiting for me to get out of his kitchen, and we both knew it, but I was prolonging the moment in the hope that Bobby would wander in so that I could say a final good-bye in person.

Our little contest of chicken was starting to be really uncomfortable, so I stuck my hand out, said, "Well, good luck," and was surprised when he reached out and shook my hand, a smile, forced though it might be, playing across his face.

"Thanks. Bye." Fred withdrew his hand, turned, and headed for the dining room, looking over his shoulder while I stepped carefully around Buster and out onto the front porch.

Where I ran smack into Bobby, who was carrying an armful of blankets and nearly fell down the porch stairs from the force of our collision.

I reached out and grabbed his arm, steadied him, and then bent to help him gather the blankets. "Sorry," I said. "I guess I was paying too much attention to Buster and didn't see you."

For the first time since I'd met him, Bobby's features seemed relaxed. He smiled and said, "That's what he's there for, to make sure everyone knows we have a guard around here. We're going to put him in the back of the car, and he likes these blankets, so he'll stay pretty quiet. I want to warm them up before we leave, so I was bringing them inside."

"That's nice. I wish I had someone who —" I laughed. "Never mind. I brought you and your parents something. It's in the kitchen in a cardboard box. On the counter."

Bobby's face reddened, and his smile lit up the whole porch. "Wow, that's . . . Thanks. You've been really nice to me. I appreciate that."

"Well, I'm glad you're going to get to make a new start, Bobby. You're smart and you're kind, and I'll bet you —" Not a good thing now to make a reference to the football team; I cut myself short, mentally wheeled and changed direction. "I bet you're going to find a lot of new friends in Florida. Listen, I've said this before but I'm not sure you really heard me, so I want to say it again. I'll probably never have another chance."

His face tensed, and I kept my gaze steady.

"Some things, some hard and painful things, are easier to live with if you tell someone. You know, a counselor or a pastor or someone like that. I hope you do that, Bobby. It's none of my business, I know, but I don't want you to live with something that's going to eat away at you if you don't talk to someone. That's all; that's what I wanted to say."

I refrained from kissing his cheek, and I started down the stairs.

"Ms. Marino?" His voice was lighter again, and his face too. "Thanks for saying that. I did. I told my dad. Jane — she doesn't know yet, though. My dad and I decided we'll tell her later. When we're in Florida. My dad's been great."

I was speechless. I could hardly imagine Fred Benson playing the healer. From what I'd seen of the man, he was more likely to bite than offer balm. Maybe all fathers had the capacity to find the grace to do what was needed in tough situations. My own did, although he usually cut it pretty close and made me sweat out the last few minutes of a crisis wondering whether he'd make one of his magical appearances or just let me twist in the wind.

"I'm glad, Bobby. You're lucky to have him in your corner." I looked around, realizing I had nothing more to say. "Well, I have to get going. I hope everything works out well for you. And don't forget that box."

Bobby blushed again, and then a shadow fell across his face as the door swung open and Fred Benson stepped outside. Wordlessly, Bobby shifted the blankets in his arms and went inside. Fred's eyes narrowed and he stepped very close to me, close enough so that I could smell the coffee that he'd drunk just a few minutes earlier.

"I don't know what you're after, coming over here this morning and chatting up my son, but we're trying to get this move done and you're in the way. So I'd appreciate it if you'd just leave." His expression didn't change as he stood looking down at me.

He had every right to ask me to go away, to let the family get on with their lives, but I knew something softer resided in his center. A man who had counseled his son through such a difficult time had a store of wisdom I hadn't seen.

"Look, I'm going, but I wanted to tell

ou that I'm really glad Bobby has you to protect him, to help him stay safe. He's been through a lot, and he's pleased and proud that you're on his side."

I started down the steps, but Fred blocked my way. "Why wouldn't I be on my son's side?"

Confused by his question, I shook my head. "I didn't mean to imply that. Just, you helped Bobby through a hard time and that's admirable. That's all."

He let go, and without another word went into the house and slammed the door behind him. I trudged through the snow to my Subaru, backed out around the moving truck, and headed home. It was hard to reconcile the gruff, angry man who'd chased me away with the person who had comforted Bobby, but there it was. Paradox was the first rule of human behavior, I thought as I drove back to Iron Mill Road.

Chapter 22

I thought about it all the way home, about what happened to Bobby, about Alvin Akron and his long-standing hatred for the Johnsons, like one of those central European countries waiting fifty years for Communism to fall so that they could start bashing their neighbors over some centuries'-old blood vendetta again. Alvin Akron, mild, sneaky, and offended, had let his hatred simmer until he'd reached the boiling point and then had cooked his own goose in it by murdering Coach.

Maybe.

He was being hung for having his prints on the Dremel wire brush, developing computer plans to use the disputed land, and being a solo hunter.

If only there still weren't too many unanswered questions. And most of them kept circling back to Michele Castro. She'd given no details when she told us that Tom Ford had been in Seattle, only some vague statement that she'd confirmed he was here. What did that mean? And what about the missing rifle, the one Will had suggested might be the murder weapon? Might he have stolen it, used it himself, taken cover in the protection of his stepsister? And it wasn't only Will's connection to Castro that was troubling. What about her stepfather? Ira Jackson's vitriol could have spilled over into a psychotic, murderous rage.

I thought about stopping at The Creamery to shake some of these bad feelings with a little conversation and some pastry. But with my mind in such a state, I might say something inappropriate. I needed to wrestle down these doubts and get rid of them, so I headed home, aware of a car behind me and vaguely uncomfortable.

I turned left onto Iron Mill Road and let out my breath when the car kept going straight ahead, toward Hudson. My house sat like a pale lemon gumdrop in the middle of the white icing covering the rolling land, and I was glad to be home. I might even shovel out the front and back walks. After I'd had some oatmeal, something hot and hearty to get me ready to go back out into the clear, bright cold.

I dumped my boots on the mat inside

the back door and stepped into my fleece lined slippers. A gift from Ed Thorsen two years earlier, they had been the signal to me of what I could expect from our relationship. I foresaw a future of slippers and copper-bottomed pans, of pretty cotton sheets and food processors, and I realized I wanted silk underwear or quirky handmade necklaces or other equally unnecessary but lovely gifts from a man with a romantic streak he wasn't afraid to show. Small details, petty even, but they helped me clarify that Ed represented a stolid safety that I didn't need.

The water for my oatmeal was just starting to boil when I looked out the window, surprised to see a car pulling into my driveway. A large figure sat in the driver's seat, but I couldn't make out who it was. And then I heard it: a loud, insistent barking. And as I looked into the back of the car, I saw Buster, scratching at the window furiously as though waiting for a signal to leap forward and rip out my throat.

Fred Benson got out of the car and opened the back door. Buster leaped out, but Fred stepped on the end of the leash and Buster was caught up short. Fred must have growled out a command, because the

ext thing I knew Buster was sitting on his
aunches and staring up at his master,
whining as puffs of white vapor clouded
around his open mouth.

As he bent to pick up the leash, I noticed
that Fred's jaw was working, his lips
moving, as though he was delivering a
stream of instructions to the dog. Transfixed and confused, I watched as he walked
to the back of the cottage, slipped Buster's
leash over the stair post, and bounded up
the three steps to the door. I was even
more surprised when he just burst in,
without knocking or announcing himself.

"Hey, is something wrong? You look —"

"Yes, something's wrong. You need to
stay out of other people's business. I tried
to tell you that, but you kept sniffing
around my boy." His eyes bulged and
spittle sprayed from his mouth. "We're
leaving town. Alvin Akron is gonna be arrested. And you're stirring up trouble
about this damn rifle thing. Just leave us
alone. Take your suspicions and shove 'em,
you hear me?"

I did not like my position, pressed up
against the sink with nothing near at hand
for me to strike back with if he attacked
me. I breathe deeply to slow my skittering
mind, and I looked around. It seemed like

hours, but I know it wasn't more than fi
seconds before he stepped closer.

"You didn't answer me. Are you gonna
leave my family alone?" A sheen slicked his
forehead, and pearly sweat sprang out on
his upper lip.

"I only wish your family well," I said in a
low, even voice. "I just wanted to say good-
bye to Bobby and bring you all a gourd.
Nothing else. I can see you're very upset,
Mr. Benson, and I know it's been a rough
time. Believe me, I am not trying to make
trouble or anything like that. Now, please
let me pass. I'm getting a little upset myself
here."

In response, he stepped even closer, so
close that his belt buckle brushed against
my hand. Now I was the one sweating. I'd
said what I thought were placating things,
hoping to get him to realize he was being
irrational and that I was indeed on Bobby's
side. But Fred Benson had gone over some
edge, and I wasn't sure that he'd even
heard a word I'd said.

"Mr. Benson, you're scaring me. Please
step back so I can move."

He blinked, shook his head. "You want
to get Bobby in trouble. Boy's been hurting all his life because people want to get
him in trouble. Picked on for no reason,

rtured. Who's supposed to take care of ᴧat?"

My chest hurt from the fear gripping me, and I wondered how I could distract the man long enough to push him aside and run to the door.

"You don't have a good answer now, do you? School said he was making things up. Years and years of making things up. Now, that just isn't right. They should have put a stop to it."

And then I knew what happened to the other rifle. It wasn't Bobby's rifle that was missing at all. And Bobby wasn't the one who had anything to do with Coach's death, except indirectly. The horrible victimization he'd suffered all his life at the hands of Will Jackson and his cohort was at the heart of it all. I felt sick at the thought of what the family had endured, sick at the way Fred Benson had decided to put a stop to it.

None of that changed the fact that I was being squeezed by Fred's desperation into a corner I might not get out of, if I didn't use my wits and fast.

"Mr. Benson, I can see how upset this is making you." Use a mediator strategy, I reminded myself. Repeat his feeling, with the same intensity he'd said it. "You got really angry that nobody had done anything to help Bobby all these years. It made you really mad that they didn't believe him. Didn't believe you too, when you tried to get help for him. But you couldn't change what happened."

Fred Benson sobbed and slammed his fist into the wall. I ducked under his arm and ran to the back door, yanked it open, and stopped cold.

In a single leap, Buster was at the top step straining against his leash, his teeth bared and his nostrils flared. The growl started deep in his throat and erupted in a series of sharp barks that made me quiver. Scylla and Charybdis. I laughed later when I realized that I thought about Odysseus and his dilemma, the proverbial rock and a hard place. Buster in front of me, Fred Benson behind. I looked over my shoulder and saw that he was still leaning against the counter, chest heaving with sobs. If I dashed through the house to the front door now, I could get to my car, get to the road, get help.

I held my breath and ran past the kitchen doorway and through the living room, floorboards creaking despite my light steps. Buster's frantic barking propelled me forward, and as I reached the oor, turned the knob, and yanked the oor open, I was grabbed from behind and nearly slammed into the door jamb.

"Let go of me," I demanded through my ragged breaths. I swiveled around, but Fred still held onto a fistful of my sweater. He grabbed my arm and held it up high, so that when I moved a sharp pain shot down into my shoulder.

"You're right about all of it." His reddened eyes flickered to the road, to my face, but his voice was sad. "Bobby told him about what happened, did you know that? Told him two days later. Coach Johnson said he'd take care of it, but four days later, after nothing happened, Bobby came to me. When he told me, I couldn't see straight. I never meant to hurt that man, not that way. But when I saw him, all those years . . . all that pain my boy endured . . ."

I lifted my leg to knee him in the groin but he stepped out of the way of my blow and then spun me around and yanked my arm up behind my back.

"You need to go to the police, Mr. Benson. Hurting me isn't going to help you." It was weird, talking to the air while I could feel his breath on the back of my neck. I wanted him to have to look into my

eyes when he decided what he was going
do next, but he held firm to my arm.

"They won't believe me. I have a reput
tion for having a temper around here. I saw
Coach's car and I parked and walked into
the woods and down to the pond."

He coughed, and I tried to wriggle out of
his grasp, to no avail.

"He should have known these kids
would do something. Bobby even told him
he'd heard they were planning something
special for him. He warned him. But the
man ignored him, just the way the school
has been ignoring him for ten years. I lost
it, I really did. I yelled at him, started
shoving him. He shoved me back, and then
he must have slipped on some mud, because he lost his balance. Oh God, the
sound. When his head hit the rock, it was
horrible."

The sob that wracked his body wrenched
my heart, but he never loosened his grip.

"So, it was an accident. That's going to
make it —"

"I ran away. It was like my mind turned
off and I just ran back to my truck and
drove off. I don't even know where I went
or how long I was gone."

Suddenly his hand fell away and my arm
was free. I started down the front stairs,

ecting heavy footsteps to follow behind
e. But only Fred's voice, soft and without
flection, chased after me. I stopped and
urned and looked at him. The man was
standing on my porch, his eyes squeezed
shut and his chin lifted, as though he were
watching a movie only he could see. His
clenched fists hung at his sides, and his
mouth kept forming the words of his terrible story.

"It must have been an hour later, I drove
back to the pond and his car was still
there, and I could see his body, floating.
Just lying there like a big doll. I heard gun-
shots in the woods, and I decided that I
had to make his death look like a hunting
accident, so I got on the hill and I shot him
in the back of his head."

Now Fred Benson's eyes flew open, and
he blinked as though waking up from a
dream. He frowned when he looked at me,
then slumped into a heap on the top step
of the porch, deflated and confused.

Torn between needing to protect myself
and wanting to help this man, I backed
away slowly in the direction of the driveway. My footsteps crunched in the snow,
and I reached one hand out behind me to
keep from walking into a tree or some
other obstacle. I wanted to tell him that I

would take him to the sheriff, that he'd better off turning himself in than runnin away or hurting me. But I said nothing just kept backing away, step by slow step.

When I reached my car, I realized to my horror that the keys were sitting on the counter in the kitchen. If I was going to get away from Fred Benson, then the only chance I had was to make it to the Kensington house a quarter mile away. I turned and started running as fast as I could through the knee-high snow.

"Hey!"

Suddenly the sound of Fred's voice shifted, and he was no longer the sobbing, repentant man who had crumpled onto my porch, but the old Fred, the one who had come into his wife's workroom and stopped the laughter in our throats when Nora and I visited. The Fred who had accidentally murdered Coach, covered it up, and now was anxious to get his family out of town, with me as his only real impediment.

I ran across the lawn, hearing his steps as he clattered off the porch. I stumbled and fell face down in the snow, and as I picked myself up, Fred closed the gap between us. He grabbed a handful of sweater and pulled me to him.

'I don't want to hurt you," he said, his breath steaming as he panted for breath. But we're leaving. I have to take my family where it's safe. You won't be able to stop us and you won't find us either, but I need a couple of hours."

He marched me toward the shed where I kept the garden tools and the lawn furniture for the winter. I tried to wriggle away, but again found myself in an arm-twisting hold that kept me moving forward.

"You don't want to do this, Mr. Benson. You're making things worse for yourself. They'll find you eventually, and the fact that you did something to me will be much worse than the accidental murder." Silently I prayed for words, for wisdom, but that was as much as I could manage. He wasn't interested in salvation at this point. Or maybe he was . . .

"You want to protect Bobby and Jane? This isn't how you do that. You'll never sleep at night, always looking over your shoulder, always waiting for the knock on the door. And you know it will come, and then what will they do? Better to have them say he made a mistake, he paid for it, now we can all get on with our lives. What are you teaching your son by hurting me?"

He growled and wrenched my arm

higher. "I'm not going to hurt you. going to tie you up in that shed and th call someone in twelve hours to come ge you. You won't die in twelve hours. Now, shut up."

We were nearly at the shed door. On impulse, I let my body go limp, despite the pain when he tried to drag me up by my arm. Would he break my arm? Something in me doubted it, and I folded into a bundle in the snow.

"Get up," he spat, and then he let go of my arm and grabbed my legs, dragging me the rest of the way to the shed door, which he kicked open with his booted foot.

Inside, dim light trickled from the single, dust-covered window. It took a few seconds for my eyes to adjust to the darkness. The smell of mold and damp plastic assaulted my senses. Spiders would be my only companions for the next twelve hours, I thought, and the notion made my skin crawl. If I was lucky, I'd scream loud enough to be heard in Brooklyn, and someone would come to find out what all the commotion was about.

Fred Benson pushed me down so that I was lying on the small patch of dirt floor, and he took his belt and wrapped it around my wrists, with my arms behind my back. I

ked at him as he knelt beside me, but he
ıly grunted and went on with his work. I
ıcked again, and a pile of barbecue tools
tumbled onto the floor, making a fearsome
noise, but it didn't even make him turn his
head.

Frantically I looked around. He found
the length of garden hose I'd so conveniently and neatly hung on two large nails
after Bobby had finished the yard work and
began to wrap it around my upper body.
Well, at least that ought to keep me warm, I
thought as I looked up and noticed the teetering pile of clay pots on the makeshift
table. If I could swing my legs a little . . .

I kicked out again, this time connecting
with Fred's hand.

"Quit it. I said I wouldn't hurt you. I'm
sorry I have to do this. Now, stay still." He
turned to unkink the hose, and in that
second I kicked the rickety table, which
sent the pile of pots clattering to the floor.

Fred yelped and loomed over me, glow-
ering.

I was about to say something when I
heard a car engine and the crunch of tires
on snow and gravel.

"In here!" I shouted. "Help me. In the
shed. Help."

I kept screaming the same words over

and over. Looking like a trapped anim[...] Fred rubbed at the grime on the windo[...] peered out, then groaned. He knelt besid[...] me, muttering as he unwrapped the coiled hose, fingers fumbling as he undid the belt around my wrists.

"Don't tell him," he said through gritted teeth. "Don't tell him."

I sat up and rubbed my wrists just as the door burst open, and Bobby, panting and frowning and holding his unsheathed hunting knife in front of him, stepped inside the shed.

"Dad, what . . ." Bobby didn't finish his question, his expression dazed, as though the truth would be different, more acceptable if he didn't say anything more or feel another emotion. Fred held out his hand, and Bobby turned the knife so that he was holding the blade and passed the handle-end to his father.

"We have to get going." Fred tried to drop an arm around Bobby's shoulder, but the boy jerked away.

"I don't get it," Bobby said, glancing from me to Fred and then back to me again. "What were you doing in here?"

Fred's hoarse laugh rumbled through the shed. "Not what you think, son. I just needed to . . . talk to Miss Marino here."

rubbed at my sore wrists, and then I realized that Bobby thought his father and I
were having an affair. As ludicrous as that
might seem to me, a sixteen-year-old boy
would be devastated by such a discovery.
Especially this boy, whose father was his
ally and protector.

"Bobby, your dad and I were talking
about the situation with the football team."
I had to get it out in the open, had to force
Fred's hand. I stepped around the two
men and headed for the doorway, ready to
run if necessary.

Warily, Fred inched forward, and Bobby
watched his father move toward me with a
frown furrowing his brow.

"You already told me that you told your
dad about what happened in the woods,
and about a lot of the things that happened
to you. Since second grade."

"Third," Bobby muttered. "It got bad in
third grade."

I kept talking as Fred Benson stepped
closer to me. "I also know that your father
tried very hard to get someone to listen to
him, so that the kids who were tormenting
you would leave you alone. But people in
the school seemed to think that whatever
was going on wasn't serious. Did you know
that?"

Bobby nodded and his eyes welled tears. He was watching his father now, gaze fixed on the big man's back. Fred h stopped an arm's length from me, his fe planted like those tree trunks Bobby had so diligently removed from my yard. His rasping, ragged breathing frightened me.

"I'm going to step out of the shed now. I'm going to stand on the front porch of my house until you two come out. Bobby, I think your dad has something to tell you."

It was an awful chance I was taking, but it was the only way Fred Benson, a man who had reached the end of his rope, which had then snapped and sent him hurtling into a dark abyss whose bottom he hadn't yet reached, had for dignity. He could reclaim his soul, but only if he willingly told Bobby what he'd done.

Slowly I turned, the hair on the back of my neck prickling with the fear of being struck from behind by a man powerful enough to have brought down Henry Johnson. I followed my own footsteps through the snow, one small step at a time, listening with hyperacute awareness for the sound of someone following me, but I heard nothing.

As soon as I stepped onto the porch and looked back at the shed, the figures of fa-

and son, silhouetted and framed by doorway, started moving, arms gesturing, flailing. Bobby pressed himself against the door jamb while Fred paced the dirt floor. Their voices were loud enough to be heard but indistinct, and I prayed that when they stepped outside, father and son would both be ready for what they had to do.

I sat on the porch step, the cold seeping up through my jeans. But my shivering had nothing to do with the temperature. I was furious, at the kids who had chosen Bobby to be the object of their misguided hostility, at the adults who had done nothing even in the face of repeated requests for help. At Fred Benson, for not only losing his temper but then going back after coldly calculating how he might cover up his terrible act. I was mad at the universe for allowing such outrageous insults to happen.

The two figures now stood facing each other, their bodies tense. Fred Benson's head hung low, his chin touching his chest. Bobby started to move away. Fred reached for his shoulder, turned Bobby so that they were facing each other again, and lay his other hand to his son's shoulder. Bobby lifted his head, as though he were looking at the sky.

And then it came. A scream, sharp than the one that had awakened m. months earlier, a soul-piercing pain knifing through the country quiet.

My stomach twisted into a knot. Fred Benson had told his son what he'd done.

Chapter 23

"Last round. King high bets." Elizabeth held the deck of cards in her manicured hands and looked at me, waiting for my response.

Seven-card stud poker gave the pot a chance to get really big, and this was no exception. This might be a nickel-and-dime game, but the money was hardly the point. I glanced at the overflowing pile of blue, red, and white chips, and at my hole cards, which lay face down in front of me, and smiled instead of groaning. My poker face — but this time, with three pretty good chances to come up with a straight in spades or a full house, I had a reason to smile.

"I'll start at a dime," I said, not wanting to scare anyone off by betting too much on this round.

I looked to my left. Nora stood behind Karen's chair, peering over her shoulder at her cards. She bent down, whispered in Karen's ear, stood straight again, and smiled.

"Hey, this isn't a partner's game," lissa said, grinning broadly. "And even was, you should be standing by me, No. We're the ones going into business to gether. I can't believe that you'd do this. You're actually going to help a girl with red streaks in her hair and a perfect French manicure, as nice and as funny as she might be, take the money of people you've known all your life?"

Karen sat back in her chair, took a sip of her Cosmo, and narrowed her eyes and checked her down cards, a smile playing at the corners of her mouth. "Nora and I decided that since we have half a functioning brain between us right now, we only count as one person. Besides, the sooner I can rake all those chips over to my side of the table, the sooner we can get to that spaghetti. I'll see your dime and raise you a dime, country girl."

Susan frowned and tossed in two blue chips, and Elizabeth shook her head and folded. I slid another chip to the middle of the table to stay in the game.

"Well, then, down and dirty, my lovelies." Elizabeth slapped me a card, then laid one on Karen and another on Susan.

Instead of peeking, I watched as my opponents checked their last cards. Susan's

...lders sagged, and I knew she had ...ning. Nora's curved eyebrow arched ...gh, and a hint of a smile lifted the cor-...ers of her mouth. She looked as though she were appraising a haute couture costume and trying to figure out where she might wear it. Karen, who might know cards but couldn't help wearing her hearts and spades right out there on her sleeve, pretended to shake her head in dismay while her eyes twinkled with mischief. I peeked at a corner of the card Elizabeth had just dealt me.

All eyes turned my way.

"King bets." Elizabeth, who now had no stake in the outcome, seemed tickled at the drama. "Possible full house, possible straight. Against Karen's possible four of a kind and Susan's possible . . . well, I don't know, but it's king's bet."

Without hesitation, I said, "A quarter."

The arch in Nora's eyebrow inched up. My heart pounded as I waited to see what they would do. Karen nodded, looked at me, looked at her cards, looked at Susan. The ticking of the mantel clock filled the room. Finally, Karen reached for a chip, held it between her fingers, then scrunched up her face and turned her cards over. "I'm out," she sighed.

Without hesitation, Susan followed s[...] "Me too. Can't fight destiny."

"Thank you, ladies," I said, tossing m[...] cards back into the deck and scooping the[...] pot of chips my way, not about to let them know my bluff had paid off. "You've been mighty hospitable to the newcomer to-night, and I surely appreciate it. Now, I'd say it's time for that spaghetti you prom-ised us, Nora. That sauce smells like it came straight from *paisan* heaven. What's the secret ingredient?"

"You think I'm giving away my secrets? This is my audition," Nora said, "so be kind to me. If you all like it, then Melissa thinks maybe I can be trusted with run-ning the restaurant."

"They're too easy. These customers would like anything you cook." Melissa smiled, and we all joined her. "But I happen to know that this partnership is going to be fabulously successful. As long as Nora doesn't have to play poker."

"Or cook the pasta." Elizabeth popped out of her chair. "Hope that water hasn't all boiled out."

"Let's go see," I said, following behind her into my kitchen. "The rest of you, talk among yourselves. We'll be back in a few minutes."

Karen pushed a deck of cards into the box. "Take your time. And don't worry about your Cosmos. We'll watch them carefully."

Susan, Nora, and Melissa laughed, and the four of them continued setting the table with the place settings Karen and I had put out on a tray earlier in the afternoon. It had taken her about fifteen minutes to declare that she loved the cottage and the little towns I'd taken her to after I'd picked her up at the train station just before noon.

I was glad for this moment alone in my kitchen with Elizabeth. I opened the refrigerator and pulled out the salad and wedge of Romano. I pointed at the counter. The gourd I used for years to hold wooden spoons, wire whisks, an array of kitchen utensils, shone with a burnished glow as Elizabeth removed the cheese grater.

"Do you take commissions?" she asked.

I smiled, nodded, waited for her to say more.

"I want one of these for my kitchen. Tuscan colors." She set the gourd back on the counter. "I'm so relieved that Will Jackson admitted that the story about Bobby was true," she said. "Bobby has enough to deal with — all those years of

nobody listening to him, suffering throu
that awful night, his father in jail, accus
of murder — but at least he won't b
called a liar. And his stepmother will see
that he gets help when they move."

"Sure, Will admitted it. After two of his
friends said he'd lost his car keys in the
woods and they had to drive him home to
get a spare. I'm glad I kept Michele Castro
honest by turning those keys in."

Eyes widening, Elizabeth said, "She's
pretty solid. She was already following up
about Will when you called her about the
keys. She told me that she'd been worried
about him forever, that she was feeling
pretty bad about not being firmer with Ira
that the kid was trouble. And she says that
Alvin Akron has agreed not to press
charges for false arrest. He swore from the
start that the Dremel bit has been lost
since maybe April or May, and could have
fallen out of a pocket when he was walking
around with all that surveyor's equipment." She shrugged. "If I was the prose-
cutor, I'd have worried about the evidence
against him anyway."

"What's going to happen to Fred?" I
asked as I pulled the salad out of the refrigerator.

She dumped a handful of linguine into

pot of boiling water and then watched the noodles sank below the bubbling surface. "He'll do ten, fifteen years for manslaughter. And his family will move to Florida, as they planned. The judge is considering letting him do his time there."

"That's pretty enlightened," I said. "It's not as though —"

"Enlightened? You sound like you were expecting dark ages and the rack. We're not —"

"Whoa. I would have said that in Brooklyn. I didn't mean anything about Columbia County. Only about the way the justice system works. Everywhere. God, you'd think I was an outsider who needed to get to know how people think and feel around here."

Elizabeth started laughing, pointing at herself and nodding. I started laughing too, partly because it was such a relief to not think that she was making a comment about my presence and its legitimacy. I might never really know this woman and what mattered to her, what she valued, but she was telling me that we had crossed some line and there was no going back.

"The croutons for the salad are in that bag," I said.

She dug into the paper bag, pulled out a

cardboard box. "Wow, straight from Dean & Deluca. Some good things do make their way from the city to our little corner of paradise."

She hugged me. It surprised both of us, but if it felt as good to her as it did to me, then it was the kind of surprise that I'd welcome into my life anytime.

Welcome to Lili Marino's Gourd World

Lili Marino doesn't spend all her time helping to figure out who killed a prominent member of her new Upstate New York community . . . She's a gourd artist who has discovered fascinating facts about this astonishingly versatile plant.

Gourds, known to botanists as Cucurbitacea *Lagenaria,* are believed by many scholars to be among the first domesticated plants, and they have spread across the globe to nearly every culture. Depending on their size and the hardness of their shells, they've been used in Africa, Asia, the Americas, and Europe as containers, eating and drinking utensils, musical instruments, masks, and money. The legends and customs surrounding this humble yet fascinating plant are almost as varied as the shapes and sizes of the gourds themselves.

Hawaii: Don't get your gourd in a t

Old Hawaiian custom dictates that gou
should be planted when the moon is shap
like a fruit. A pot-bellied man should pre
pare the ground by digging a hole for each
seed and then carry the seed as though it
were a heavy gourd. He must open his
hands suddenly to drop in the seed. If he
twists his hands, the result will be a twisted
gourd.

Kenya: Bitter heart, bitter gourd

Gourds can be either edible or poisonous.
To distinguish between the two, Kenyan
farmers scratch the gourd's surface and
sample the flavor. A bitter taste indicates
that it should not be eaten. Poisons extracted from the pulp of certain gourds are
used to control cockroaches and other in-
sects. One Kenyan tribal group believes
that a bitter taste is directly related to a lack
of purity in the heart of the person who
planted the seeds.

Haiti: A gourd for your thoughts?

Gourds were once the national currency of
Haiti. The standard coin today is still called
a *gourde,* worth about three cents in the
United States.

Gourd Pendant

The great thing about creating your own gourd pendant is . . . it's whatever you want it to be! The colors and designs can complement your clothing or your mood or reflect your heritage. And it's easy and wonderfully satisfying.

You'll need clean, dry scraps of gourds, sandpaper, and a fixative (polyurethane is simple to work with). Part of the fun of making gourd pendants is experimenting with different materials to create designs: acrylic paints, leather dyes, colored pencils, marker pens. You can include pyrographed (woodburned) designs, glue on beads . . . the possibilities are truly endless.

The first thing to do is put on your mask. If you're new to gourds, please be aware that you should always wear a paper mask, sold in all hardware stores, to protect you from gourd dust and mold. (Serious gourders often use a respirator mask.)

First, cut the scraps into the shapes you want, using either a sharp utility knife, like an Exacto, or a miniature electric saw. Then sand the sides and the inner surface, which is usually the back of the pendant.

You'll need to drill one or more holes for the thong, cord, or chain from which the pendant will hang. Drilling two holes usually means that the pendant has a better chance of lying flat and not twisting when you wear it.

Now you're ready to create your one-of-a-kind jewelry. You can draw a design with pencil and then paint. You can create a pyrographed design, or you can just start painting. I love using acrylic paints for pendants, because the colors are so rich and vibrant. Leather dyes give a wonderful wash effect, a lot like watercolors, and I use them on many of my whole gourds.

When you're finished with this step, give the pendant twenty-four hours to dry completely. Then it's time to spray on the polyurethane, a two-step process. First spray the back. It's best to use a light coat, so that the poly doesn't run and pool. Let it dry for half a day. Then spray the front. Here it's especially important to use one or two light coats.

Once the poly is completely dry, you can add embellishments, if you like. I've glued beads and colored glass onto pendants, and even used twisted wire to create accents in my design.

Finally, cut the leather thong or twisted cord to double the length you need, and allow enough extra to tie a knot. Slide the thong through the holes, make a knot, and enjoy your unique gourd pendant.

Visit me at MaggieBruce.com to see some gourd pendants. Happy gourding!

Maggie Bruce

The employees of Thorndike Press hope you have enjoyed this Large Print book. All our Thorndike and Wheeler Large Print titles are designed for easy reading, and all our books are made to last. Other Thorndike Press Large Print books are available at your library, through selected bookstores, or directly from us.

For information about titles, please call:

(800) 223-1244

or visit our Web site at:

www.gale.com/thorndike
www.gale.com/wheeler

To share your comments, please write:

Publisher
Thorndike Press
295 Kennedy Memorial Drive
Waterville, ME   04901